NO ONE TO HELP HER

A totally gripping crime thriller full of twists

KATE WATTERSON

Detective Chris Bailey Book 3

JOFFE
BOOKS

Joffe Books, London
www.joffebooks.com

First published in Great Britain in 2022

Cover art by Nick Castle

ISBN: 978-1-80405-454-3

PROLOGUE

It was a cold night with ice on the roads, and a thin wind whistled through bare branches, making them dance like grasping claws against the filtered moonlight.

February was his least favorite month.

Fred Dawson didn't care for the late shift. It ruined any chance of having a social life. He didn't get to play pool on Thursday nights, and there was no chance of asking a girl out on a date. An early lunch would be the best he could swing, and that spelled no chance at romance. So he worked his three to eleven, then went home, drank a couple beers to unwind, slept until midmorning, had a bite all alone, and repeated the routine.

At least he had a job, he reminded himself morosely.

He only spotted the body because of the purse.

The purse was lying in the middle of the road — which he found unusual on a rural county highway — and his headlights caught it. The sleek, black leather looked expensive to him as he drove past it, and he decided to pull over and walk back to pick it up. He was trying to imagine why any woman would toss her purse out the window.

He spotted the hand first, just on the edge of the grass, fingers curled. He wasn't too sure he was seeing clearly, and he used the flashlight on his phone to hesitantly walk closer for a better look.

The woman was sprawled face down on the shoulder of the winding country road, and there was a glossy dark pool around her head. He wasn't an expert, but she sure looked dead to him.

"Oh Jesus," he muttered.

With shaking fingers he punched in 911.

Not that it was going to help her.

CHAPTER ONE

The killer was sweating, disbelieving that he'd just so callously done what he'd done. He sat in his kitchen in the dark and wondered why he'd taken such a chance with his own life.

It might be slipping through his hands.
What could he do about it now?
Maybe enjoy the moment.

* * *

Two in the morning on a cold, lonely byway in the sticks was not his idea of a good time, but Detective Chris Bailey worked for the sheriff's department and as far as he could tell, his hours were set by the crime, not by a clock.

In this case, it appeared to be a murder that had called him out.

Rotating lights, multiple vehicles, and two uniformed deputies standing in the road awaited him. The deputies would normally be directing traffic, but there certainly wasn't any right now — not in this location at this time of night. They'd no doubt been the ones to respond to the call, and there were a couple of other vehicles he recognized.

The warm bed he'd gotten out of to answer this call — with the equally warm woman in it — was part of the price he paid for being a law enforcement officer.

One of the deputies pointed. "Hey, Bailey. Over there. It isn't pretty."

The wind really had a bite to it as he slammed shut his car door and walked in that direction, switching on his flashlight.

No, it really wasn't pretty at all.

On the side of the road sprawled in the grass was a woman's body, hair disheveled, blood everywhere, her open eyes gleaming in the fleeting moonlight but seeing nothing.

A single high-heeled pump lay obscenely alone in a pile of last year's fallen leaves tinted with frost. He didn't see the other one — she was barefoot.

The coroner wasn't any happier to be there than he was. Dr. Loren had waited and his collar was turned up, and he had replaced his rubber gloves with real ones. Compared to the northern climes, it didn't often get cold, but they were a lot less prepared down in Tennessee when it did.

"I would say good to see you, Detective, but it is never good news when we meet, is it?"

"That's a fair assessment of the situation. What have we got here?"

"Five gunshot wounds. She bled out here. There isn't rigor yet. She hasn't been here long."

"Are you serious?"

"Am I ever not? So I would guess whoever did this pulled over, forced her or somehow got her out of the car, and shot her from behind, but you're the detective and that's your job, not mine. I'm the one that turned her over. She has definitely been declared deceased, and I am confident you will get a determination of manner of death to be homicide from the medical examiner."

The doctor that served the county in his position was astute and to the point always.

Chris nodded, not happy all the way around. "I have never worked a case where someone shot themselves more

4

than once, much less that many times, and from behind would be a neat trick, so I think homicide is the forgone conclusion."

"She was wearing heels and no coat. I'm guessing she wasn't just walking down the road."

"Not in this weather." He was, if he said it in true country boy style, freezing his ass off in a leather jacket and jeans and boots.

"It's yours from here. I'm heading back to bed."

"Thanks, Doc."

They formally shook hands, which was standard for this particular man because he was old school.

Chris watched as they loaded the body into the van and went to interview the witness, who was sitting in his truck on the side of the road. He was too young to find a body on a county highway and definitely shaken. The truth was Chris knew Dawson's older brother pretty well because they had gone to high school together. "Thanks for waiting, Freddy. Doing okay?"

"Not really." He did look pale, making the freckles across his nose stand out. He wore a coat that probably wasn't sufficient for the unusual cold, and his red hair was caught back in a ponytail.

"The sheriff's department really appreciates you calling this in."

Fred looked at him. "Of course I would, but man, how do you do this job? I'm never going to be able to unsee it."

Chris actually wasn't positive how to answer that question, so he asked instead, "It seems like her death happened very close to the time when you found the body. I need to know if you noticed any vehicles that caught your attention when you were driving down this particular road. Please think carefully."

"Not really." He shook his head. "It's late, and I think I passed maybe one car."

"Do you happen to remember what kind or what color, that sort of thing?"

"Um, okay, give me a second." He did seem to try and collect himself. "A black sedan, I think. I wasn't paying attention, but I only noticed because it was going pretty fast. I was just off work and ready to go home and drink a few beers and then go to bed. I keep it slow because I don't want to hit a deer, and at this time of night, I see them cross the road pretty often. I thought to myself they were being pretty stupid speeding."

"So headed south?"

"Yeah."

"Nothing else unusual?"

"Just that purse in the road. I'm pretty sure there's a nightmare in my future now. The next time I see something that seems off to me, I think I'll just drive on."

"You did the right thing, because it really helps us to be on the scene as soon as possible. Time and nature deteriorate evidence. Go home and have some cold ones and drink one for me, will you? This is now my problem."

"I think I'm going to stop bitching about my job. I sure as hell wouldn't want yours."

The kid had a point. Working his last murder case, he did get shot twice, so there was a downside to his occupation, and his partner, Carter, had also taken a bullet. "It isn't all sunshine and roses, but it does have some satisfaction going for it when we catch the bad guy."

"Good luck. I don't know who would shoot someone a bunch of times and leave them at the side of road, but I don't like the idea of them being out there."

He watched the truck pull away and figured he might as well go home too, because the crime scene was too dark to reveal any secrets not captured by the forensic crime scene investigators and their special cameras. He'd go over the report when it was all available. It was damned late, and he could go ahead and sit in the warmth of his house and start making notes.

He and sleep were not the best of friends, so he might as well.

Anna was still in bed when he walked through the door, but most people would be at this time of night. However, his little dog greeted him with a wagging tail and bright eyes under that unruly curtain of long hair.

He patted her head. "Hello, Moppet."

She was hardly a manly canine, but endearing for all that, and she followed him from room to room in a true show of affection. He appreciated it, because even though the latest romantic interest in his life spent the night occasionally, she did have her own busy life, and the dog was good company. Never complained or nagged at him for working such long hours and only barked when someone came to the door, which he actually valued, like having a personal doorbell.

He went over to the refrigerator and got out his own beer so Fred Dawson could enjoy the one for him guilt-free, and sat to scribble down some notes before he forgot anything. He always kept a pen and a pad of paper handy so he could do just that if something about a case occurred to him, and hey, he was a bachelor, so he just left it on the kitchen table all the time.

The beer gave a satisfying pop when he cracked it open. He took a long drink and then considered what he knew so far, pen in hand.

Five bullets when just one might have taken care of the problem? The killer was angry.

"Is it day drinking, if it is . . . let me see, almost three thirty now in the morning? Or are you still operating on the day before, so it is just really still late evening to you?"

He glanced up and saw Anna in the doorway, leaning against the jamb, just wearing one of his T-shirts. She looked attractively rumpled, which was without a doubt his fault considering what they had been doing before that call came from dispatch.

"I don't work a regular schedule," he informed her with a hint of ironic humor, "so it can go either way. I'm sorry if I woke you."

"No, that's fine. How bad was it?"

"The scene? I'm processing." He paused, then said honestly, "I don't like who I'm dealing with at all. To my mind, if one bullet would do it, why would you continue to fire four more times? You're the psychologist. Angry, or focused and making sure?"

She was a social worker but also had a master's in psychology and an agile brain when it came to reading people. He was always interested in her take on why people did what they did. She'd helped him out on a case or two by giving him a slant on motivation. It wasn't his job to find out why; he was more geared toward whom, but profiling helped narrow the field.

"I need more information. Who is the victim?"

"No identification yet. Young woman and it seems obvious she was with someone in a car because she was well-dressed but did not have on a coat. They left her on the side of the road after taking the contents of her purse."

"Robbery?"

"No. I'd say she was in that car willingly."

"Hmm." Anna walked over — she had nice legs, currently bare, so it was a pleasure to watch — and sat down, her expression contemplative. "I'd say an argument on the first guess, but I'm not you."

"That's why I'm asking. I'm studying the crime committed and how it was done, while you might give me your assessment into why. I think this case needs insight, and I'm on a learning curve here."

Dryly, she observed, "You seem to be doing fine since the FBI wants you."

They had offered him a job after the long application process, and he was considering taking it.

But first things first.

He agreed. He jotted down. *In the car, so the victim knew and trusted her killer.*

"Boyfriend?"

"Well, not a good one if he was, but that might be my guess. However, that's quite a violent reaction to a disagreement," Anna said.

"It has happened before."

"I know. I wish I couldn't say that, but I do. Have you ever dealt with children when a parent has killed the other parent? I have. It isn't an easy experience. We are first responders, not to the crime, but to figure out what happens next to the survivors."

As much as Freddy wouldn't want his job, he wouldn't want hers. He said quietly, "I firmly believe there are angel wings somewhere down the line for you."

She had lovely, dark eyes, and her gaze was always straightforward. Anna just looked at him. "So, we are both awake in the middle of the night. Should we maybe go back to bed? This will still be a problem in the morning, but we could get some sleep after?"

"After what?"

She stood. "Let me make you forget about this new case for a little while. We were interrupted by that call."

He was on board with that. She had a passionate nature, and that was a drawing card for him. "Sounds like just the therapy I need."

CHAPTER TWO

The killer sat up in bed, sweating profusely, his mouth dry.

Bad dreams. That had never happened before. What the hell was that all about?

She'd deserved it for interfering in his life.

They all did in his mind.

* * *

There was no doubt the house needed work.

Fine with him.

Mick Reynolds had wanted a property on a wooded lot with or near water, and this place was pure Tennessee with fifteen acres and a large pond that was stocked with fish. The air of abandonment didn't bother him too much, and he could overlook the dated interior, for that could all be changed. He even liked the layout for the most part, but it didn't matter; he was much more interested in the setting. Still, it did have vaulted ceilings in the living room and a big stone fireplace, and the second floor was a loft that would make a perfect office with an incredible view of nothing but trees.

It was near to perfect as far as he could tell and, with updates, could be stunning.

He'd turned to the realtor. "You're sure I can get internet service here so I can work remotely?"

"Absolutely. There's satellite, and they've been working on running fiber optics in this area."

A bald eagle soared overhead right then, silhouetted against brilliant blue sky, and a soft breeze whispered through the trees.

It seemed like a sign.

"Let's put in an offer then."

Two days of negotiation and a cash offer and he had an acceptance for the property on Willow Lane about fifteen miles from Willamette. The price was ridiculously low, so renovations should be a breeze, and he could do a lot of it himself. He could wield a hammer and paintbrush with the best of them, and in the meantime, it was livable.

That was two months ago.

This drastic change in his life was much needed. The high-powered job in Chicago did not make for an existence he enjoyed, and he'd invested his money wisely, not to mention started his own company on the side.

He was ready to take the leap from corporate to private. That degree in business he'd earned at a prestigious school would hopefully pay off big time. If it didn't, he could go back into the melee, but he'd found he didn't like living in a big city.

At all.

In theory it had sounded like something he'd enjoy. Nightlife, convenient restaurants, meeting new people . . .

No.

He'd lived it for six years, and this particular country boy was glad to be home. He'd waited to tell his parents he'd found a house until the new bed and mattress were delivered. It had come just that morning.

A place to sleep. That made it official.

His father pulled up in a pickup that had seen better days, but then again, he always drove a vehicle until it just plain quit. He climbed out and looked around, taking his time before walking over.

"Nice place, son. I always liked it." His dad was just like him, looking at the land, not the somewhat neglected house with the front door that needed to be replaced. "That's not really a pond but a small lake. Good find. Forget the house, you can change all of that, but you can never change the location."

"My thoughts exactly." Hands in his pockets, Mick felt relieved because Ray Reynolds was a direct man, and if he didn't agree with the decision, he would hear about it. Even at his age, he did want his father's approval when he made decisions, and buying a house was a fairly large one.

"I have a friend who is a contractor, and he's good. I'll give you his number. He can take care of the renovations."

"That would be great." That saved him looking around for someone for the big jobs he couldn't handle or maybe didn't have time to do. If he was working this the right way, it might be the latter. The business enterprise had done quite well so far, not necessarily to his surprise, but better than he expected would be the way to put it.

"Have you by any chance talked to your sister lately?"

They were standing by the front porch, which clearly needed staining when the weather was warm enough, not to mention new screens — the whole property needed some work, not just the house. Mick shook his head. "I sent her a text when the closing was scheduled, but she never responded. I was kind of surprised. She must be busy."

"Must be. Anyway, supper at six and you're always invited."

"Thanks, but now that I have the keys, I ran to the grocery and plan to try out the stove. It passed inspection, so I assume it works. I'll take out some beer and start thinking about what needs doing and just spend the evening listening to music or something like that. I packed up my car with some essentials, so I have a frying pan and dishes."

"The door is always open, but enjoy your evening, son." With a wave he got in his truck and pulled away.

He would. A week with his parents was enough to appreciate that while he loved them, at twenty-eight years old, seven days was more than enough.

Well, he thought he'd enjoy his evening.

His cell phone rang, and he and he answered it without checking the caller.

"Hello?"

"Michael Reynolds?"

"Yes."

"This is Detective Chris Bailey."

The county sheriff's office? Why the hell would they want to talk to him?

"I obtained your number from your former employer who told me you had moved back to Tennessee. I wonder if we could meet? I don't actually have a location for you at this time."

He'd called the Chicago office?

"What is this about?"

"I would very much prefer to talk to you face to face."

No answer to his question, but he couldn't think of a reason to refuse. "I guess it is fine. I'm just unaware of any law I have broken."

"If you have, I am also unaware of it. I just need some information. You can come to the county office here in Willamette or I can come to wherever you are."

"Here's the address." He rattled it off, since it wasn't like he hadn't read it a million times — or so it felt — recently, as he signed all the final paperwork just this morning.

"The Kilmer place? Okay. It's about twenty minutes away."

Whoever the detective was, he was local. To instantly recognize the address indicated he really knew the area.

The implication of wanting to talk to him was still unexplained, but he was innocent as far as he knew of any infraction.

So fine. He had to admit he was curious.

Information on what?

While he waited, he made up the bed in the downstairs master with clean sheets and the new bedspread he'd purchased that day and racked his brain for any reason law enforcement would want to talk to him.

He came up blank.

* * *

They were an odd couple.

Carter drove. It just worked out that way usually. His partner was senior to Chris, no doubt about that, a by-the-book detective who had been with the department for years and had a lot more experience, but they had come to a gradual understanding that their different methods of approaching cases worked fairly well together.

By-the-book-strict met hunches and intuition and a shoot-from-the-hip approach. It seemed to be a good combination most of the time. Two different perceptions of the same crime created balance.

They pulled up and parked, and Chris got out and shut the car door. "I'm not looking forward to this."

Carter agreed in his pragmatic way. "There are some unpleasant aspects to what we do for a living."

"Then let's get on with it."

The place was set on a beautiful piece of property, the house all cedar and stone, well-suited for a single male and absolutely not suited at all for a couple with young children. It had a small lake that was a hazard for kids, and the nearest grocery store was in town twenty miles away. It had a long driveway, so they'd have to walk and wait for the school bus on a county road. There was a reason it sat on the market for a while after the previous owners, who were retired, died within a year of each other.

He'd have loved to have bought it, but it was too far from the office and he had a cabin on the river to give him his fix of peace and solitude, so it was a no go for him.

The man who answered the door was close to his age, just a few years younger, also blond, hazel eyes, with a lean build, and unfortunately his features were familiar and his coloring was right.

They both produced their badges. Carter was the one that spoke. "Detectives Carter and Bailey. We just have a few questions."

"Come on in." Michael Reynolds looked uncertain, which told Chris he had no idea what the problem was, so they were going to be about as welcome as a case of the bubonic plague, but there was no help for this visit. "It's pretty cold out there."

The only furniture in the living room was an old couch and two recliners that had also seen better days. Reynolds stood near the couch. "I just took possession. My furniture is in storage. This came with the house because the people selling it didn't want it. If you know of a place to donate it, I'm going to do that when mine arrives. But have a seat. I admit I have to wonder why you're here."

Chris chose one of the recliners and it was pretty comfortable, so maybe the family made a mistake.

Carter was the one who usually began interviews. He was the distinguished older guy in a pressed shirt, dress slacks and a jacket, and Chris dressed usually in jeans, boots and a button-up shirt, but no tie. Carter took the other recliner. "There's a database that can be accessed by law enforcement for anyone who decides to provide their DNA to those companies that will then give you information on your genetic background. It seems you have done that, correct?"

Michael Reynolds sat. "Yes, I did. How can that possibly be of interest to anyone but me?"

"We can use it sometimes to be able to track a perpetrator, or in this case, maybe a victim, by connecting the dots."

"What?"

Chris leaned forward. "We have an unidentified female victim of a homicide. Her DNA when we ran it matched yours very closely, and the results said 'sibling.' How many sisters do you have?"

"Just one . . . are . . . are . . . you serious? Amanda?" He went white, a suddenly shaking hand running through his hair. "Oh God, my father just asked me this afternoon if I'd heard from her, and I told him I was surprised I hadn't because I texted her about the house and she didn't reply. I can't believe this. A . . . did you say *homicide*?"

This kind of moment was what Chris dreaded. "I did. It seems like it might be your sister. The body was found in this county. We just didn't have any identification or a missing person report, so we tried everything we could to figure out who she was before contacting maybe the wrong family."

"You were the only one we could directly connect," Carter supplied in backup.

Michael Reynolds put his head in his hands. "I don't even know how to deal with this. You're sure?"

"We are sure we have a victim and need to identify her so we can move forward with the investigation. Any information you can give us will help immensely. We'll unfortunately need someone to positively identify, as she's still in the morgue. If it isn't her, you'll go through an unpleasant experience, but if it is her, it'll be even worse. I can't sugarcoat it." Carter was always straightforward. "We need someone to do it."

"I'm shaken." He stood up and walked across the room to the fireplace and took in a breath. "I'm literally shaking. I don't know. I would reluctantly, but I have a feeling since my father is a down-to-earth man, he might want to see her to believe it. He might insist on doing it or going with me. I can't even think of how to tell my parents."

"Either way, we need some help."

"I'll talk to him. What happened? Tell me she wasn't raped, because I can't handle it."

"No." Chris was also relieved that hadn't happened. He hated those cases. "No evidence of sexual assault. This victim was shot and left on the side of the road. Was she seeing anyone?"

Silence.

He understood.

Finally he spoke. "She mentioned a guy on and off, but it wasn't serious as far as I can tell. She's two years younger than I am, and we were close but hardly shared our everyday lives. We talked every couple of weeks on the phone."

"His name would be enough. We can find him."

"My sister lives in Nashville. Why would she be here without telling my parents?"

He was unfocused, and Chris couldn't blame him. If something like this had happened to his only brother, he'd be all shaken up as well.

"We are trying to establish that and who she was with, and that is why we are here." Carter was ever the calm voice of reason.

He visibly regrouped, taking in a deep, steadying breath. "I don't know his last name. All she told me was John."

"And she met him how?"

"I didn't ask, and she didn't offer."

So all they had was a common first name and a speeding black sedan, and both of those bits of information could mean nothing.

But Chris was almost one hundred percent sure they'd at least identified the victim.

"Her best friend might know more about him. I have her number, so I'll call her." Reynolds exhaled audibly, his voice catching. "I'll go do the identification and then I'll tell my parents when I'm sure. This feels very surreal to me."

Chris thought that was how to approach it. "That sounds like the best way to handle this to me."

CHAPTER THREE

There was a fine line between guilty satisfaction and the feeling that there was still unfinished business.
The killer had thought it over and couldn't figure it out.
He recognized that fact.
It all came down to how far to go to find what he needed.
Or was it what he wanted? Hard to tell the difference.

* * *

It was a dilemma to a certain extent.

Samantha Davidson stepped off the curb in the chilly air and hurried to her car across the street.

She'd been hoping Mick Reynolds might give her a call now that he was back, but his cryptic message — she'd been in a meeting and couldn't answer it — left her undecided on how to respond.

Unfortunately I need you to call me.

If it weren't for the words 'unfortunately' and 'need', she wouldn't be so uncertain.

Their high school through college romance had blazed to life and then died to ashes, but it had occurred to her more than once that they'd both been so ambitious it stood in their way. Too young, too determined, too immersed in a desire to move on from a small-town upbringing.

Yet not headed the same direction.

Still, she hadn't fallen in love with anyone else since that ill-fated romance. Not even close.

However, that didn't sound like a message that meant he wanted to revisit old times. It was almost insulting.

He'd left his number, but undoubtedly, he'd gotten hers from his sister. She was a little surprised Amanda hadn't let her know Mick had asked for it.

She had a nice house in an older neighborhood, built in the thirties. She loved the classic craftsman style with a wide front porch with a swing, and it had been nicely redone before she bought it and had a smooth lawn with mature trees. In the summer she sat out there and enjoyed a glass of iced tea as children rode by on their bicycles on the quiet street. Older couples owned the houses on either side, and both kept immaculate yards, so she'd come home more than once to find someone had mowed hers as well, since she was fairly busy.

Nice folks, as her grandmother might point out.

She was happy for the most part, but hearing that Mick was moving back to Tennessee had stirred a longing for more that she'd dismissed six years ago. It was true she was fine on her own without him. That she'd proven, but . . . still.

She'd missed him all that time. Maybe it was a case of first-lover syndrome.

Or that a part of her was really just not over it.

After she walked in, she set her purse and briefcase aside on the table in the entryway and put on some quiet music — Bach was always soothing — and poured a glass of wine before she called back. She chose a full-bodied Chardonnay, because she needed some fortitude for this.

Then she punched in the number.

"Mick?"

"Samantha."

"You left me a message?" It was formal, but she wasn't sure how to handle it.

"I did. Are you home? If the answer is yes, I'm coming over."

He sounded off, but then again, she hadn't talked to him for quite a while.

"Hello to you, too."

"I'm sorry. You aren't going to like any part of this conversation we are about to have, and I'm really off balance."

That was starting to become clear just from his terse tone. She could easily remember his clean-cut good looks, compelling smile and confident air, and he was usually considerate.

Even in bed. She wished she didn't remember those nights and the passion they once felt for each other, but life moved on and so it went.

This wasn't remotely him to act this way.

At a loss, she asked slowly, "Yes, I'm home. What are you talking about? Why am I not going to like it?"

"I'll be there in about twenty minutes."

He abruptly ended the call. She sat there in her kitchen and stared at her phone at a loss, wondering what just happened. She wasn't even aware he knew where she lived, unless maybe Amanda had given him the address for some reason.

The last time she'd seen him had been over a year ago, very briefly at a Christmas party given by a mutual friend when clearly neither knew they were both going to attend. It had been on the awkward side with murmured greetings and a swift retreat on both sides.

If he was coming over — without an invitation — she wanted to at least change into something more comfortable than her work skirt and heels. She eschewed her drink for enough time to go upstairs and put on jeans and more comfortable shoes, but left on her feminine silk blouse. She had to admit she did check her hair in the mirror briefly.

Why? She really didn't want to examine that question too closely.

She went back downstairs to her glass of wine, and true to his word, she heard a knock on her door right at the expected time.

Still wondering what prompted this urgent need to talk to her, she answered it. "Uh, can you tell me what's wrong?"

He looked like something was very wrong, his face tight. "You're drinking wine. I could use a glass if you don't mind. God knows I need something."

His wavy blond hair was slightly disheveled, those vivid hazel eyes not quite meeting hers, and there was no doubt he was tense. She could see it in the set of his wide shoulders. Tall, lean, muscular, he was strikingly good-looking, maybe even more so than when they'd first started dating a decade ago. "Let me take your jacket. I don't mind at all. I have the feeling I might need to refill mine for some reason I hope you will explain."

"I will." After he shrugged out of his coat, he followed her into the kitchen.

The frisson of disquiet was definitely not welcome. This was not a friendly "I'm back in town" visit.

Wordlessly she got out a wine glass and poured from the already open bottle and handed it to him. He sat down on one of the barstools at the island and said plainly, "I just left the morgue."

Whatever she expected him to say, that was not it.

He gazed at her. "I had to identify Amanda's body."

She stared at him in utter shock. It was a miracle she didn't drop her wine glass and have it shatter on the floor. "What?"

"Yeah, I know. Truthfully, I want to cry whether grown men are supposed to or not, but I'm just too numb to do it."

She wasn't. She and Amanda had been friends literally since kindergarten. Instantly her throat tightened and her eyes welled. "She's . . . dead?"

No. No. No. She couldn't take it in.

"Yeah. I couldn't believe it either until they opened a drawer and showed me the body. Shit, I still can't."

She had to sit down next to him because her legs were suddenly shaky. "What happened? She had a car accident?"

"No. That's why I'm here. What do you know about John, this guy she's been seeing?"

* * *

He was never going to get past the experience of standing there in that cold, sterile environment and recognizing his sister's familiar face.

Not ever. Hardly as he remembered it but lifeless and still. Forever.

She'd been shot five times.

Someone had shot his sister *five* times.

What the hell, Mick had to ask himself.

Samantha was as stunning as ever — that hadn't changed. Her slender body in jeans and a silky shirt, auburn hair loose around her shoulders. But now there were tears pouring down her smooth cheeks, and he'd expected the reaction. She and Amanda had been very close, which was why he knew her in the first place, why that acquaintance had turned into a love affair that had lasted for years, and also why this needed to be done in person.

It wasn't like he didn't want comfort too, but what he really needed was some answers.

"John?" he prompted quietly. "I don't know anything about him, and she was murdered. My impression is that the detectives who gave me the unwelcome news think she knew her killer."

"Murdered?" Her expression showed her horror. "What?"

"She was shot, and her body left on the side of the road."

Utter silence. He understood.

Finally, she spoke in a thin whisper. "I can't believe this." Her eyes were a true emerald green and glossy with tears.

"We agree on that."

She took in a shuddering breath. "Okay, let me under-stand . . . John did this?"

"I don't know, but the detectives investigating this asked me and I realized I don't know much about him. First name is about it."

"I'll try to remember what she told me. I've never met him."

It wasn't like he never wanted to hold her in his arms again, but these were definitely not the ideal circumstances. He envied her ability to cry, and she was breaking down. He touched her wet cheek instead in an offer of solace.

He wasn't doing any better, just unable to express his trauma in the same way.

"I think she met him through a friend. I don't know his last name either." The words were choked out.

"What friend?"

"Sandy, I think." She rallied and exhaled as she swiped at her cheeks. "Yes, Sandy. Amanda and I met with her for drinks one night. I think I have her number in my phone because she texted me to say thank you after I paid the bill. It was only a few weeks ago."

That was exactly what he was looking for. "Can you give it to me?"

"Yes. Well, maybe. My hands are shaking."

There was no way to blame her for that.

"I completely understand. I keep waiting to wake up from this nightmare."

"Wake me up too, please." She picked up her phone, and it did take a couple of tries due to trembling fingers and tears, but finally she managed to find the number.

He immediately sent it to Detective Bailey.

There, he'd accomplished something anyway. He was hardly a detective. He knew the world of business fairly well, but finding a killer was out of his skill set.

But he was willing to aid in any way he could because, under the grief and shock, he was angry, bereft and a thousand other things he couldn't quite process.

Bailey texted back immediately. *I'll follow up on this lead.*

He simply showed the display to Samantha.

She swiped at her eyes with the back of her hand again. "I can't take this in."

"Yes, I know." He took a healthy drink from his glass. "I still have to tell my parents. I'm not sure how I'm going to get through that."

"They don't know yet?" She shook her head in disbelief, her soft hair moving across her slender shoulders. Her coloring was so striking, and there was no doubt in his mind if she'd chosen to become a model she'd have done very well. She had a delicate allure that was infinitely noticeable.

She was hands-down beautiful.

"No." He explained why the detectives found him first. "They couldn't identify her but connected it to my DNA. Whoever killed her took the contents of her purse, so no ID. That's how they discovered who she was."

"Do you think maybe a robbery?"

"No. She knew who did it. She wasn't wearing a coat and I am not a forensics expert, but she was probably already dead when they shot her the last four times according to the assistant medical examiner I spoke with. It was motivated by more than just the urge to rob her."

He should never have been so frank, and his only excuse was he was out of his element by about a million miles. When her eyes widened, he apologized quickly. "I'm sorry. You didn't need that detail."

"I wish you didn't know it either." She touched his arm, just a gentle glide of her fingers.

That was the other thing. Her physical appeal aside, she was a nice person. No wonder Amanda had always valued her as a friend.

No wonder he had fallen in love with her.

And never really fallen out.

Their senior year in college, he'd scraped enough together to buy her a ring, but she never knew that. She'd made it clear she wouldn't leave Tennessee for Chicago, and he'd gotten the job offer of a lifetime for someone his age just about to graduate, so . . .

But he'd kept that ring.

"I have no idea if it would help or make things worse, but I'll go with you to tell your parents if you think it is a good idea. I've known them almost all my life." She looked and sounded sincere.

It really was a generous offer. His mother was going to be devastated to an extent he only barely comprehended. His father would take it on the chin and feel probably like he did, furious and helpless and that the loss was just as much an arrow through the heart, but his mother was going to lose it. "I think that is the only good thing I've heard since two police officers arrived on my doorstep. Neither my father nor I will be able to help my mother take this in. You might really be what she needs. He's not going to cry either. Don't get me wrong, the tears are there, just on the inside for some reason."

"Strong men who hide how they feel. Are you kidding? Do you think I don't know you?"

If she really did, he was in trouble. She'd know he was still hung up on her.

"Thanks. I think it is a good idea. I don't know how tactful I am under a crisis situation."

"I don't think any of us do. Not for a revelation like this. No one should have to tell their parents this sort of news."

Grimly, he assessed the upcoming evening. "I agree. I might need another glass of wine. You can drive if your offer stands."

CHAPTER FOUR

It was a conundrum.

The killer liked that word. It was sophisticated and indicated a dilemma that could not be solved easily between conscience and what needed to be done.

Enough said.

Since he'd embarked on this, he might as well get full measure of his purpose fulfilled.

He pulled up to the house and studied it. It was dark now, and no lights. No car either.

Good. He could deliver his housewarming gift and be on his way.

* * *

In her line of work, Anna listened to a lot of sad stories.

Her mother told her often enough she was a saint, which she wasn't. For one thing, she was sleeping with a detective who was sexy as hell and yet had an abstract analytical view of the world, and she didn't mind the situation. Her marriage had certainly not worked out, and she was resigned to the fact that she'd made that mistake, and while she wasn't sure Chris Bailey was a perfect decision either, she felt the gamble was worth it.

This particular story was maybe worthy of his attention.

Mrs. Dunn was eighty years old and had taken on raising her six-year-old great-granddaughter, which was why Anna checked in once every two weeks, just to make sure it was going well. When little Dorothy was placed with social services because her mother died from a drug overdose, the older woman had petitioned for custody, and frankly, Anna had been dubious. But she still had a sharp mind and a nice house on a quiet street, and in her opinion, the child was better off with family if possible.

She did make regular visits just to make sure all was well.

It had been in one of those morning meetings that Helen had told her of her daughter's and son-in-law's deaths, and how the case had never been solved, even though it had been determined a double homicide. She'd taken in her granddaughter, who was also quite young at the time, and now she wanted to do her best for her great-granddaughter.

"I couldn't stop Lily with the drugs," she said with resignation, slowly stirring some sugar into her coffee. "It started when she was about sixteen, and I didn't realize it. By the time she was in college, I think it had slipped past her control. It was a shame because she was very bright, but the trauma from her parents' deaths left a mark. She dropped out after two years and went to work as a waitress and then became pregnant with Dorothy and did her best to stay clean, but once the baby was born, she just went right back to it. She never recovered from the murders. I dealt with it differently, but I haven't recovered either, to be truthful. They are gone and I can't change that, but no one was ever held accountable."

It was impossible to not recall the conversation she'd had once with Chris about how he wanted to specialize in cold cases. "If it doesn't upset you too much, what happened?"

The older woman looked away for a moment, removed her spectacles and wiped her eyes, but then she replaced them and her voice was steady. "They were tied up, left in the garage, and someone started their car and closed the door.

Rather awful, if you ask me, to know you were going to die that way. Whoever it was burglarized their house but didn't harm Lily, who was asleep, I can give them that, but it takes some Christian faith to forgive them for the rest of it."

That was certainly true in Anna's opinion. That was calculated and deliberate murder.

"Can you give me the date?"

"Of course, honey. If you think I don't have that etched in my memory, you'd be mistaken."

She left there and thought it over as she drove home. Then she called Chris on his cell. "Dinner? I'll make Italian. I have a favor to ask of you, and maybe you'll be interested."

"I'm interested in you and Italian food, so you are already ahead of the game."

"Murder is hardly a game."

"Okay . . . clarify?"

She knew she could get him drawn in. "I'll explain over tortellini."

"I believe we have a date then."

They were playing it by day-to-day. Sometimes she invited him and sometimes he invited her, but no schedule. Casual dating and memorable nights. Lovers, but with no hint of any commitment on the horizon from either side.

After a failed marriage, it suited her idea of romance. Great sex and some enjoyable companionship was the right dynamic. She'd had both with Trey, but the promise hadn't turned into permanence, and she wasn't interested in making that mistake again. In the case of her ex-husband, she'd also ended up disillusioned and was never sure exactly who was at fault.

Chris Bailey was a more straightforward proposition.

No promise of forever. She wasn't sure he ever would with her or anyone else. He was one focused man. The intensity was part of the fascination, but that must be her weakness, since Trey was a talented defense lawyer and he was fairly much the same way.

For all she knew, she was as well.

The truth was it seemed the relationship was working for both her and Chris, and that was all she cared about.

So she just left it.

"You maybe could help someone I like very much."

"I'm more than willing."

It wasn't hard to tell she'd stirred his interest.

"An unsolved case involving two murders."

"You're serious?"

"I am. Well, you certainly know I am since this involves a child's welfare."

"You don't have to say more than that to me. What time?"

"Six?"

"I'll see you then."

She stopped by the store and picked up the ingredients for the sauce and a salad and at some point realized it was sort of a bribe. She really wanted him to solve this unfortunate puzzle because Mrs. Dunn deserved closure. If she could give it to her through Detective Bailey, she wanted to do so. There was no question she was probably handing him an impossible task, but by his own admission, that was the kind of challenge he wanted.

He arrived close to the appointed time, bringing a nice bottle of chianti, dressed as usual with a casual denim theme and boots, his blond hair slightly disheveled since he tended to run his fingers through it when he was thinking, a habit she'd noticed.

She didn't mind running her fingers through it either, usually during a pleasurable activity he was quite intense about as well.

"Smells pretty fantastic in here. I hope you don't mind that I brought the moppet." He indicated his little dog. "She's home alone way too much."

"I don't mind at all," she replied truthfully. It was a sweet little creature and, unlike some small dogs, rarely barked. "You are both welcome anytime. Come on into the kitchen and I'll tell you the story while I finish the sauce."

* * *

Chris admired the blue-black sheen of her raven hair as she stirred the contents of the pan on the stove. Anna's beauty was understated, but to him it was compelling. She wasn't a bombshell, but she was certainly noticeable, and the symmetry of her features reminded him of classic paintings of refined ladies. Straight nose, long dark lashes he knew were real, and the sensual shape of her soft lips . . .

He was a fan.

She wasn't voluptuous exactly, but she had nice, firm breasts and some definite curves. There was no question they were compatible in bed, and on a personal basis they seemed to connect as well. If he could help her, he would.

The first time they'd met hadn't been congenial, but then again, her problem hadn't been with him, he'd discovered later, but more an unavoidable interaction with her ex-husband due to a case.

"Okay, talk to me."

"Open the wine, please. You are used to discussing things like this and I'm not."

"Fair enough. Glasses?"

She pointed at a cabinet. "If you'll pour, I'll fill you in on what I know."

He got out a glass for her. He'd brought beer, because he really didn't do any other alcohol than that except occasionally some of Lynchburg's finest, but that was rare. He was literally on the job all the time. He opened the bottle and poured her a glass, and he hadn't been exaggerating: whatever she was fixing smelled amazing.

Anna Hernandez had quite a few talents he admired. He passed on the glass of ruby liquid and cracked a beer and leaned against the counter.

She flashed him a smile of gratitude and took a sip. "If you want to solve cold cases, I believe I found one for you."

"I'm not exactly sitting at my desk twiddling my thumbs — whatever that might be, I've always wondered what the hell that meant — but, go ahead."

She considered him across the counter. "I have an elderly woman taking care of her great-granddaughter. Her daughter and son-in-law were murdered, ostensibly in a robbery, by being tied up and locked in their garage with a running car. It is unsolved twenty years later. She raised their daughter and now has taken on her child. I want her to have an answer. She is such a sweet lady."

It was an admirable attitude, but her good intentions weren't enough.

"That does constitute deliberate malicious murder. This county?"

"I don't know."

"I'll find out."

"I know you will. Why do you think I asked you?" She lifted those arched brows.

"Twenty years ago, I was in grade school, but Carter might have worked it."

He really might have. He'd been promoted young too. There were questions he could ask.

"Thank you."

"You don't have to thank me. Do you think if there's someone out there walking around thinking they got away with it that I don't want them to be caught and held accountable?"

"Nothing could be clearer — what I know more is that it's the last thing you'd want, and you would be just the man to catch up with them. That is why I felt free to ask you."

He gave an exasperated sigh. "It isn't a favor. It is what I do."

She gave him a gaze full of challenge. "And you are good at it. I know it isn't simple, but I can't believe something so heinous is unsolved."

"I agree. Your passion is always compelling."

"Oh, why do I think our subject has shifted?"

"Because we are about to have a delicious dinner and I don't always want to live in my world, or even yours. I want to have dinner with a beautiful woman and hope she invites me to give my opinion on the firmness of her mattress."

She laughed. "I believe you've tested it out already."

"I'm doing an in-depth study." He grinned.

"I'll be anxious to see all the charts and graphs."

"I promise a full report, ma'am." He watched her move efficiently between the stove and the counter, where she'd been chopping vegetables, enjoying the view and relaxing at least a little. The shooting victim really bothered him, but maybe now they had a thin lead if they could track down the elusive boyfriend, if he was even that.

All he knew was he did not envy Michael Reynolds this evening. Having to tell anyone of the death of a loved one was difficult, but the parents of a child who was murdered was about as rough as it got, especially if they were also your parents. In addition, if you had to visit the morgue and identify the body on the same afternoon and it was your sister — hell on earth.

He'd called the number that Reynolds had sent him, but there'd been no answer, so he'd left a message and as of yet had not received a response.

Tomorrow he and Carter were going to Nashville to search Amanda's apartment if they could get someone to let them in, which in a homicide investigation was usually not a problem. Her keys along with her identification had been taken presumably by the killer. Reynolds hadn't known if his parents had a spare set or not, but he said he'd ask.

Chris had to give him credit for shouldering the task. No one wanted law enforcement knocking on their door, so it was better coming from someone they knew, but from experience, breaking the news just wasn't a pleasant experience for either party.

At that moment his phone rang.

"Get it. I understand. No one probably calls you unless it is important." Anna was succinct.

He appreciated her attitude and pushed a button. "Detective Bailey."

"Um, this is Sandy Rolla. You need to talk to me?"

"I have a few questions, yes. Your friend Amanda Reynolds was seeing someone named John, and according to another friend of hers, you introduced them. Can I have his full name, please, and perhaps any other information on how to find him? Where he works or lives?"

"Can I ask why?"

He didn't answer questions, he asked them. "Yes, because on behalf of an ongoing investigation by the county sheriff's office, I need that information, please."

It took her a moment, but she got it that he wasn't going to give details. "John Newsome. He's a friend. I don't have his address, but I can give you the name of the company he works for and a phone number."

"I'd appreciate it."

He noted the information, and when the call ended, he glanced over to see Anna looking at him steadily, an introspective expression on her face. "I take it that's a call you were glad to receive."

"It may make my life easier, or it may not."

"You do realize you're a hunter and I am a gatherer."

"I skipped psychology classes, so feel free to elucidate."

She tilted her head, studying him from across the kitchen. "You try to annihilate the problem and I try to fix it."

"Annihilate is kind of a strong word. How about remove the problem?"

"Your last case, you killed the killer."

That was true and a matter of public record. "Can I point out she'd killed five people in cold blood, shot me twice, and shot my partner? I believe the consensus was she was a very dangerous person."

He wasn't happy about how it all had played out, but she'd started that deadly confrontation. A quiet arrest would have been better.

"I'm not arguing that at all. She was delusional, impulsive and a proven menace, and so it was clear self-defense.

Her own daughter was afraid of her. I was just stating our approach to problems is quite different."

"Good. Then we might have a dynamic that balances out."

"I suppose that's one way of looking at it." Anna lifted a brow.

His real issue with their tentative relationship was she was — to him anyway — clearly still involved emotionally with her ex-husband. Otherwise, she wouldn't care that he'd moved on, but she did, and she wasn't quite ready to let it go.

To a certain extent, he was ambiguous about it because Chris wasn't sure he wanted long term anyway. If everything went as planned, he'd be leaving for Quantico soon, so a short-term association with a passionate, intelligent woman he liked was fine with him.

He was taking that aspect of his life day-to-day right now.

"I always try for a clear view and succeed some of the time."

"I don't think you do too badly, from your track record."

"I'm hardly perfect either, as you pointed out."

"As a psychologist, I have to ask this. On an emotional level, does it bother you that you fatally shot someone — not morally because it shouldn't — but emotionally?"

"I don't think so. I never put her in that position; she put me there."

"From what I understand, that's true. I've never been unclear on that, but people react differently to volatile situations."

"She and I did not do well in that one."

"No."

"We are trained to act in a certain way if someone is firing a weapon in our direction."

"So you should be. It is a dangerous job."

"It was that particular evening." He didn't think he had an emotional problem with what had happened, but he'd rather not dwell on it either. Whether it was justified or not, killing another human being was something he'd rather put past him, so he changed the subject. "I see you have the plates and silverware set out. I'd be happy to set the table."

CHAPTER FIVE

It wasn't like the killer didn't feel some remorse. It crept in now and then in dark moments, uninvited and unwelcome like a drunken relative at the dinner table.

Ignored, it would just go away eventually.

He could put up with it in short bursts but not tolerate it for long. Then anger crept back in, as did a desire for evening a score in a game his opponents didn't even know they were playing.

The first round belonged to him.

* * *

The room was utterly silent.

Mick was clearly not sure what to say next either, so he contributed to that yawning lack of sound. He'd done his best to simply state the facts as he knew them. Samantha was surprised at how dispassionate he sounded when in truth she knew he was torn apart, but concentrating on being calm and collected seemed to help him. He was a sensible and considerate person, he always had been, and so she knew he was processing this, figuring out how to handle it the best way possible for the sake of his parents.

"I don't believe it." That was his father, his face tight when he finally spoke. "They have the wrong person."

"I had to go to the morgue to identify the body." He said it gently but with audible emotion. "It's her."

"It can't be."

"I didn't believe it either until I saw her. Plus, they wanted a positive identification." Mick steadied himself so his voice was completely without inflection.

His mother just looked paralyzed, staring at him.

Samantha fought tears. She was there to help, not weep all over the place and make it worse. It was just shocking and hard to absorb, and Alison had gone deathly white, which was hardly a surprise. It was hard to even imagine what it would be like to lose a child, especially to senseless violence.

Samantha went over and sat down next to her and took her hand. Very softly she said, "I'm in disbelief, too. This can't have happened."

"You're sure?" It was a weak whisper as Alison Reynolds looked at her son, her fingers tightening over Samantha's.

"Mom, I'm afraid so." Mick briefly shut his eyes. "I'm sorry."

"Who? Why?" His father demanded. "What are they doing?"

"I know they are looking. They found me, didn't they? I met the detectives investigating the case, and they seem to know what they're doing. I don't know if they'll ever deliver a why, but hopefully they will deliver *who* did this."

"I just want my daughter back." Alison rose, visibly trembling. "Excuse me."

She unsteadily left the room and Samantha wasn't sure she'd helped at all, but she'd tried anyway.

"I want to talk to them." His father was adamant.

"I have both their numbers written down for you." Mick had obviously expected that request, because he took out a slip of paper and handed it over. "Bailey and Carter. The medical examiner's number is also on there. I knew you'd want all of that."

"They should have contacted me first."

"They made the connection through me. They didn't know who you were until they talked to me."

The truth was both father and son were very alike. Determined men who didn't enjoy anything out of their control, and Samantha got that was how they operated.

A tragic car crash was bad enough, but an accident. Murder was different. Malicious and not a careless mistake.

"I'm going to go check on your mother." His father looked away but then back again, and it was poignant. "Mick, I'm with your mother: you're sure? I don't know what to say."

Samantha understood because she didn't quite comprehend it yet either.

"I wish I wasn't."

When his father left the room, Mick stood and came over. He reached for her hand and said quietly, "Let's go. Thanks."

Samantha murmured, "Thanks for what? I didn't do anything."

"There's nothing you can do. There's nothing I can do."

At least he recognized it.

"No. So forgive yourself for that."

"The thanks were for not making me do this alone. I believe that's the hardest thing I've ever had to do in this life."

She really couldn't imagine how it felt, even though she'd been right there.

He went on, and it seemed he was thinking aloud more than anything. "I could have let the police do it, but I don't know, I thought this was better. Maybe I was wrong. I'm not sure I'll ever get over it, but it had to happen some way. Surely it was better than having two strangers deliver the news."

But probably harder on him.

"I hope I never have to find out."

"I hope that for you, too."

They walked out to her car side by side, and he looked resigned and distant. Not that she could blame him. She felt the same. Disconnected from reality because most people did not know anyone who had been murdered.

She'd rather not belong to that elite group.

Disbelief was part of it. However, *why* was the most of it. That she couldn't get.

"Besides John, do you have any clue? because I don't."

He slid into the passenger seat and shook his head. "I don't. She was my sister, not my confidante. She would tell you things I'm sure she'd never tell me."

"I'm not convinced that's true. She never said much about John, if he is even significant."

"Someone else?"

"I don't know why she'd keep secrets from me *or* you."

"I'm curious myself. According to what I know, the police seem to think she knew whoever killed her. She was comfortable enough to get in their car and take off her coat. Why was she down here without saying a word to me or my parents?"

"Or me."

"Or you. That's something else I don't understand. I am at a loss all the way around."

It was dark now, and she knew he'd had an extremely difficult day. She pulled out on the road and headed toward her house. "You can agree or refuse, I won't be offended either way, but we both should eat something, so I could make some sandwiches if you'd like to stay for what will pass for a very casual dinner."

"Dinner? I don't have the slightest idea what to do next. That sounds reasonable, but the world doesn't even make sense to me at this point."

"I couldn't agree more."

* * *

It surprised Mick he was able to eat at all, but while his mind rejected the thought of the mundane business of consuming food on a day like this one, his body apparently thought it would be a good idea.

Samantha simply made grilled ham and cheese sand-wiches and put together a salad. They ate at her kitchen table, no frills, no small talk to fill in the gaps.

If he'd gone directly home, he probably wouldn't have eaten at all.

The look on his mother's face would haunt him forever.

"That was something I suspect I needed, so that was a good idea." He carried his plate to the sink and rinsed it, stowing it away in the dishwasher.

Just that simple act reminded him of their last year together in college before he graduated when she'd essentially moved into his apartment: the companionable evenings, the memo-rable nights, laughter and hurry in the mornings before going off to classes, sharing the shower, meeting friends for drinks at their favorite off campus bar . . . simpler days, certainly.

Were the circumstances different, he might have asked her if she was seeing someone seriously, and if the answer was no, whether or not she might want to have dinner with him again, but he didn't have the heart for it at the moment.

Romance was the last thing he was able to handle right now.

"Not exactly haute cuisine, but I don't think either of us is in the mood to enjoy that anyway." She looked pensive and reflective, resting her chin on her fist. "I should thank *you* for staying. I don't know if I would have even bothered with dinner. I'm really worried about your parents and keep thinking I should call Amanda to check on them. Obviously, I'm not taking this in very well in a rational way."

"It isn't a rational series of events."

"No."

"I'll check in on them, but I think they need some time to absorb this. I know I do." He just shook his head. "It will eventually sink in because I don't have a choice. I thought we should leave because I think they need to deal with this together as husband and wife. They don't need an audience, and if I were there, they'd worry about me, too. I just needed to tell them."

"Of course you did." Her gaze was sympathetic.

"There are things you never see coming. I count today among them."

"I agree. Do you want to stay the night?" She hastened to say, her cheeks taking on color, "Not that way, I just meant for company."

Maybe they weren't past it, either one of them, but this was certainly not how he wanted to rekindle that old flame.

Dryly, he said, "Oh I'd love to stay the night 'that way' sometime if you are ever interested again, but tonight is not the optimal choice. I think I'm going to go home and have a glass of bourbon like any boy from this great state would do, watch mindless television and fall asleep on that old, discarded couch. Maybe in the morning this will all just be the bad dream I mentioned."

Her smile was faint. "I hope so, too."

"Good night."

It was a ridiculous thing to say, but it was at least polite. This was hardly a good night.

He went out to his car and got in, wondering once again why Amanda, who was always such a thoughtful person, would come back home, where her family lived, and not say a word about it, especially to him, who had just moved back from another state. Her death, according to the police, was pinpointed to a very specific time because the body had been discovered so quickly by a passing motorist.

Why was she on a deserted county road at that time of night?

It did not make sense.

There was a reason out there; he just couldn't see it.

He'd think about it and maybe in the morning call one of the two detectives and explain how unusual he found that behavior.

Driving slowly along roads surrounded by leafless trees in the dark, he mulled it over, a thin wind whipping at the branches. The slant of secrecy — he couldn't come up with a better word — bothered him immensely.

What also bothered him was driving up to his house and seeing the lights on. He had not left them that way to his knowledge, but he'd been rattled enough by the visit from the detectives. They were on now.

What the hell?

There was exactly nothing to steal, so that part wasn't a concern, but maybe he had flipped on the lights and was so thrown about a trip to the morgue he didn't remember it. Of course, why would he? It had still been afternoon.

The front door was ajar, just an inch or so but enough to notice. Again, he wondered if he had left in such an abstracted state, he hadn't closed it completely. This house was new to him. He hadn't even spent a night there since it was virtually empty, so it was easy enough to see someone had been there in his absence.

He hadn't turned on the lights or left the door open.

The visitor had left him a gift on the kitchen counter.

The house was silent, so he assumed they were gone, but he stayed aware as he went to look.

Why?

He found his answer in his sister's driver's license, credit cards and auto insurance card, all in a neat pile sitting there on the counter. He went ice-cold after he registered what he was seeing and the implications, and he stepped back from the stack like it was a coiled-up venomous snake.

He went right back out to his car and got in and, despite it being nine o'clock, he called Detective Bailey, who didn't pick up, but he was able to leave a message. "I think I have something you might be interested in. Someone broke into my house and left me a definite message about my sister's death."

Then he called Samantha. "I think if the offer is still open, I'll take your couch."

CHAPTER SIX

Since he couldn't be a fly on the wall, the killer had to use his imagination.
How would he feel?
At least anger and helplessness.
That was the goal.

* * *

Chris was unaware of the message from Michael Reynolds until he got up restlessly at two in the morning and looked at his phone.

He would have called him back right then but reminded himself not everyone was wide awake at this particular hour and that the man had had one hell of a yesterday that still needed to be expounded upon.

So instead, he worked on the cold case Anna had handed to him.

He found it easily enough. It was pretty brutal. A couple of the last name Springer who had a young daughter. They were tied up and deliberately killed by someone leaving them in a garage with a running car, but the child was left sleeping and unharmed.

Not the way he'd want to go. Not violent but knowing what was coming wasn't pleasant. That was sadistic to his mind.

So he did just what he wanted to do for the FBI: he started digging for similar cases to see if he could come up with a match. He had access to databases that could match patterns.

He found one, in Kentucky. That made it cross-jurisdictional but close enough it could be the same perpetrators. Robbery, the same method of murder, and the children were left alone.

It was more recent, and they'd taken guns besides anything else of value according to the brother of the deceased husband.

Connecting the dots would be his pleasure if he managed it, because he really didn't like the nature of the crime. Yes, whoever it was left the children alive, but those unattended children had to wake to the horror of finding their deceased parents.

Had to be the same culprit — or culprits, because he thought it would probably take two of them to tie up both the husband and wife, but maybe not. Maybe one person could accomplish it if they threatened to kill the children and made the wife first tie up the husband and then took care of her, made them walk into the garage and, before they realized what was going to happen, got into one of their cars and started the engine.

Crimes like this were why he was involved in law enforcement.

In the morning — which it was technically by now, though hardly office hours — he'd call Nashville and talk to Agent Wright about the similarity of the crimes and find out if the FBI was aware of it being a pattern, since he couldn't really investigate the one in Kentucky. He could contact Kentucky himself, of course, but it depended on the department, how cooperative they were, and who handled the case. The FBI could usually get things done if there was any indication of serial murders.

He'd traveled this road before with cases across state lines, and the feds were invaluable help. They had resources his mostly rural county didn't have.

Anna had specifically brought this up, and he really saw her point. The woman she mentioned had lost her daughter and son-in-law, then her granddaughter, and was now caring for a child who would probably end up in foster care considering the woman's age. By the time the girl was eighteen, her great-grandmother would be ninety-two. If she lived that long.

Yes, he would pursue this as best he could.

He'd keep digging, and maybe he'd come up with a clue or an angle that had been missed. All thanks to a certain Ms. Hernandez, who was currently asleep in her bed, and that he wasn't there also spoke volumes about his problems with sleep. He should be still next to her under the sheets, her warmth improving the chill of this winter night.

Instead he contemplated the anatomy of murder in her tidy kitchen and wondered just how he was going to track them down.

If this was serial, he could find them, or at least he was fairly confident he could.

* * *

At midday she picked up her phone and made the call.

It was time.

Anna issued the invitation via a message and received a text several hours later of acceptance because the recipient was an assistant district attorney with a demanding schedule.

There was no question she missed her best friend and she knew Stephanie felt the same way, but it had been a tumultuous couple of months, or if she was honest about it, past few years.

For both of them.

Considering how long they'd known each other and all they'd been through together, it was time to patch things up as much as possible.

If it was possible.

What she didn't expect was how hesitant Stephanie appeared when she walked into the restaurant at five thirty that evening. She spotted her at the corner table, came over and sat down opposite. "Nice of you to ask me. It's good to see you."

That stilted response from a lawyer who could argue cases in front of grand juries and dealt with judges and even political figures was telling of how far they'd grown apart.

Friends since kindergarten. All through school together. College roommates. Maid of honor at her wedding . . .

This needed fixing.

"A drink together. We are both busy." Anna said it mildly. "I don't want us to grow more distant. My olive branch, as it were."

"Neither do I." Steph carefully shrugged out of her coat and set it aside on the next chair. "It will be nice to catch up."

"We probably should clear the air. I'll start. I'm aware of you and Trey."

That was abrupt, but Anna acknowledged she had a tendency to just say what was on her mind and Stephanie knew that well enough.

She really was. Too aware, but that was an ongoing problem and not necessarily Stephanie's fault. She completely blamed her ex-husband.

Quite the opposite to Anna, her lifelong friend tended to weigh her words, so she didn't respond at once. Finally, she said, "Never while you were married. He did nothing wrong. I can promise you that."

She believed it, to a certain extent. "He thought about it."

"I think you should give him credit, because if that is true, and neither you nor I know if it is, when it comes down to it, he didn't."

She was arguing with a lawyer, but Anna knew a lot about people. "Ethics aside, if he even considered it when we were married, then that counts."

"I would never have done that to you."

Anna agreed completely. "I know. The question is, did he know that and that's why nothing happened?"

Stephanie laughed without mirth. "This black-and-white world you have always lived in, please buy me an entrance ticket. You've always seen things through this clear lens, and I don't think the rest of us do. I deal with judges almost every day. They are called judges because they have to weigh in with an opinion. That means they personally think it over and make a decision dependent on what was presented, and what they think should happen next. I never know. This is a gray world."

"Are you in love with him?" That was about as black and white as it could get.

"Are you?" Steph shot that right back in challenge.

Anna very much wished she could say no unequivocally, but she couldn't.

At that inopportune moment, the waitress arrived to take their order, so neither question was answered.

She ordered a glass of Chablis.

Stephanie ordered a glass of sparkling water with lemon.

They knew each other very well. Normally she would also have a nice glass of wine, but instead she'd ordered water.

Why?

With a certain twist to her stomach, Anna wondered if she knew the answer without even having to ask, but she was, to a fault, upfront. "No alcohol for a specific reason?" She could ask even more directly the pressing question, but Stephanie might just deflect, so she just said it as a fact. "You're pregnant."

"I guess we really are clearing the air."

There was no way to analyze her reaction quite yet to that revelation. On a logical level, she shouldn't care one way or the other. Emotionally, it was different. The idea Trey and Stephanie might share a child did set her back, she had to admit it.

Stephanie correctly read her expression. "I'm so sorry if you aren't fine with this. Not sorry about the baby, but there has never been an intention to hurt you."

She meant it. Anna knew she did.

"I don't know what I am." That was truthful enough. "I suppose it would be foolish of me to assume he'd never have children with someone else."

"But you didn't expect it to be me."

"Actually, I think I did." This conversation had to happen sooner or later, so it was almost a relief. "The minute the two of you met, he just no longer belonged to me. You were with Daniel at the time, so he went ahead and married me anyway, but his heart just wasn't in it."

Stephanie's expression was very neutral when she responded. "I did not split with Daniel because of the slightest indication of interest on Trey's part, please believe me on that score. It had nothing to do with him. I split with Daniel because he is a self-centered ass with an inflated view of himself, and he failed to mention to me he never wanted to have children. You know this."

She did. And Trey definitely was a man who wanted a family, so in her opinion, Stephanie had struck gold there.

And was Anna still in love with him? Yes. A part of her always would be. But she had to weigh reality, and the truth was it was most certainly out of her hands and had been for some time. There was no point in being angry at either one of them and a waste of her inner energy.

She summoned a smile. "Your decision about Daniel was correct, and you knew at the time I agreed with you and I still do."

There was no doubt Stephanie was noticeable with her fall of blonde hair and striking dark-blue eyes, so men were drawn to her because she was beautiful, but she was also intelligent and most importantly, genuine. No deception, no artifice. She was a very decent person, and while Anna had lost Trey, there was no reason to also lose her.

It was important to Anna's own well-being to acknowledge their friendship was something she valued enough to make an effort to forgive and forget.

The waitress brought their drinks. She picked up hers gladly and watched Stephanie take a sip of water. She decided to take the high road as best she could. "Okay, that's done. When are you due?"

"We don't have to talk about it."

"I believe I just asked you."

Stephanie regarded her, and there was some clear wariness there. "Late June."

"So when we were all working together on the multiple murder case?"

"You'd been divorced for a while. Over a year."

"And you were interacting quite a bit together. Trey must have seized the day."

"Actually, no." Stephanie just shook her head. "Since we are being honest with each other, never once did he do anything to make me think he was interested in me that way. But we both agree he's attractive and intelligent, and as you well know, I really do want children."

Anna did know that. "And so getting together was *your* idea?"

"The alternatives didn't appeal to me."

It took a moment and several sips of wine to take that in, but at least they were talking. "I am sure there was no objection on his part."

"The three of us have interwoven lives for certain."

"I believe there are four of us now if we include your coming child. Maybe five, who knows."

"Five?"

"I believe you know Detective Bailey."

* * *

It wasn't better or worse than what she'd imagined, but getting this conversation behind her would be a relief.

Stephanie St. James still had to admit to some confusion. "Why is Chris Bailey included into the mix? That case was resolved."

"We're seeing each other, and I've asked him to look into a case I believe your office might have to be involved in if he comes up with anything."

Her brows went up. *They were seeing each other?* "I'm interested all the way around. What kind of case? Elaborate?"

"It's a cold case Chris is looking into, at my request. Murder and robbery that left a child orphaned. When she grew up, she had a little girl of her own but then sadly died of an overdose. That little girl is now in my care."

"That is a sad story. No suspect and no arrest?"

"Unfortunately, no. The great-grandmother wanted custody. She's far too old — I mean it should not be on the table — but we really do our best to keep children with family if we can. When she told me how her daughter and son-in-law had been murdered and she'd raised her granddaughter only to have her die from drug abuse, I wanted to help her find closure. I asked Chris if he might look into it. I'm passionate about this."

Anna was passionate about everything, as far as Stephanie could tell. "I agree anyone that resilient deserves justice. To have raised three generations? She must be remarkable."

"She is. Little Dorothy needs someone like her and has pretty much lived with her for her entire life, so we've left it that way with regular check-in visits."

"And Chris Bailey agreed to investigate? From what I know of him, he will be as serious about it as you are." She paused. "You're seeing him? Like on a personal basis?"

Anna just shrugged. "A very pleasant experience at this point, but it seems to me likely he's moving on to federal law enforcement, so I will be someone he looks at as backtracks in the snow."

"Well, it doesn't snow that much here in southern Tennessee. Tell me more about the case."

"Locked in a garage and killed by carbon monoxide poisoning."

Stephanie only dealt with cases that had criminal charges pending, so unless law enforcement brought them into her view, she had no idea. "Not under my microscope. When?"

"Years ago and no suspects."

"Okay, I guess that is why it doesn't register. Law enforcement has to bring it to me. Hmm, what does Bailey say?"

"He'll check it out, and I promised him your attention if he found anything."

"Did you? I'll be interested. A case that cold? He has time for it?"

"His sleep habits are eclectic."

She was sleeping with him? In shades of a time gone by when they really talked to each other, she would already know the answer. Stephanie asked, "You know this?"

Anna looked noncommittal. "I do."

"I see."

So she knew it firsthand. That was interesting, and Stephanie could see it. Chris Bailey was attractive, and he could handle Anna's upfront approach to life. "Good choice. First impression is a country boy, second is that he's razor-sharp, and Darlene would tell you he isn't hard on the eyes."

"Darlene?"

"She works for the sheriff's office in dispatch or something. We haven't met, but we talked on the phone that memorable night he and I spent together at his cabin when he played rescue when I was stranded. That is how she described him."

"He's never said anything to me really about it."

"He's a polite and decent individual in my experience from interacting with him, and you obviously have a pretty high opinion as well, so let's agree he wouldn't."

"Is decency required in this instance?"

"I've already assured you we slept in separate bedrooms. That is if he slept at all, and if you're right, maybe he didn't. I went to bed and to sleep when he was still awake. When I woke up, he was at the table drinking coffee, so how do I know?"

Anna looked more like the girl she remembered. Lighter, still the determined fighter, but like they were coming to some sort of peace, which was all Stephanie wanted and why she'd agreed to the meeting.

Anna toyed with the stem of her wine glass. "I guess you and I have quite a history, don't we?"

"I'd prefer we not forget it." Then she asked frankly, "Can you forgive that we are having a baby?"

"Trey and I didn't go there for a reason. He made a mistake, but so did I, and I guess we both knew it pretty soon." It wasn't a yes but an acknowledgment of sorts.

Stephanie would take that.

Not a real answer, but if it smoothed troubled waters, it worked.

She just nodded and drank water when she would most definitely have preferred something stronger for this conversation, but it had gone better than she expected.

CHAPTER SEVEN

It was as if the course of his actions had percolated like old coffee grounds in his grandmother's electric coffee pot, boiling up and then settling down, and the result was a toxic-tasting bitter brew — not the desired result.

The killer had tried therapy as he got older, the impulses needed to be addressed because he wasn't concerned for other people — only for himself.

It had helped somewhat, but there was no way he could be completely forthcoming. In retrospect it was a waste of his time and not worth it, but saying most of it out loud allowed it to sink deeper and wedge there.

At the time there had been no trigger to make him act. He'd been on hiatus.

Biding his time.

Things had changed.

* * *

Detective Carter wore a red tie over a white shirt and a nice dark suit. "You just bought this house, correct?"

Mick nodded. "Yes, and how many people in the course of showings and inspections and whatnot had access to it recently is a question I can't answer. Though it isn't helpful,

I'm not sure I even locked the door. As you know, I barely have any furniture in yet, and otherwise just a suitcase with my clothes. I wasn't worried about anyone taking my worldly goods."

Bailey sat back in his chosen recliner, his face contemplative. "Not staying here was a good decision." He was casual again in jeans and boots, his badge just pinned to his shirt. "Someone sent you a message. What we have to do is figure out why."

"No." Carter disagreed. "All we need is who."

That the two men operated differently was fairly evident, but as a team, maybe their opposite approach was effective.

"Since I have absolutely no idea who would want to kill my sister or why, I'm just bewildered, I guess. Is this directed at me in some way? I just moved back from Chicago, and I was there for six years. Before that I was at college for four years in undergrad, so not really here except holidays and the occasional weekend trip for the past ten years."

So why personally taunt him with that delivery, and how would they even know his address? His *very* new address.

"It stumps me what the intent might be. Do your parents have a feud with anyone that you know of?" Carter looked intent.

"My parents," he said carefully but with unconcealed bitterness, "are the nicest people in this world, and I can't even imagine someone who would get back at anyone by murdering their only daughter."

Bailey, who wasn't much older than him at a guess, murmured, "I wish I had your faith in the grace of humankind, but someone certainly did kill her, and we are going to find them. Any information you have will always be considered carefully. We will take everything and have it checked for prints in the lab, and see if we can come up with a lead. In the meantime, I would lock my doors."

"And maybe get a security camera," Detective Carter suggested. "You don't have any close neighbors. Even without what has happened, I would recommend that anyway."

After they left, he thought it over and decided that was probably not a bad idea. Maybe he would do just that if someone who obviously had a malicious agenda felt free to walk in, and on his part, he'd like to see them nailed to the wall. It would be satisfying to do that himself.

With real nails and a real wall.

There was no doubt that he was having an issue coping with his reaction to what had happened, and aside from the detectives, he did not want to tell anyone about the macabre delivery, especially his parents.

Except he had told Sam. Well, obliquely. Now he was worried about her. All he'd said was he thought someone had broken into his empty house. What if he was followed to hers? This was all so unsettling. Maybe he shouldn't have gone to her house and just chosen a motel instead. In retrospect, probably, but he was hardly at his best. The bad news, the detectives, the visit to the morgue and having to tell his parents . . .

That hadn't even occurred to him — usually he was more level-headed — but in his defense, it had hardly been a usual day.

So he called her at work. Without preamble, he just said, "Look, I think we should spend the night together."

"Do you?" There was a pause. "Since I recognize your voice, I didn't just hang up at that suggestion. Mick, what else could possibly be wrong?"

"I drove to your place last night and never thought about someone following me there. For some reason they are paying attention to me. I have no idea what is going on. Two detectives just left here yet again, and my impression is they don't know either. At least not yet."

"Um. What?"

"No, you don't understand. I'm thinking it over because I'm having a hard time thinking about anything else. What if I led them to you?"

"To me? Can you be clearer?"

"No. Nothing is clear." He was telling the truth there.

"I'm not objecting exactly, but I think there are some details you have left out, and I don't blame you considering everything, but will you fill me in over dinner at least? I promise I can do better than last night."

"I'll bring steaks or something like that. Don't worry about it . . . that I can do. When you walk to your car, be careful and aware, that's all I ask. Can someone go out with you?"

There was a pause. "You are scaring me."

"I hope so. My sister was killed and we have no idea why. I can't think of how it would have a single thing to do with me, but what if it does? Someone dropped me off a gift last night, and it had to be whoever killed her. It was the contents of her purse. The police just left."

Shocked silence.

He was stymied himself.

Finally, she said, "Oh God, you're serious? That's why you knew someone broke into your house? You didn't tell me that before."

"I was on overload. I just needed some sleep. Let me apologize for not thinking more clearly. It actually would not have occurred to me if the detectives hadn't asked me if someone might have a vendetta against my parents."

"Your parents are wonderful."

"I agree. But it raises the question, what if someone has one against me? They took the trouble to break into my house and leave me that disturbing delivery. And no, before you ask, I have no idea who it might be."

"One of the CPAs is about six foot-four and built like a solid brick wall. If it will make you feel better, I'll ask Jack to walk me to my car."

"Good." He was still trying to make any sense of this and was having absolutely no luck with it. "Call me when you are getting ready to leave and I'll meet you at the house. Right now, I need to go back home and see how my parents are doing."

Her voice was somber. "Not well, I imagine. I'm still in a state of complete disbelief. I'm going through the motions but not really able to concentrate."

There was no doubt he understood that. He had roughly a million things to do but not the ability to focus enough to do them at the moment.

"I'll see you later then."

He ended the call and realized he'd forgotten to shave that morning, then decided he didn't even care.

As reality set in, he thought today might even be tougher than yesterday, and that was a high bar.

* * *

The story of Amanda's murder had made the news. Samantha's mother had called her, and several clients had mentioned it. Her brother, James, stopped by the office to find out if it was true — concerned for her and, because he was friends with Mick, asking about the family.

James sat down in a chair by her desk, his expression reflecting her own unrest. "I heard and couldn't quite believe it. How are you holding up?"

"Sad. Shaken. Furious. Helpless. How's that for an answer. I was there when Mick told his parents. It was not an experience I'd care to repeat."

"I thought about calling him, but I have no idea what to say. What *do* you say in this sort of situation? A natural death is one thing, but this situation is not at all easy to deal with." Then he frowned. "You went with him? Is there something I don't know?"

It was a fair question. "He needed some information he thought I could maybe provide, and while I couldn't directly, hopefully I helped. I went along for moral support and to see if it might help Amanda's parents. He'd had to identify her body at the morgue. He was shaken and that is not Mick, so I offered."

Her brother agreed. "No, that's not Mick, but I can hardly blame him. If something like that happened to you, I would be off the rails."

They were decently close, but he was hardly verbal about his feelings very often, so she was touched. For James that was quite a declaration. "Same here if it happened to you. He slept on my couch last night, and I suspect he will again tonight. If you want to talk to him, that's where he'll be."

"Your couch? Why would he? I thought he just bought a house."

"Someone broke in and left him the contents of his murdered sister's purse." It still gave her a chill.

"Are you serious?"

"Unfortunately, yes. I don't have to be law enforcement to guess that was the killer. What would you do? I'm thinking he didn't feel safe, and his parents needed to be alone to process. We'd just been there together, so he called me because I knew what was going on, and he came back over to crash on the couch. Nothing romantic about it."

"I guess that makes sense if any of it does."

"Nothing makes sense to me right now."

"I meant he still has a thing for you anyway, so a natural choice."

She just looked at him.

"Samantha, he wanted you to follow him to Chicago. You didn't do it." James simply lifted his brows. "Instead, you stayed here and went into the financial world to make your own way."

Like that was her fault.

"That was quite a while ago, and he never asked me to go with him. He just left."

"He got one hell of a job, who could blame him for taking it? And as for the asking part, that isn't as easy as you think. The polite phrase 'no thank you' could have been your answer. Or it could just have been a flat-out no."

Her brother was a good-looking guy with the same russet hair and green eyes as her, and she'd never sensed in him any uncertainty. Growing up, the girls had always made comments to her about how attractive he was, so she was skeptical he got a no very often, but then again, he was also upfront.

"I'm not doubting you, but maybe Mick could have just talked to me."

"Or he could have been twenty-two years old, and you were even younger, and he just didn't know what to do, so he took the job."

Was she really getting this lecture? Six years later?

"Well, I didn't know what to do either. He was leaving and I still had to finish college."

"Now you can talk it over again. You're both older and wiser."

Was she wiser? She wasn't sure, she thought wryly. "It is hardly the time."

"Like hell." James kept a hard line.

"Has there been some sort of conversation no one has ever told me about?"

"Sam, I've known Mick as long as you've known Amanda. Even longer since we are a few years older. That this has happened . . . I'm trying to take it in. All I'm saying is he probably needs you right now, and I'm guessing you have already come to the conclusion you need him, too. Take note neither one of you has ever gotten seriously involved with anyone else."

It wasn't like she didn't agree, but mutual grief hardly seemed like a way to rekindle a long past romance.

When he left, she just sat there at her desk and thought it over. Her older brother was an engineer, not a psychologist, but he was an intelligent man and when he spoke, she usually listened to what he had to say.

In this case he could be right or dead wrong, but in the meantime, there was nothing remotely romantic about their situation.

Hopefully the Sandy connection had helped the investigators.

Amanda wouldn't conceal anything normally, so it was very out of character for her to be secretive about her private life.

Something was off. Why would someone deliver to Mick the contents of her purse after she was murdered? A Good Samaritan would have simply called the police or called him if they recognized the name. Or more likely would call her parents if they knew who she was, which obviously they did.

He also had just bought that house and they knew that as well.

As she sat and thought about it — instead of working like she should — maybe he was right. He was involved in some way.

How he was part of it did escape her, but she was not a detective.

CHAPTER EIGHT

It was clear there were loose ends that needed to be addressed.
    The killer was good at details.
    Which was very bad for his quarry.

* * *

They could have done it over the phone, but Chris drove to Nashville to see Special Agent Wright. That was fine with him. It gave him time to think, and they needed to touch base anyway about his application with the FBI.

He had his doubts about a final approval for the job even though there had been a tentative date set for when he would start.

He had fatally shot someone not all that long ago, and that was rare enough that he wondered if he would now be rejected, even though an offer had already been made. He'd been cleared by the state review board; an officer had been downed in the incident, and he'd been shot twice himself, so he'd returned fire.

The suspect had not survived to go to trial and be found guilty of murder, so the circumstances were all gray around the edges, although she had shot two police officers.

However, that didn't change the situation that he had now killed someone in an exchange of gunfire. It was a question they had asked during his official interview. Had he ever fired his gun during an apprehension? At the time, the answer had been no.

Now it was a resounding yes.

Wright would hopefully know the answer about whether the job offer still stood, plus he needed her help on the cold case.

Her office was a place he'd been before, and they knew each other well enough from a previous serial case that had crossed state lines. She was the one who had suggested he apply for an agent position in the first place.

She was at her desk and greeted him with a genuine smile and gestured at a chair. She was middle-aged and business-like, and he admired her poise and intellect.

"Sit down, Detective, and tell me why we are having this meeting. You've been quite busy since our last one."

He sat. "Not by choice."

"But we do this for some reason. Talk to me."

"I really want help from you for a cold case, but can we first discuss the fatal shooting . . . not to be flippant about it, but does that also kill my chances with the Bureau?"

"My opinion is no. It was cleared. Maybe increases them, but I don't get to make those decisions. You addressed the situation, and the suspect had killed multiple people and shot both you and your fellow officer. I can't see what you could have done differently."

He didn't either. "It was dark. I didn't specifically shoot to kill, but I certainly wanted to stop her."

"You accomplished that."

His smile was rueful. "Yeah. Let's talk about this cold case, then. The method is almost exactly the same. Can I get some help with the Kentucky connection? I called, and the detective that handled a similar one was gone and the detective who inherited it really wasn't interested in talking to me. My impression was he was on the busy side and didn't too much care about something that happened so many years ago. I'm small potatoes, but maybe you aren't. It's a copycat or a repeat offender. The MO is almost exactly the same. If the FBI asked, maybe it would fly. I'm interested for quite a few reasons."

And Anna had asked him, and while their relationship was mainly sexual at the moment and casual otherwise, they did like each other. She was on the intense side — there was no secret as to what she was thinking — and she was compassionate and insightful, both qualities that made her very good at her job.

To please her, to help an older woman find some inner peace, to heal a child, and for his own satisfaction, he wanted to solve the case.

"You care." Agent Wright looked at him with seriousness. "That's why you'll make a good agent. I'm pushing for it and trying to keep you in Tennessee, but I can make no promises. The process is the process. The shooting might make it take longer, as they do their own review before assignment. In the meantime, I'll talk to Kentucky and get you the information they have."

"Thanks."

"That recent homicide in your county, you are handling that, right?"

"Me and Carter, yes."

"If our office can help, let me know. That's one I want you to solve. That falls into the category of overkill."

"It gets worse. Someone broke into her brother's house and returned the contents of the victim's purse. He's wondering if the killing is aimed at him, and I can't say I disagree. No well-meaning person would handle it that way if they just found it. Set it on the front porch but don't leave it on the kitchen counter. I'm guessing the killer."

"I agree. This brother of the victim, he has no idea?"

"None, and I believe him. He just moved back from Chicago and, unless he's a very good actor, has no idea what's going on. He's the only reason we identified the victim. She'd been in the morgue for nearly a week while we worked on it and connected their DNA. She lived and worked here in Nashville."

"It sounds like you have two very interesting investigations going."

"Yes, and your help is always appreciated."

He drove back to Willamette, pondering the conversation and wishing for leaves on the trees again. Spring was on its way, since there was a haze of red starting to show, and there were a few crocuses poking up and blooming, spots of yellow and purple on the roadside.

If he had to guess, the fatal shooting of a murder suspect might affect his future plans in a negative way, but he wanted to stay in Tennessee and that had never been a given in federal law enforcement anyway.

There was a point when a man had to shrug and just accept that what happened with the shooting had happened, and so it went.

On the other hand, he couldn't accept that someone had shot a young woman five times and left her body on the side of the road, and it was still his job to do his best to make sure they were held accountable for the crime. Now that they had a lead, he and Carter were set to interview the man she'd been seeing. They had just tracked him down.

Sort of.

John Newsome had an interesting occupation.

He was a private investigator.

It opened an unexpected angle to this investigation. Could Amanda Reynold's murder be related to her boyfriend's occupation?

Chris had every confidence between him and his partner they'd figure out if he was a realistic suspect or not. And it was always possible he had an answer to that question. They had a name and knew where he worked.

While Chris was in Nashville, Carter was handling that aspect.

He called Carter once he was back at his desk.

"John Newsome was unavailable. So that lead didn't pan out. I'm on my way back to the office."

Carter was Carter and presented everything in a very prosaic way. Chris had to take a moment. "Can you give me a few more details?"

"I knocked politely on the door of his residence, but when he didn't answer I went around back and looked through the window. It looked like he'd departed in a hurry. There was a half-eaten sandwich on a plate on the counter. I called the firm he works for, and he hasn't reported in for over a week, and he's usually meticulous about it."

Chris put his palm to his forehead and rested his elbow on the desk. "So we may have a suspect or another victim."

"I'd say that's possible."

"I guess we need to ask the deep, dark question — what would spark this kind of reaction over two people just casually dating? As far as I can tell, that is all they had in common."

"There's more to it. We just don't have a grasp on it yet," Carter said.

"Sandy would be the place to start. I have her number thanks to Samantha Davidson. This person knew both Amanda and Newsome and introduced them. Were they dating, or involved in a professional manner?"

"Excellent question. I definitely think she might want to help us or stay aware, because so far *she's* all we know they have in common."

He had a point. "I'll contact Sandy Rolla again," Chris said somberly. "I never asked her why she introduced them, I just said I knew that was how they met and if she knew how we could get in touch with him."

* * *

Samantha lived on a quiet street across from a small park in a very nice older house, with a wide porch which in the summer would probably be a lovely place to sit and drink a cup of coffee in the morning or a cocktail in the evening, but Mick shivered in the February chill as he climbed the steps.

Or maybe it was just because his entire day had been bleak and cold.

His father had insisted on going to the morgue. It wasn't like he was surprised, but he could have lived without a repeat performance of that particular unwanted experience. He'd known his father would want to see for himself for finality, and so he'd offered to drive because it really was not pleasant, and he knew his father would be stalwart on the outside but devastated on the inside.

He carried the bag of groceries up the steps along with something else, and Samantha opened the door before he even had a chance to knock. "Come on in. As you can see, I made it home just fine. You brought a gun?"

"I doubted you had one. I thought you were supposed to call me before you left work."

"Since we left at the same time and he walked me out, my colleague followed me home and waited until I was safely in the house."

"I'm glad he was that thoughtful. Not that it is any of my business, but just a colleague?"

"Happily married with three children. A nice guy."

That answered his question, the one he should never have asked.

The night before, he hadn't paid too much attention, but her living room — which contained the couch he'd slept on — was warm and cozy, and she'd started a fire. The walls were painted an indigo color that contrasted with the bamboo floors, and there was a patterned rug, a walnut coffee table and a very nice landscape painting that looked like an original above the mantel.

She'd dabbled in art in both high school and college. He had to wonder if it was hers.

"I like your house. I doubt I commented last night," he said in an effort to be normal as he followed her into the kitchen.

"Thank you. You had a pretty reasonable excuse. I doubt anyone would argue it. I assumed you'd like a glass of wine again because today probably was not any better than yesterday. I know I do."

She did have two glasses and an open bottle of Cabernet set out on the polished counter.

The answer was easy enough. "I had to pay another visit to the morgue. Does that answer your question? I guess I just assumed you had a grill." He took the steaks out of the bag.

"I do. It's cold out though."

She looked amazing in jeans and a casual ivory blouse that was a contrast to her strikingly rich hair. He'd always thought the old masters would have loved to paint her. She had the right curves too, not too opulent but very noticeable. He could attest that she turned heads in a bikini, including his.

"I have a coat. The cold isn't a problem."

"Why did you have to go back to the morgue?"

"My dad."

"Okay, I can see that." She opened a drawer and got out a grilling fork and set it down. "He's that kind of man. I don't think for a minute he doubted you were telling the truth; I think he just didn't want to believe it."

He couldn't argue that point. "I know, but I had to go back. Trust me, I didn't want to do it a second time, but I didn't feel I could let him go alone."

Her expression softened. "I wouldn't want to either, but you did it for him."

"Well, he's my father."

"How's your mom?"

"I don't know. She hasn't really spoken. This afternoon she asked if I wanted a glass of tea. That's the extent of the conversation we had."

"She's in shock and denial."

"I get that big time."

"Did you tell them about your unwanted visitor?"

"No." He wasn't about to go there with his parents. "I told the police. They are going to try to lift prints. Who knows what might come of that. The wallet was leather, so they weren't sure they would be able to. Plus, it would only point at someone with a record if they were stupid enough to not wear gloves."

She splashed some wine into both glasses. "I can't imagine Amanda knowing anyone like that to the point she'd trust them enough to get into a car with them. I'm so . . . baffled." Then she added, "And angry."

"I know *I'm* struggling to make sense of any of this."

What an understatement. He honestly thought both his parents had aged ten years in the past twenty-four hours. The drive back home after the mortuary had been filled with utter silence, but Mick was at least glad he was the one driving because as capable and robust as his father had always been, he looked weary and pale, like an old man.

Arrangements had to be made, and that was just an unfortunate truth. Those decisions belonged to his parents. He was there to offer moral support as best he could.

What a damnable situation, he thought darkly.

He was there with Samantha just to stand in the breach if somehow his sister's murder was tied to him; he couldn't imagine how it would be, but until the detectives figured it out, he wasn't going to risk being the cause of harm to anyone else he loved. His father was perfectly capable of defending himself and his mother. Ray Reynolds was a backwoods farmer who also had served in the Army Reserves for twenty years. Mick had been taught how to fire a .22 rifle when he was ten years old.

It was cold on the deck as he grilled, the wind biting, but the steaks turned out nice and charred, and like a good southern girl, Samantha really knew how to fry potatoes, crispy and perfect.

It was a quiet evening, with disquiet inside, but that was hardly a surprise, and he was able to at least appreciate her company.

"This new company? Tell me about it," she asked, changing the subject.

She at least did sound interested.

"It's a marketing enterprise, and it is already flying to an extent I couldn't do both jobs, because they both took up so much time. It seemed a natural move. I'd much rather work from home and skip the tie and suit and those tedious board meetings."

"And here I thought that was what you wanted." She looked at him across her farm-style kitchen table where they sat, her green eyes serious, long lashes shadowing her cheeks. She had a dining room, but they had opted for cozy rather than formal.

"I believe while you and I communicated in certain ways, in others we didn't." His smile was wry. "I certainly wanted to succeed, but the corporate world isn't exactly my thing. I need trees and water, not concrete and skyscrapers."

"The lake didn't help? Michigan is *big* water."

"Not enough when you are spending all your time in an office or navigating traffic."

"Hmm, I can see that."

He admired the curve of her mouth, her lips tipping upward just enough to hint at a smile.

There was no doubt he remembered way too much about their previous relationship. The taste of her, the whispered words exchanged, and how she felt in his arms . . .

And this was not the time.

In his opinion, they were both not at all in the right place.

"I did it for quite a while," he said pragmatically, listening to the thin wind outside. "Not really for me, but I was determined enough to stick it out until I had a chance to escape. I'm not a city boy. I can wear a suit, but jeans probably suit me better. I do know the difference between decent bourbon and a really good one, but don't mix me a high-end martini in some fancy bar."

"I have a city job and country point of view.'" She sipped her wine. "I mostly handle farmers. They bring boxes of receipts and I don't say a word of criticism for their bookkeeping, I just sift through them and figure it all out. They are busy men who view the process from a different angle. They work daybreak to midnight and let us sort out the details of their business. They don't have the time. They aren't afraid to trust a woman with their money, and some of them make quite a lot of it. They let me handle that and go back to their fields."

He agreed, since he'd grown up here. "So it goes, only so many hours in the day. Farmers are the quiet warriors, the consistent gamblers when it comes to weather and commodities. It is a more dangerous job than almost any other, and no one realizes it. Dealing with a six-hundred-pound grumpy sow with a litter of piglets isn't easy, the weather is never in your corner, and you may not survive an overturned tractor. My father never complains, just does what needs to be done."

"I agree. He's a remarkable man."

He was a remarkably upset man at the moment, but then again, Mick was as well.

"It is understandable he didn't say much today, because what is there to say?"

"I'm working around that myself as well. I want to suggest something to you, but I don't know what the right words might be. How about you do not need to sleep on my couch?"

CHAPTER NINE

He wasn't home.

Dark house, bleak woods, deserted driveway.

The message had been received, but it wasn't like the killer didn't know where to look.

* * *

Sam wasn't exactly sure what she was doing, but it didn't matter; she was doing it anyway.

Open invitation to her bed.

It wasn't like they weren't lovers before.

It wasn't even that she wanted that specifically, but at this point she hardly wanted him to have to camp out on her couch because he was worried about her. The comfort of having him right next to her wouldn't hurt either.

He just looked at her speculatively. "You are going to have to cut me some slack here because I'm hardly at my best. Please realize I still firmly believe you are the most beautiful woman I have ever met, both inside and out. I can't reliably sleep next to you in the same bed without lascivious thoughts."

It was a nice compliment and tinged with humor that eased the tension because he was right: how could either one of them know how to act? "I do have a guest room, but I use it for an office and I have stuff piled on the bed. We can pretend we are like at a church camp in northern Wisconsin or something for a night, right?"

"You think so?" Unequivocal skepticism. "Your couch is fine. I'd like to believe I'm a gentleman in the old-fashioned interpretation of the word, but I don't know if you could count on it if I was in a comfortable bed with you. There's nothing wrong with my memory of what it was like to make love to you."

Make love. They certainly had been in love for quite some time. Those years in high school. Two years in college . . . there was a lot of history.

"I think we might have the same problem."

Her brother was right: she had never really moved on. She looked at him with his just-so fashionably wavy blond hair and those vivid eyes and felt the familiar thrill that she'd just not experienced with anyone else.

It was unsettling now that he was back. When he was far away and ostensibly enjoying his new life in the big city, she'd accepted it. Now, not so much. The reality was acute and startling with him sitting right in front of her and the discussion of the night ahead.

"I wish you hadn't just said that."

It was difficult because she knew they were both in need of comfort to the extent they'd suffered a loss, so falling into each other's arms seemed like a natural choice, but was it a wise one?

Probably not.

She didn't care. "So, sleep together rather than you guarding me from the couch?"

"Am I being propositioned?"

"I think you are the one that called me and said we had to spend the night together."

His mouth quirked in a rueful curve of his lips. "Once the words were out, I realized how it sounded but it was too late. I'd said them."

"And apparently I agree."

Open invitation.

"I really didn't mean it that way, but trust me, there's no objection here."

He really was so attractive, not just physically either. Michael Reynolds was an intelligent, compelling man, and the truth was she'd missed him. Once upon a time they'd loved and laughed together, growing from adolescents to adults, feeling their way as they made decisions, some good and some questionable.

Like now?

She didn't know. "This is just the worst timing ever."

He didn't dissemble. "There's no way I would argue that, but with the caveat that getting to see you again is the only positive in a very big negative."

It seemed possible they were thinking along the same lines.

So he wouldn't have called her otherwise? She'd wondered when she'd heard he was moving back if he would ever contact her, but she'd assumed they would cross paths through Amanda.

Not like this.

"I don't even know how to deal with it."

"I can't think about it." He stood and offered his hand. "If you meant it, maybe we can make each other forget for at least a while."

He hadn't kissed her in six long years.

But she remembered it only too well. His scent, the persuasive feel of his mouth against hers, and how he pulled her up against his body . . .

She was certainly willing to give that a try. As therapy, it was tempting.

* * *

Sex was a matter of silent physical communication, reliving memories he'd thought were never going to happen again.

He'd fantasized about it now and then in the dark hours when Mick really missed her, he had to admit that.

The reality was much better.

Smooth skin and sighs, and afterward, a close embrace. The pleasure was incredible, and he needed the intimacy.

"So, I know you. There's no one else in your life right now or you would never do this." He smoothed back her hair in the breathless aftermath, the first one to speak. Statement, not a question.

Samantha stirred against him. "No, you're right, I wouldn't. I assume there isn't someone back in Chicago pining away for you either."

"Nothing serious enough for that." He could have added *not since you*. Instead, he asked, "Would Amanda betray what I always thought were some serious principles?"

That startled her. He could feel her reaction because they were still so closely intertwined. "Cheat on a lover? Is that what you're thinking?"

"I don't know. To me it was clearly a crime of passion. Someone was angry with her."

"I don't think she would. Ever." She stared up at him, with the sheets tumbled around her shapely body. Her bedroom suited her personality in his opinion. A woven rug on the floor that picked up the faint pattern of delft blue in the wallpaper, a four-poster bed he was currently enjoying very much, all elegant in a renaissance style. It was definitely a very feminine room. "You know she wasn't like that. I could, of course, see her break up with someone if it wasn't working out, but she didn't say anything to me."

"What you might tell a close female friend might be different than what you'd tell your older brother, so I thought I'd ask."

"I have been trying to think of anything unusual that she said to me or that I noted as different about her."

His arms tightened around her. "I have the same problem. Like I should be doing something, but I don't know what it is, and even if I helped, it won't alter what has happened."

"Unfortunately, that is the truth." She rested her head on his bare shoulder, her lashes lowering.

Moments later, her breathing altered into the rhythm of sleep, a slow exhale and then a pattern he recognized and just listened to as she relaxed completely against him. He remembered their first time, in his bedroom on a sunny June afternoon, his mother gone on errands, his dad in the fields so they were alone, and how he'd finally persuaded her to go just a little bit further than they'd been before.

Was that really ten years ago? And here they were again.

The night was quiet, the wind low, and there were faint stars blanketing the sky. Pleasant physical contentment was a contrast to his mental unrest, but it helped to at least balance the equation, and he thought Samantha had offered her bed instead of the couch for the same reason.

Hopefully coupled with a true desire for his presence in this setting, but he was just glad to be there for a myriad of reasons.

Especially when he heard the sound of breaking glass.

It was faint, and if he'd been a little closer to drifting off, he would have missed it.

He slipped out of bed and yanked on his jeans because stark naked was exactly how to sleep with a beautiful woman but no way to confront an intruder.

As unromantic as it was, he had carried his weapon with him up to the bedroom. He was decent with a handgun, but he preferred his rifle, so he'd stayed a farm boy in that way despite the suit-and-tie job in the big city.

He picked up the gun and gently shook Samantha's shoulder. "I think someone is breaking in. Stay here, but if you hear anything alarming, call 911. Tell them to not shoot the bare-chested blond guy with the rifle, okay?"

"Mick." She sat up in sleepy alarm, sweeping back her disheveled hair. "Don't go down there."

"The entire reason I'm here is because I was afraid of something like this. Let me see what is going on."

Well, obviously not the entire reason.

He went quietly into the hall, and he'd been hunting enough with his dad that he knew how to move without giving his presence away, but of course his car was in the driveway, so anyone paying attention to his life — or to Samantha's — would realize he was spending the night.

This had to be linked to him somehow, thanks to the macabre delivery of his murdered sister's belongings to his home, unless it took coincidence to a new level, and this was a random break-in.

He very grimly doubted it.

Cautiously going down the dark stairs, he realized there was a light on in her nice kitchen when he remembered her turning everything off before they went upstairs.

He cocked the weapon, because this was clearly a problem and his visceral reaction was to solve it the old-fashioned way — shoot first and ask questions later — but he didn't hear or see anyone, so he eased up to the doorway to see the reflection from shattered glass on the floor and feel an eddy of cold air.

The real question was: where were they?

The answer proved to be gone.

But the visitor had left a gift again.

A shoe sitting amidst the broken window shards on the floor. It was stylish and had a heel, so obviously a woman's, but he didn't recognize it, so it meant nothing to him on first sight.

Except he knew it did carry some sort of message.

He didn't even care about the time. He sent Detective Bailey a text.

CHAPTER TEN

There was the man, and then there was the killer.

Separate entities.

That he couldn't resist bothered him. Self-control had gotten him through life so far and it should be almost an art form by now, but it seemed to be fading away like a memory he wanted to put behind him.

Some things he remembered just too well.

Those recollections tested his ability to pretend to be just the man.

* * *

They had a second victim.

Chris turned to Carter, who had arrived just a few minutes after him since he'd been in a meeting about another case when the call came in. "We suddenly have an active killer."

This time the body was dumped haphazardly in a ditch by a farm lane, much to the dismay of the elderly man who had discovered it when going by on his tractor to another field.

"Who would do this?" Theo Packer, the elderly farmer, demanded, his face gray from the unfriendly temperature and shock. "She's just a kid. It's February, but we're still a working farm. I check on my cattle every day, and I just found her lying there."

Judging from her clothing and the discarded backpack, Chris would judge a college student, early twenties or so, no coat, that backpack empty, and shot five times. He'd counted.

She had long, smooth, brown hair, a tattoo of a butterfly on her left arm and no make-up that he could tell, and she was dressed in gray sweatpants and a T-shirt with a figure from a cartoon on it. A little yellow bird. Woodstock from Peanuts standing on a doghouse.

Not exactly outdoor attire for February.

To an eighty-year-old man, she probably did seem like a kid.

"Who, sir, is exactly what we intend to find out. The coroner should be here soon. And though it doesn't seem to me the crime itself was committed here, a forensic technician will determine that for certain."

The old man shook his head. "I can't tell my wife about this. Not on our property."

It would probably make the news, but neither he nor Carter made that observation. A second murder that was so similar and close to the first one might force the sheriff — who did not like media statements — to acknowledge that there was a problem. He was, after all, in charge of public safety. It was extremely uncertain if the killer of the two young women was actually from his jurisdiction, but maybe the rural setting provided a place to dump the bodies.

Hills, trees, water and farms. Peaceful place, but bad people still did bad things, Chris thought with dark intro-spection. He knew Carter would just dismiss his desire to figure out why and go for the facts that gave them the ability to point a finger at who. "Have you seen a dark sedan around here you didn't recognize? With plates maybe from another county?"

It was the only clue they had.

"I don't know." Theo Packer rubbed his jaw. "I'll think on it and ask the neighbors. I'm not quite myself, son. There's a dead girl by my lane and two detectives talkin' to me. I got up this morning thinking about whether I wanted toast or an English muffin with my eggs, not anything like this happening."

It was easy to understand the disbelief. Chris didn't have it anymore, but then again, he'd chosen this job. "If you do remember or find someone that does, we'd appreciate a call."

"We'll be off your land as soon as possible and the coroner's office will take the body," Carter added.

Packer shook his head, still in evident disbelief. "The coroner? Son, I can tell you from where I stand right here that girl is gone from this earth."

"It is how we do this. I'm a law enforcement officer and cannot officially pronounce her dead. Only the coroner can."

"I see. I suppose that's why we have one." The words were said with glum resignation. "I've always asked myself why anyone would want the job."

The man in question arrived then in the official van, accompanied by a sheriff's deputy to escort the body to the medical examiner's office. There would be an autopsy since this was clearly a homicide.

Dr. Loren got out and walked over. "Didn't we just see each other, gentleman? At least it isn't the middle of the night."

"Doc." Bailey shook his hand, as did Carter.

"Let's see what we have here." He took his bag and climbed into the ditch to kneel beside the body, pulled on a pair of gloves and went to work. Chris never enjoyed anything about this process, so he walked down the lane looking around for anything unusual and not at all hopeful of finding anything. He only went a few feet before he saw a cigarette stub hung up in the weeds.

It looked like it had been very recently discarded. He turned around and walked back to ask an important question. "Do you smoke cigarettes, Mr. Packer?"

"No, son." He shook his head. "Quit that years ago. Bad habit."

Carter caught on and pulled a pair of gloves from his pocket. "Fresh?"

"Looks like it to me. Cold rain yesterday afternoon. It's been dropped since then."

"It might mean nothing. For all we know he stopped alongside the highway and picked up a stray butt and dropped it on purpose for deflection."

"Let's hope he isn't that smart." Chris watched as his partner picked it up and dropped it in an evidence bag.

"And doesn't know much about DNA if it is his." Carter was pragmatic. "That would be a nice break."

Chris looked over to where the coroner was working. "I hate to say this, but since the killer — and I can't imagine who else it would be — is targeting Michael Reynolds for some reason, maybe he should be our first visit with a picture of this victim. All her identification is gone, that backpack — which I assume belonged to her — is empty . . . if he knows who she is, we can make some progress in a connection."

Carter raised his brows. "Or the person who is doing this plans on tormenting this new victim's family in the same way."

"We need to find out her identity as soon as possible." It was stating the obvious.

"I agree. We can take a crime scene photo to Reynolds and see his reaction."

That response and the way it was phrased were interesting. "He's a suspect in your mind?"

"Everyone is, and keep in mind Reynolds moves back and this starts happening. It doesn't mean there's a connection, but there sure might be. We are taking his word that someone left his sister's wallet and ID in his house, and his story about the shoe."

"I don't know." Chris meant it. "I saw his face at the morgue."

"Good actors exist."

"I think we need to look at other angles."

"*All* angles."

"When have I ever disagreed with that?"

"You are more idealistic than I am and don't want to believe he'd murder his own sister. The block I've been around has a wider perimeter because I've been doing this a lot longer than you have."

It was true to the extent that he thought Michael Reynolds seemed truly stricken. "Do I believe he might have a role in this drama? That I don't discount. Is he the killer? I don't think so. I do think he is our ace in the hole, however, to maybe finding out who is. This victim is also missing one shoe. What the hell?"

"I've asked myself that every day since I started this job," Carter said with ingrained cynicism. "Every single one. Let's see if we can confirm his alibi."

* * *

The fact that Chris hadn't called didn't bother her. Anna was used to very independent and focused men, and she was like that as well. That she was still processing her conversation with Stephanie was distracting, though.

Was she jealous she and Trey were having a baby together? Maybe jealous was the wrong word.

Hard to say, but probably a yes.

The question was of what exactly. Her relationship with her ex-husband was over and her choice, not because she wanted it that way, but because she recognized a lost cause. There was no point in staying married to a man who wanted someone else. End of story.

Not quite. He'd apparently gotten his wish, and that was what she was envious of. While she understood life wasn't fair by any means — in her job she dealt with terribly unfair situations every day — she still wanted to get her wish too. But what was it that she wished for?

Was Chris Bailey the answer? He was complex and she seemed to gravitate toward that, and certainly the sexual part of their relationship was satisfying. However, there were some fundamental aspects they just hadn't discussed, mostly because he was leaving for a good four months of training with the FBI, not to mention there was no guarantee he'd be assigned to a field office in Tennessee.

If he even got the job. The shooting last fall, he'd mentioned in an offhand way, might nix his chances even though it had been ruled justified under the circumstances.

Obscure odds for any future for sure.

Not to mention she wasn't certain a permanent situation was what she wanted. Her first try hadn't worked out, so she was leery of a second.

To her surprise the subject of her thoughts walked into her office at that moment after a perfunctory rap on the door frame. "I need to spend the evening with an intelligent, attractive woman. You look very promising. Available?"

Chris looked . . . taut. It was in the set of his shoulders, and his smile was forced, she could tell.

"Bad day?"

"Let's say it wasn't perfect. Without going into detail, I had quality time with the coroner for the second time in the space of a few days."

"Oh. Lasagna or tacos? You need comfort food." Sometimes she turned into her mother.

"I'm thinking tacos. You do Mexican food like no other, but your choice. If you'll cook, I'll eat. I know I'm going to have a glass of bourbon to soothe my troubled mind."

She'd wondered if she was going to spend the evening alone or not. "My place, then. Bring the moppet."

"That sounds like a date to me." He lingered for a moment. "I found a lead for that cold case you told me about. Let's see if it amounts to anything."

"Thank you for looking into it. What kind of lead?"

"Anna, I said I would." He shrugged. "Let's see if anything solid enough for a new investigation comes of it. In the meantime, taco night sounds fantastic to me if you don't mind."

"I think it sounds fantastic as well. I like to cook, you know that."

"I'm on a learning curve." His smile was quixotic. "More information gathered the longer we know each other."

"By a detective? I'm doomed to have to behave myself."

"Oh no, don't do that." That smile morphed into a boyish grin. "Feel free to continue your decadent behavior, Ms. Hernandez. What time tonight?"

She still had a dozen things to do. "Seven too late for you?"

"Nope. Me and the moppet will be there."

He left, and it wasn't even a minute before Gina, one of the other social workers with an adjoining office, came in. "Damn, he's really cute. Spritz me with your perfume or something, will ya? I need those pheromones to attract someone like him."

Anna gave a muffled laugh. "Well, I offered to cook him dinner."

Gina rolled her eyes. "Oh, great. I can make meatloaf and that's about it, and it isn't good either. *I* can barely eat it. Cooking classes might help?"

"When a detective that investigates homicides has a bad day, I think you can safely say it's bad, so maybe tacos will help."

"I can only barely imagine his sort of bad day and I don't want to even try. Cheer him up this evening, and don't give me details that will depress me about my love life or lack thereof." She turned to leave.

"He has a lead in that case involving the surviving child placed with the great-grandmother."

That stopped her. Gina was always in the loop. Her eyes widened. "The orphaned girl of the drug addict with murdered parents that landed on you? Are you serious?"

"I hate to say this, but he's not only cute, he's also pretty amazing at his chosen profession."

"That case disturbed me so much."

Anna couldn't agree more. "I try to not get too emotionally involved, but it happens anyway. This case isn't easy."

Gina crossed her arms. "Like I haven't heard that before."

"I wish we hadn't."

"What's the lead?"

"I have no idea." Anna had to shake her head. "He's a man that asks questions but does not answer them. It seems to be a hard and fast rule."

"An enigma, then? Hmm, interesting." She quirked a brow. "Please tell me he has a brother who is single or even a cousin half as good-looking?"

It was hard not to laugh, but Gina was doing it on purpose. It made the job easier. Despite the sometimes grim day-to-day, she did appreciate her colleagues. The people who worked with her were caring individuals or they would not go through the grind. "A brother, yes, but no details. He might be a Franciscan monk for all I know. As for eligible cousins, I can ask, but as it has been established, I doubt he'll give up that information."

"A girl can dream, can't she? Keep me posted."

She departed, and Anna sat there contemplating the ironies in life. She wouldn't even know Chris Bailey if he hadn't been investigating a case involving a young man in her charge who had been left adrift by the murder of his family. Chris had been shot twice by the suspect before the fatal exchange of gunfire that ended in his favor. He still had some very vivid scars from the confrontation, so she was reminded every time they were intimate.

And her ex-husband and best friend were having a baby together.

She picked up her phone and called her mother. Sometimes you just needed to talk things over with someone who would truly listen.

CHAPTER ELEVEN

It was nice to have a reliable source.

Buy a girl dinner and a couple of drinks, coax information out of her, and if she's only moderately attractive, it is not hard to do.

"Detectives?" He was hardly feigning interest.

His date nodded. "They were asking about my friend Amanda. I'm so upset and shocked over this."

"I would think you would be." He was drinking a martini. Top shelf gin, because the killer really thought he deserved it. "What did they ask you?"

"About what she could be looking into that might require someone like John Newsome."

He was afraid of that. Pleasantly, he asked, "What did you say?"

* * *

It was disconcerting to have two detectives knock on her door.

Samantha opened it to an extended badge from one well-dressed man probably in his fifties and a much younger one with his pinned to a denim shirt. The older one did the introductions. "Ms. Davidson? I'm Detective Carter and this is Detective Bailey. We spoke on the phone. Can we ask you a few more questions?"

She recognized his voice, so she nodded and stepped back. "That's fine. Please come in."

It wasn't as if she had anything really to tell them that she knew of, but then again, if she could help, she would. She led the way to the living room, sat down in a chair and looked at them inquiringly.

"You were asleep when the window was broken in your home?"

That wasn't a question she was expecting. Of course, she wasn't expecting this visit at all.

"I was." It was impossible to not feel confused at why they would ask her. It was a bit personal to admit she and Mick had been in bed, but she was talking to two police officers, not her grandmother.

"So you didn't hear it happen?"

"No. Mick woke me and told me someone was breaking in. He said to call 911 if I heard anything, and though I wasn't all that happy about his decision to go downstairs, I could tell he was going no matter what. I waited and heard nothing until he came back up and told me what he'd found. By then I believe he'd contacted you."

The window had been replaced and the glass swept up, and she'd reconsidered her decision to not opt for a security system. This was a safe neighborhood, but maybe it wasn't a bad idea after all.

"I'm not asking because we want a play by play of your evening, but do you have a sense of how long it was before you fell asleep and he woke you up?"

They had just had passionate sex and her life was upside down, so it wasn't like her regular routine by any means. She had no idea.

The light dawned and she had to stare at them both in shocked realization of why that might be important. "You think it is possible *Mick* broke the window? Why?"

"We actually don't have to find out the reason, just who might have done it. We move on from there." The older one sounded disturbingly calm and reasonable. "Please consider this conversation from our point of view. Opportunity is crucial. We cannot read the minds of individuals, but we can discern who could possibly have been there at the scene of the crime and committed it."

She supposed that if anyone had opportunity, Mick qualified, but the idea of it was ludicrous, to her anyway. "I've known Michael Reynolds for a long time. He's a genuinely good, decent person. He and Amanda got along better than most siblings in my experience. He'd no doubt die to protect her from harm, so you need to look for someone else."

It was the young one who said very politely, "The insight is appreciated and noted, but could you answer the question, please?"

"I don't know exactly." It was unfortunately true. "He was definitely still there when I drifted off, but I didn't note the time."

They thanked her and left then, but she had the sinking feeling it was easy to see their line of contemplation. Mick moves back and suddenly all this happens and he's the common denominator. His sister is killed, his house invaded, her house vandalized while he's there . . .

She called him, not really sure what to say. "Hi."

Surely she could do better than that, so she added, "I was just wondering if you were okay."

"Not the best day of my life." He sounded tired and resigned. "I had to go with my dad again. My mom couldn't handle it."

To make arrangements now that Amanda's body had been released. She couldn't handle it either. "I don't blame your mother."

"I don't either. Not the greatest experience I've ever had, but it was better that my dad didn't have to go alone, because he would have."

She didn't disagree. Ray Reynolds would. "I get it. Should I cook and we take them some dinner?"

"I think my mother's excuse was she was making meat-loaf and mashed potatoes, so she'd just stay home."

That was understandable and heartbreaking. "I could make dinner for you, then, unless you are eating with them."

"Samantha, after last night, do you think I'd leave you alone?" He sounded disbelieving. "My father isn't entirely aware of everything, as he has enough to deal with, but I have told him maybe something is going on we don't completely understand and to be on his guard."

She didn't understand it either and kept her tone even. "Yes, two detectives came to visit me."

"I guess I'm not surprised. At least they are doing their jobs. Look, my furniture was just delivered, and I have no idea what to do with it. Apparently, your house is no safer. Dinner sounds great. Come here? You can tell me where to put the couch and coffee table. Maybe we can have a normal conversation, or at least give it a try."

"Okay, I'm willing to pretend normal. I don't think I have the address to your new house. I know it is outside of town." She almost said Amanda had mentioned it, but she stopped herself in time. Thinking of her in the past tense hadn't quite settled in. The sorrow was throat-tightening.

"I'll text it to you."

"I guess it is a date, then."

Not for a great reason, maybe, but then again, their renewed relationship was based on mutual loss at the moment.

And some memories of the past that weren't forgotten. The physical attraction certainly still existed, but they both had evolved into adults, and as life changed, so had they. Sex had been intense, no lighthearted teasing smiles included, but that could easily be the circumstances.

This might be a huge mistake for them both, but then again, as her brother pointed out, she hadn't really moved on either.

And the night before, they hadn't even discussed birth control. That was her fault for making it clear he was welcome in her bedroom, but he hadn't seemed concerned about it either. In her mind it was a shared responsibility. Maybe he assumed she took birth control, but as he'd pointed out, he knew she would never have slept with him if there was someone else in her life.

An unplanned pregnancy would be reckless behavior, but at least they were no longer in college or even worse, high school, and at that time they had been careful since they both knew they had future plans.

Not so much last night. No caution.

* * *

He wasn't sure which box the dishes might be packed in, but Mick managed to find it once he unearthed a blender he didn't he remember he had and some juice glasses with a plastic pitcher.

The plates were underneath in neat stacks, not packed by him but the moving company, and he found the silverware in the third box labeled KITCHEN.

Success.

No napkins, but he had paper towels.

He did have a dining-room table, six chairs around it, most of his living-room furniture and a new rug. The rest was in the garage in tall boxes, except that new bed.

Maybe he'd actually get to sleep in his house at some point.

So far that hadn't happened.

Samantha arrived with a casserole dish and a bottle of wine at six o'clock and greeted him with a soft hello. By then he'd been able to put toilet paper in the bathrooms and a rug on the kitchen floor. It had been worth the money to pay to have a cleaning crew come through and do all the dirty work, and though it was still unfinished, the place was clean, the walls were painted, the floors were polished, and it was starting to become livable.

The movers had carted his heavy desk upstairs to the loft, the one he had inherited when his grandfather passed away, so now he had at least part of an office and wasn't working remotely from his phone.

"I like this." She seemed to genuinely admire the interior. "And outside, it is gorgeous."

"I was looking for something quiet with a view."

"I think you found it."

Whatever she brought apparently needed to go into the oven and he had to admit he had no idea how to work it yet, but he did know how to open a bottle of wine, so he let her figure the oven out on her own while he went to work on the bottle. "You can give me lessons later."

"It just needs to heat up." She bent over to mess with the digital panel, and it was a very nice view of a shapely posterior in his humble opinion. Apparently she figured it out, for she made a sound of triumph and the display on the front lit up.

"I have yet to unearth wine glasses. I hope a plastic cup is okay. Unpacking isn't going according to plan."

"Of course it's fine. I can see why it isn't going along smoothly." Tonight, she wore a soft blue shirt and jeans, her silky hair falling over her shoulders.

He poured her a glass. "That's an understatement." He passed the plastic tumbler of wine to her. "Can you just tell me so we can get it out of the way: what did the detectives want?"

At least she didn't lie to him, for he got the expected answer. "I think to find out if you could be staging it all, the broken window and the shoe, and even finding Amanda's wallet and the contents of her purse in this house."

So he was a suspect in his own sister's murder?

Her beauty was indisputable, but Samantha was also intelligent, and she frowned before she went on. "At first I wondered why they were asking. Then I realized they might look into that because of the timing."

"Lucky me." His tone was level, but there was no levity in it.

"Why would someone do this to you?"

"If you think I haven't been trying to figure that out pretty much every waking second of the day, you'd be wrong. I'm more with Detective Bailey's point of view. If we figured out the why, it might lead us to the who."

"Hopefully they'll do their job and accomplish that."

He had the same wish, because the last thing he wanted was for them to waste their time looking at him while Amanda's killer walked free. On the other hand, they probably needed to consider anyone and everyone.

And yes, it was his word only that both events had happened the way they had.

"I moved back." He picked up his inelegant glass and took a drink. "I'm trying to think of anyone that might want to do this. I never imagined I had an enemy like that. This is some extraordinary vindictive retaliation if that is the motivation."

She'd thought about it, he could tell. "It does seem like someone is taunting you, and why escapes me."

"I have pointed that out to the police. I haven't lived here for a long time."

They were silent, just looking at each other.

After a minute, she said slowly and very quietly, "What about Shawn Whitman?"

"Whit?" That took him off guard.

"Yes."

He couldn't, or didn't, want to believe it, but maybe it had been there in the back of his mind. The kid he'd known since kindergarten and his friend for years? They'd played sports together in high school. Gone camping, even dated some of the same girls and laughed about it in congenial commiseration when it didn't work out.

It stopped him cold. After a moment he asked, "Why would you think so? And that is an intellectual question, not one that dismisses your hypothesis."

Samantha took her time to answer, sipping her wine thoughtfully, but her gaze was direct. "I've always wondered about him. I couldn't tell if he was just competitive with you or obsessed with you."

Shawn Whitman was a concentrated individual, or he had been back in the day. They hadn't really seen each other in quite a while but occasionally texted, communicated on social media, and certainly Shawn knew he was moving back.

He had to ask, weighing this point of view. There was no doubt he respected her opinion since they'd known each other so long. And so well. "Obsessed is an interesting choice of a word. What do you mean?"

"I'm not sure how to define it exactly. Like he just wasn't as good-looking as you and fell short of being as smart too, but that wasn't quite it either. He did everything you did — played the same sports, liked the same girls, even drove the same kind of car. He chose the same university and joined the same fraternity. Look back, Mick. When you decided that it was taking too much of your time and were better off without that kind of social commitment that being Greek required, he quit too."

"So we made some of the same decisions."

"I see it as you made the decision and he did the exact same thing but only because *you* chose that course." Those green eyes — he'd always and still found them so striking — gazed at him with evident conviction.

An interesting assessment, but he wasn't sure it was accurate. "It was a long time ago, and I can't see him ever hurting Amanda. He always had a thing for her as far as I could tell."

"Yes, and she shut him down because she agreed with me. What he had was a thing for *you*. She told me she believed he just wanted to sleep with your sister and that's why he was giving her the full court press."

He stared at her, disconcerted. "She never said anything like that to me."

Samantha simply shook her head. "It seems to me you're the one that pointed out there are things you would tell a friend and not say to your older brother, especially if it might be upsetting to him to hear it. That wasn't her."

No, that wasn't her, but he was very disturbed this conversation had ever occurred without his knowledge. Not that he needed to be included in their private discussions, but considering what had happened to Amanda, maybe someone should have said something to him.

"Do you really think he could be part of what has happened?"

Samantha nodded, her expression unhappy. "I'm sorry, but I do think it is possible. You might not have seen it, but I did. When we started dating, he hit on me almost immediately. I wasn't tempted or flattered because I sensed it had a lot more to do with you than me, even though I was only sixteen years old." Her smile was tremulous. "Besides, I liked you a lot more than I liked him. Intuition? I don't know."

"I guess I didn't know that either." He tried to keep the accusatory inflection from his voice. "Did it occur to you to tell me?"

That won him a reproving look. "To what purpose? I'm my own person and made it clear I wasn't interested. End of story. I handled it."

He didn't want to argue, it was the last thing he needed, but he had to point something out. "I believe I would have looked more closely at our friendship if I had known. He was well aware I was in love with you."

She looked at him with suddenly luminous eyes. "You do realize that is the first time you've ever told me that."

That did take him aback. "What?"

"That you ever felt that way. Even in college, even when you suggested we live together that last year before you graduated, you didn't say it."

He about dropped his glass, which wouldn't really have mattered since it was cheap plastic and all that would happen was an unfortunate spill on the recently cleaned floor. *Was she serious?* "Samantha."

"No." She shook her head. "I waited for it, but it never happened."

"Surely you *knew* how I felt."

"I hoped I knew."

"So I'm an idiot." Statement, not question.

Casting back, maybe she was right. He was too much like his father, who just did not believe in endearments or any display of affection, but just assumed you understood how he felt.

"No, you're the most intelligent man I know, but not wonderful at expressing yourself."

"My apologies. I don't think I realized I had that particular problem." He meant it. "All those times together, I really never said it directly to you?"

"Verbally? No." She amended her words. "Physically you did just fine."

I did love you. I don't think I ever stopped.

"Thanks," he said dryly, but he was really thinking about Shawn now, weighing the possibility, wondering if that always friendly competition had a veiled animosity behind it that stemmed all the way from childhood. "I guess I can't discount the possibility. If I'm a suspect, surely Whitman could be as well."

"He is in my mind, because there's clearly some malice involved in tormenting you with . . . I don't know what else you'd call them, but trophies from your sister's murder."

He took a moment to consider. "The problem is I can't really point a finger at him based on the flimsy facts that a long time ago he made moves on my sister and hit on my girlfriend and he's competitive and played the same sports."

Samantha didn't agree. "I think *I* could make a compelling argument that they should at least take a look at him."

"What if we are wrong? There goes a lifelong friendship."

"You don't look at it the way I do. I see there goes a lifelong, one-sided, obsessive, jealous relationship. Mick, remember when you got your SAT scores back? I was there for that conversation. He was relentless about finding out your score on that test compared to his and that you wanted to tell your parents before anyone else really pissed him off."

"Samantha, that proves absolutely nothing."

"You aren't looking at this through the same eyes as I am."

"I'm getting the message loud and clear you aren't his biggest fan."

She said flatly, "Neither was Amanda. I wonder if he knew that."

CHAPTER TWELVE

The beauty of it was there was no direct connection.

Of course, they'd look for it, but they would probably never find one.

A concerted effort would be made, and there would be absolutely nothing. Small county police officers would sniff around and give up. They were overworked as it stood. Tax dollars only went so far.

It was a canny strategy, and he had every confidence in his ability to pull it off.

* * *

Agent Wright had at least come through.

He had the case file from the cold Kentucky murders and was studying it at his kitchen table, making notes, when his cell rang. It was Carter, who had been in court testifying that afternoon. His partner didn't even bother with a greeting. "I may have a lead on the identity of our second roadside victim."

"I haven't been flagged by a missing person report." Chris had been checking frequently just hoping for a break.

"No, but Doreen apparently got a call this afternoon from a woman asking how to file one and how long the person had to be missing for us to start to look. You know that sometimes she's just plain worth her weight in gold. She explained how to do it and she wrote the number down as she talked to the caller. The woman said it was about her daughter, and the age sounded right."

"Are we going to wait until a report is filed, then?" Chris really didn't want to be the one to make that phone call. He'd done worse things in the course of being a law enforcement officer, but speaking to the family of a missing loved one was not at the top of his favorite list, especially when they had an unidentified victim. He'd done it recently in the Reynolds case and he didn't relish repeating the experience so soon.

"If they are worried enough to call, then hopefully they'll come into the office in the morning, and we can talk to them then."

"Sheriff Lawrence can talk to them if we think the report matches our victim. For their sake I hope it doesn't, but someone somewhere is wondering what happened to her." Chris certainly wondered about her. The lonely victims haunted his every waking moment, and he knew he shouldn't deal with it that way, but there it was.

"What we need is to connect the two of them *if* there is a connection. If they were both abducted, it could be anyone. No coats in February and each missing a shoe? He's taking one of their shoes off." Carter didn't give an inch.

"A signature."

"It seems like it to me. What it means is as muddy as a rising river after a hard rain. We have to catch them, not understand them."

On that pivotal point in every investigation, they always disagreed. "If we understood how the killer works, we might catch him quicker."

"You say him. In our last two homicide investigations the killers were women, which I agree is unusual, but it happens." Carter never thought along the lines of trying to understand the perpetrator.

True enough, but this was a very different case. "No, it's a male. It's cold-blooded and methodic, not to mention he can carry their bodies." Chris had a hard time seeing a woman managing it.

"I don't argue that with his last victim, but with the first one, he killed her right there."

"He's evolving. Like once you decide to take a leap off a diving board into a deep pool and discover you don't drown, there's more confidence in your ability to do it." Chris had been considering both cases. There were handwritten notes all over his table. "It is the same killer. You and I both know it. Five shots when one did the job, the shoe, the body left by the side of the road? You don't have to be us to figure that one out."

"If we can tie this latest victim to Reynolds—"

"I bet we can," he interrupted moodily. It was nagging at him. "But I don't know in what way. My impression is he's way too smart to try to pull our chain. He might be smart enough to get away with it, but why would he ever even try? I've checked into him and he's intelligent and successful — if for some reason we don't see he wanted to kill his sister, then I don't really believe he'd deliver to us her wallet and the other contents of her purse, much less her shoe in the way it happened according to him."

It was true. Why draw more attention to himself? Just let it be a mystery.

"Deflection?" Carter was never going to follow his point of view. He just didn't think it was necessary.

"Too obvious."

"It's hard to understand psychopaths. Why you try escapes me."

Chris didn't argue that point. "I doubt he is one, but that is true enough."

"I guess we'll see what to do next tomorrow. If they don't file a report, maybe this particular girl that prompted the call is alive and well, but we'll still have the same problem with a Jane Doe victim."

And finding out whom she might be.

Then pursuing whoever had done that to her.

Call ended, Chris just sat there, thinking it over.

"Are you always so abstracted anyone can just open the door and walk into your house?"

His mother's voice. The moppet started to bark happily, embracing his unexpected visitor. He glanced up. "I've been meaning to put up a sign that says 'Bad Guys are Welcome' so I don't have to hunt them down. They can just come to me."

"It might simplify your life." She was dressed in a demure but flattering soft gray dress, so she'd probably been to a church event. She was devout. He wasn't particularly, which won him disapproval. Philosophically he reminded himself that parents were probably never going to approve of you one hundred percent, so he needed to reconcile her disappointment over him not choosing to become a minister like his grandfather, with his own way of contributing to the good in the world by catching criminals.

She might — or might not — approve of Anna. Of her occupation, she would most certainly, but they both had very forthright personalities and that either made for a good combination of like-minded individuals or a possible clash. He knew for certain his strait-laced parent would not approve of them sleeping together, but thirty-one was beyond old enough to make that sort of decision all on his own. He rarely discussed his private life anyway.

"Not that I'm not happy to see you, but why the visit?" He stood, wishing he didn't have crime scene photos scattered across the surface of his table. They were grim even to someone who had to look at it as part of the job, so they'd developed a certain analytical detachment. He moved so he was between her and the not-so-pleasant display.

She was hardly a fool and caught on. "I just wanted to see you and I was in town. Let's go into the living room since I guess I don't want to see what you are so determined to keep me from seeing."

"Crime scene photos. And you're correct: you don't want to see them. After you." He gestured at the arched doorway.

"You really want me away from those photographs."

"Why have nightmares if you don't have to travel that road?"

At least she listened and followed his suggestion. She settled on the leather couch, her hair stylishly framing her face. "I can't argue that point." There was no doubt she looked like the wife of a bank president, blonde and trim, and apparently intent on something that made him cautious. His parents lived not exactly next door, but she liked the church in Willamette and made the trek anyway on occasion.

"So, how's Dad?" He called now and then, but they were both busy and their conversations usually revolved around golf or the world of finance, neither one of which he was particularly interested in. His father wasn't into the nuances of investigating crimes either, but he was supportive of a move to federal law enforcement. They talked but didn't necessarily understand each other all that well.

"He's fine. Looking forward to spring as we all are. I don't know why February seems to go on forever since it is the shortest month. I don't think you mentioned you were seeing someone."

Ah, so that's the purpose of the visit.

"Was I supposed to?" He said it mildly. "She's a social worker, and we met because of a case. She's been married before, so I doubted you'd approve of that."

"I'm not that judgmental." She actually looked offended. She was, in his opinion.

"You never liked my relationship with Sara," he pointed out.

"You were living with her but had no intention of ever marrying her. She finally understood that, and it's why she left you. It had nothing to do with me liking her or not liking her. I didn't approve of the arrangement."

He digested that, couldn't actually deny the logic, and finally sighed. "I liked her company, but maybe I didn't feel strongly enough for a deeper commitment. At least she left me the moppet, and I am fond of her."

His mother patted the dog's head because of course the animal had joined her on the couch, settling down and resting her head on her paws. "She is a sweet little thing." His mother looked at him very directly. "Do you think you're in love with this new woman in your life?"

Of course, at that critical moment, someone else came through his front door.

"Chris?"

Anna.

This evening just got better and better.

* * *

The kitchen table was scattered with paperwork and photos, and his laptop was open and the screen up, but Chris wasn't in sight. Anna deposited her bag of groceries on the counter and wondered why the moppet didn't rush in to greet her either.

"Hi." He came into the kitchen, and she would describe the expression on his face as disconcerted. He gave her a swift and very perfunctory smile. "My mother and I are in the living room if you'd care to join us."

His *mother?* That explained it. He really hadn't said much about his family, but Chris didn't often offer information. She'd learned that from the very first moment when she'd met him last fall. Over the holidays as they'd started to see each other more, she'd expected to maybe meet some of his family — she'd introduced him to *her* mother — but it hadn't happened on the other side.

"I'd like to meet her."

"Oh, I think she feels the same about you," he added in a low mutter. "That's a warning, by the way."

She just gave him an amused look and followed him into the living room. Her mother wasn't for the faint of heart either and he'd managed that just fine, so she wasn't all that worried about it.

Mrs. Bailey proved to be gracious and maybe on the inquisitive side, but she didn't ask anything Anna considered truly nosy, more just curious. She did ask if she went to church, which was personal, but that was easy enough to answer.

At that, Chris gave his maternal parent a very direct look.

Not having any idea where their relationship might be going, Anna answered readily enough. "I do." It was true.

A few minutes later Mrs. Bailey departed with an airy wave of her hand and her son walked out with her, so Anna went back into the kitchen to pull out the taco meat, shredded cheese and homemade salsa for dinner.

"Sorry about that religious question. If I had known she was stopping by, I'd have at least warned you," he said when he came back in.

"She was fine." Anna was learning her way around his kitchen, so she pulled out the one platter he owned.

"All I can say is she wouldn't care if you were Muslim, Greek Orthodox, Catholic, or Wiccan even probably. As long as you worshipped on a regular basis, she'd approve."

"Wiccan? Hmm? I might consider changing over."

He leaned against the counter and folded his arms. "You've put somewhat of a spell on me."

That was about as close as he'd ever said anything that indicated weight about their relationship. He wasn't the only one avoiding it either. She was just as culpable and maybe even more gun shy. Casual companion and interesting conversation to offset the evenings alone, sexy man in bed, distant detective during the day, she was fine with that.

Anything more, she wasn't sure, and he wasn't either as far as she could tell.

In the meantime, she'd make dinner and then thoroughly enjoy their evening.

Except that wasn't exactly destined to happen. Chris went to clear the table as she got out plates and napkins and he set aside his computer. As she neared the table, there were still a scattered set of pictures on it and she stopped cold, almost dropping the plates. "What is this?"

He turned around and quickly took the dishes from her shaking hands. "I'm sorry. I should have moved those first. They are crime evidence. I know they are disturbing."

Her mind was struggling to absorb the images. That wasn't in question. "Why . . . why do you have those? What happened?"

"Why do I have them? There was a shooting, and we are investigating it. Once again, I apologize. I would have put them away if my mother hadn't just suddenly arrived. Trust me, I did my best to make sure she didn't see them, and I would have done the same for you."

He had no idea. Anna said hollowly, "No. Let me see them again."

"What?" He was visibly startled, the plates balanced in his hands. "Why?"

She felt suddenly cold all over. "I think I know her. Let me make sure I'm not making a mistake."

"You know who she is?" He sounded disbelieving.

"I think I do."

"We don't have any identification for this victim." He turned at once into the detective, sharp and interested. "That would be incredibly helpful. If you're sure you want to, please look, but they aren't pleasant. Years of doing this now and it always bothers me."

"Well, I don't want to, but I think we just agreed I should." She appreciated the warning, but though the subject of the photo certainly didn't look the same as when she was alive, those features were familiar.

He silently set down the plates and then handed her the photos.

It didn't take long to understand why he'd warned her. The images were going to haunt her dreams and not in a good way. Pallid skin, closed eyes and graphic gunshot wounds.

It wasn't pleasant, but she was able to say definitely, "Oh God. Yes, I know who she is."

* * *

This was proving to be an evening Chris hadn't anticipated.

He certainly didn't expect to catch a break *this* way, but then again, Anna's pale face told him that was exactly what had just happened.

She looked *stricken*.

No one should ever have to look at scene pictures when it came to a homicide. They were a clear statement of man's inhumanity to man — or in this case, woman. He'd chosen to walk a path where it was necessary to face the brutal reality, and Anna Hernandez had chosen to nurture children and offer support to families in stressful situations. She didn't need this.

So he gently took the pictures and set them aside. Facedown.

"Go ahead. Who is she?"

"Her name is Natalie Fields. I placed her in foster care years ago. She did really well and last I knew was in community college." Her dark eyes were luminous with tears. "I can't believe this. She was such a troubled girl who really fought for a normal life, and I thought she had found it. By her own choice she'd stayed in touch with me."

He cared about all of that — he cared about justice for every victim — but information was what he needed. "We have a case I'm working very similar to this one. Anything else you can tell me might be helpful. It is usually quiet around here, so while we have our fair share of crime, not that many homicides. This county is struggling with a drug problem. Could that be a factor in her death?"

Anna was resilient by nature, he'd already discerned that. She composed herself and shook her head. "I don't know. At one time she really did have a problem. She was clean last I knew. When I say 'in touch,' she just dropped by my office now and then. She wanted to be a teacher."

"Can you give me her information? If I can find a link between the two cases, I might have a true lead."

"Given the circumstances, I think I can turn over her file. Her mother left the state after we removed Natalie for neglect and abuse. She was the one to get her own daughter hooked on meth. She was arrested multiple times, and Natalie was left on her own."

If that was who the victim truly was, who was the mother who called and talked to Doreen?

"Did she still live with her foster parents?"

"As far as I know. She struggled through high school but graduated and I would expect didn't have enough money to live on her own. They were very good to her."

So they might be concerned enough to try and figure out what to do if she suddenly went missing and considered her a daughter. When he got the records, he could find out.

"That might help. Now, can we try and set it all aside for the rest of the evening? You and I are very devoted to our jobs — I don't think that is in question — but we deserve some down time like anyone else. I want to forget the bad for a while and focus on taco night."

CHAPTER THIRTEEN

How interesting it was how life could go in a circle. The hero and the heroine could meet again, the perfect romance resume, except it wasn't perfect, now was it? He'd abandoned her, or had she just not been as devoted as he thought she was?

That he might be the key in bringing them back together was ironic in a completely macabre way.

He'd taken the first kill to a wayside stop on a remote county highway.

And kept a convenient bit of evidence.

* * *

Blue skies outside, morning frost giving way to a chilly sunny day, but he still felt gray within.

He was making progress on the house anyway and it took his mind off . . . everything, or at least deflected Mick's concentration from the bad to the good.

The living room was arranged nicely, and Samantha was largely responsible for suggestions on how to do it for the best flow and aesthetic effect, because let's face it, he was male and just wanted comfort above all else, so a woman's touch was welcome when it came to style. The couch was in a good spot for being able to see the fire and the flat screen television, plus look out those tall windows to the woods, with side tables near the two nice chairs he'd bought and a floor lamp for reading in a strategic corner by the built-in bookcases. It was cozy, whereas if he'd handled it alone, he doubted he would have achieved the same effect.

He'd taken her to work to drop her off and watched until she walked through the front door of the building where her firm had their offices, the subtle sway of her hips a reminder that they'd slept together again, this time in his new bed, which was certainly a memorable way to spend his first night in it.

Was taking up where they left off a good idea? He wasn't sure. In six years, people changed, and he wondered if they both just needed comfort and this was one way to find it, or if the old flame had just flared back to life because it had never died out.

It was an interesting question.

He'd wanted to come home, and maybe she was part of it — he was so off balance that he couldn't be sure.

He hoped that what was happening wasn't somehow because of him, whether or not it was his fault. He wanted to protect her and his parents and figure out who was doing this, but he really had no idea how to do that.

While he didn't doubt Sam's instincts about Shawn Whitman, it was not enough to make a law enforcement officer take him seriously, and he wasn't sure himself it was a viable theory that Shawn could possibly be responsible for Amanda's death.

Had it been summer and the windows open, he probably would have heard the car, it was so quiet there. As it was, the knock on the door made him start, and it was telling he hesitated to open it, something that would never have really occurred to him before recent events.

The outer door had a full-length glass panel in winter which was replaced with a screen insert for warmer weather. Right now, since it was February, at least there would be glass between him and whoever was knocking. He was seriously thinking about getting the locks professionally changed today.

Two men were standing there.

Were they welcome? He wasn't sure.

The good news was they were familiar and not a threat — at least in a physical way. He opened the door. "Detectives. Come on in."

"Thank you," Carter said. "We have just an inquiry or two, Mr. Reynolds."

He had a few of his own, so that was fine.

"Nice." That was Bailey, the young, blond one who looked like he should have ridden in on a horse and swung out of a saddle, his gun holstered at his hip, as he registered the changes in the foyer and living room. "The place is shaping up."

"Thanks," Mick agreed, looking around. "My furniture was scheduled for delivery yesterday and the movers had no idea my sister would be murdered, so they brought it all anyway. Neither did I, by the way."

No doubt about it, they caught the edge to his tone.

Carter wasn't interested in an assessment of the new furnishings. "I assume Ms. Davidson told you we talked to her. We actually are trying to make progress on your sister's case and wondered if you could help us with another homicide. Do you know a young woman named Natalie Fields?"

He didn't but thought it over to be sure. He'd moved away a decade ago. "No. The name doesn't register."

"Do you mind if we show you a picture? It isn't pleasant, but you've experienced that recently."

That was the grim truth, and they were right, the picture was *not* pleasant, but he didn't recognize her. Mick shook his head. "I don't know her."

"She was killed exactly the same way as your sister."

"I can see that." He looked at both of them. "Then find the bastard before he does it again."

"We are trying to do just that." Bailey's look was level. "There has to be a connection."

It sounded like both a promise and a warning. "If I could supply it, trust me, I would. I fully realize, mostly because of your visit to Samantha, that you are drawing some sort of parallel between my return to Tennessee and my sister's death. After someone brought me — maybe the shoe was intended for Samantha, I have no idea — those items linked to the murder, I'm wondering that too but have an advantage you don't." He stopped and then said tightly, "I *know* any involvement I might have is involuntary."

"We are just here because the two homicides are so similar." Detective Carter observed, his expression impassive. "If you knew the second victim, it might influence our investigation."

He hated to do this because the picture was very disturbing. "You might ask Samantha if she recognizes the name. I dropped her off at work a few hours ago and am going to pick her up at five this afternoon. I'm really reluctant to leave her alone since, if this is aimed at me somehow, she could be a target."

"Well, someone seems to be paying attention to either you or her."

Or her?

It wasn't like it hadn't crossed his mind. He said after a moment, "We were high school sweethearts, as the phrase goes. It lasted through college until I graduated. I left, and she stayed. That was six years ago."

"But here you are, barely back in town and spending your nights together." Bailey didn't look anything but thoughtful.

"I've asked her if there was someone else and she said no. I can promise you Samantha would never lie about something like that, if you are thinking of a jealous boyfriend."

"I admit killing your sister seems extreme as retaliation, but following the thought process of someone who chooses murder other than a rational course of action is a bit of a convoluted process."

"No." Mick shook his head decisively. "I hadn't even spoken to Samantha before you brought me the news about Amanda. I only got in touch with her because I wondered if she might know about who John would be since I didn't and still don't."

"We do." Bailey said it succinctly.

"And?"

"We'll be back in touch."

* * *

Samantha walked out of the building and saw Mick standing there by his car, hair ruffled by the breeze. His leather jacket and jeans gave the impression of laidback, but he wasn't. He straightened the minute he saw her and walked over, his expression unreadable, but the set of his shoulders spoke volumes.

"You are probably dressed too nice for the place I have in mind, but do you mind if I just take you out for dinner?"

The truth was she didn't mind at all.

"That's fine. Please tell me nothing else has happened."

"Yes, and I can't give details since I don't have any. We can talk about what little I know over a cheeseburger and a cold beer? How about the Lakes?"

It was iconic in the area and looked unprepossessing unless you were local and knew how good the food would be. The weathered exterior and rusting tin roof were deceptive.

When he opened her car door, she slid in and couldn't resist. "I think you took me there for prom."

He shrugged. "I was a poor high school kid and deny the food isn't good. You were overdressed then, too."

"Well, we seem to be revisiting history all the way around, so that's fine by me."

He drove them to the restaurant in silence, his expression remote. They parked in a lot filled mostly with pickups and SUV vehicles and went into the dimly lit interior to the sound of a country song playing from an old-time jukebox and the hum of dozens of conversations. Luckily there was an empty booth in one corner, and they chose that, as there was no such thing as a hostess at this particular establishment.

No need for menus. There was a chalkboard on the wall behind the bar that listed the special of the day and otherwise they pretty much limited the offerings to burgers and fries or onion rings.

Not fancy, but then again, he'd no doubt eaten at a lot of posh places in downtown Chicago. The food in this place was like coming home and probably just as good.

He was a farm boy from Tennessee at heart, and Samantha had to wonder if all along she'd known he'd be back.

And they could talk here, and no one would care enough to eavesdrop. Their waitress was an older lady who recognized him. "Mickey. Haven't seen you in a while."

"Beware, I've moved back. You'll be seeing me fairly often, I suspect." His smile was instant and made him look very much like that young man all those years ago.

Carla was as down to earth as they came, and her age was hard to determine because she dyed her hair jet black, and it was no secret she smoked cigarettes out in the parking lot on her breaks. But she was very good at her job and a friend to most of the patrons, who were regulars. The old farmers loved her, and they didn't even have to place an order. She did it for them when they walked through the door.

"Cheeseburger for you and a beer." She apparently remembered that about him too and looked pointedly at Samantha. "You'll want the patty melt, but coleslaw not fries, right? And white wine."

"Right," Sam confirmed with a slight smile. As she sauntered away, she leaned forward to whisper, "How does she remember?"

"I have no idea."

It was a nice feeling of normalcy to be in a safe environment where people were eating, talking, a burst of laughter now and then . . . especially after the past few days.

"I'm going to do to you what you did to me. Just tell me." Samantha was very direct. "I'm dreading whatever it is you have to say, so can we get it over with, please?"

"Bailey and Carter paid me another visit trying to connect a second murder to Amanda's death. Apparently, it happened in a very similar way, and they wanted to know if I knew the victim. I didn't. Her name was Natalie Fields. Does it ring a bell with you?"

She thought about it, but nothing registered. "No, I don't think so."

"Brunette, younger than us, though that's a guess, a tattoo on her arm?"

She stared at him. "You didn't have to go to the morgue again, did you?"

"No. They brought pictures. Unpleasant to say the least."

"You aren't catching much of a break." She meant it, inwardly horrified at the idea he had to go through that for the third time, though if she really looked at it, so did the detectives. None of it could be pleasant to anyone, but Amanda's death was immediate to him. At least for law enforcement it was a job, not the death of a family member.

"I think you might have to look at them too, so just a heads up."

That wasn't good news. "Why?"

"They asked if maybe the connection to me was because of you. Keep in mind they are trying to dissect this, and currently we are the only leads since Amanda is my sister and your close friend and both our houses have been visited. I think we are all they have right now."

"How could I—"

He interrupted. "They've met you, so they understand there's a chance a jealous ex-boyfriend might be out there. I'm wondering too. A lot of people thought we'd get married right out of college."

She was one of them. "Well, you never asked."

"I bought the ring."

His beer and her glass of wine arrived right then with a theatrical flourish from Carla, who gave them each a look with a worldly eye that said she understood there was some dissention. She left without a word.

Quite honestly, Samantha had no idea how to respond to that. It took a moment and a sip of wine, but she finally decided on: "I didn't know."

"I was twenty-two and you were twenty. Even looking back, I think we were too young. There was a lot of growing up to do for each of us. At least I was mature enough to not ask."

There was no reply to that.

Unfortunately, he added, "But I wanted to."

The way the light, artificial it might be, slanted off his features and enhanced the color of his vivid eyes reminded her way too much of how that high school crush had evolved into a love affair she had never gotten over, and it wasn't just his undeniably attractive physical appeal.

Since they were being straightforward, she told him, "I guess I wasn't as mature. I would have said yes."

Silence except for the jukebox playing in the background.

"There's no jealous ex-boyfriend." She had conviction in her voice when she broke it. "They need to look elsewhere."

"You're sure? I could see someone becoming obsessed with you."

"Or you."

"Shawn again?"

"Did you mention it?"

He just took a sip from his glass and then shook his head. "To Bailey and Carter? No. That is your theory."

Fair enough. It was. "Mind if *I* do?"

"Sam, you are always entitled to do whatever you wish to do. Every move you make, it's your call. I don't have a say either way."

She regarded him over the rim of her glass. "I know you feel that way and it isn't just words. I think that's why I fell in love with you in the first place. I know this sounds sappy, but you are a reasonable and nice guy. Not perfect, that doesn't exist, but—"

"Hey, you are ruining the moment if you go off on my multiple flaws." The interruption was accompanied by a wry grin. "I accept the compliment you ever fell in love with me in the first place."

And still was.

She didn't elaborate on that. It wasn't exactly news to her, but she was face to face with it now. There was a hesitation, but they needed to discuss it sometime, and now seemed appropriate since it was not in the heat of the moment. "Since we are talking about it, maybe I should point out I am not on birth control." She added, "I haven't been for six years."

That stopped his fingers smoothing the condensation on the side of his glass. He gave a slow exhale. "I don't suppose I'm thinking as clearly as I should be right now. I can honestly say that it didn't occur to me to even consider it one way or the other. I didn't assume you were but didn't assume you weren't either."

"It's just as much my responsibility, but I thought I would mention we haven't exactly been careful the past several nights."

He regarded her steadily. "We aren't in high school or in college now. How would you feel if it happened?"

"An unplanned pregnancy? I could handle it." *Especially if it was your child.* She didn't say it out loud. He was right: neither of them was in a normal state of mind currently.

"Unplanned I suppose is the operative word. Maybe we should stop by the drug store on the way home." He amended, "Unless you want me to go back to the couch."

"No." She said it softly. "I don't want that at all."

CHAPTER FOURTEEN

The first discovery had been a near miss, the second a sure thing and the third one seemed to be so far unnoticed. The killer watched the evening news and saw nothing.

It would come, they'd make the connection, and the waiting was more anticipation than anything else.

* * *

Dinner alone unless he counted the dog, who sat hopefully at his feet under the table in case he absently dropped something off his fork, which had been known to happen when he was on the computer. He was well aware he should sit down and enjoy his meal and not work through dinner, but when he was flying solo like this evening, he had a tendency to get distracted.

Now that he had the information on the Kentucky case, he'd made a tenuous connection to the cold-case murders in Tennessee.

The wives of the couples that were victims, while they had different maiden names, were first cousins.

That fell out of the realm of coincidence for him and might explain why the perpetrator or perpetrators of the crimes let the children live. As he sat and thought about it, the method of killing also said something. It was still murder, but they'd let the victims go quietly into an unconscious state, so there was no overt violence.

They knew the killer.

A family member? He would make that his first guess, except surely someone in the family would note the two cousins had met the same fate by the same method. Admittedly puzzled, he sat there and wondered. He could see easily why law enforcement hadn't immediately made the connection. Different states, different names, and years apart, but the family should have made some sort of noise over it.

He was sitting there pondering when his phone rang.

"I know I wasn't officially invited, but want some company?"

The response included some exasperation. "Anna, you are always welcome. The moppet was looking at me as if she was wondering where you were."

"Long day. Pizza?"

Considering his unappetizing dinner that he'd forgotten to eat had come out of a can, he was up for that. "Sounds great. I'll order it."

"No, I've already done that, and I'll bring it. Whether you said yes or no, that was my dinner plan."

When they hung up, he shook his head and told the dog as he pointed at his plate, "I wouldn't even give this to you, but there is pizza crust in your future."

She arrived with his favorite — sausage and green pepper with black olives — and he was surprised she had taken note of it without him saying anything, because the truth was he wasn't all that picky usually. Cooking wasn't his favorite pastime, so he appreciated anyone who wanted to take care of it for him.

He had other things on his mind.

They finished eating and were clearing the plates, his focus on the unusual case and the new information. "Why do you think, Ms. Psychologist, a family would not point out to law enforcement they'd had four members murdered the same way? Given, it was in separate states, but it's still unusual to me because the crimes are almost exactly the same and hardly usual."

She stopped and stared at him. "Is this the cold case?"

"Well, yes."

"You do realize you expect people to always follow your train of thought without any introduction of the subject at all?"

She looked really noticeable this evening in a steel gray cardigan over a scarlet blouse and dark slacks, the swing of her ebony hair framing her face. He reached out and touched her cheek, sliding his fingers down along the elegant line of her jaw. He dropped his hand and just looked at her. "I believe Carter has pointed that out to me more than once. Thoughts?"

"My thoughts are I'd like a second glass of red wine and to sit back down to hear whatever you've uncovered before I try to give an analytical opinion. I never thought I'd like to hear more about multiple murders, but tell me."

She'd brought a bottle of Chianti and refilled her glass and came back to the table, taking a seat and looking at him expectantly. He really did want her opinion, so he opened another beer, glad she was there. Whether he agreed with her assessment or not, somehow it helped to hear his musings out loud. He'd much rather follow his train of thought with an attractive woman on a snowy February evening — a front had blown in and wind was whistling outside under the eaves — over after-dinner drinks than with Carter or Lawrence in the sheriff's office.

He sat opposite and propped his elbows on the table. "Okay, here's what I've found so far. Two identical murders in two different states quite a few years apart, the children left undisturbed but both sets of parents killed in the same way, and the wives were first cousins." He paused because he really was puzzled and didn't enjoy the confusion. Chris spread his hands. "Granted, one case was in Kentucky and one was here in Tennessee, but how could the family not report the connection? They had to know. It's bizarre."

Anna looked reflective and took her time. "Maybe they know who it is." She added slowly, "No, maybe they *suspect* they know who it is. They just don't want to say it out loud. You know folks down here. Family is pretty important. I realize these are modern times, but these are still the hills and hollers. I deal with it every day. If you don't think I'm treated like an interloper, you'd be wrong. Oh, I was born here in this state so as native as anyone, but I'm foreign because of my heritage."

He didn't disagree. He'd lived his entire life recognizing that mentality. "All right, I'd kind of worked that out as well. Thanks for the affirmation. What you and I both think is the family just doesn't want law enforcement to pursue this."

"Except for there's a child hanging out in the breeze and an old woman with no answers and maybe not a lot of time to find them. She deserves closure."

It wasn't like he was inclined to give up. "I've come this far. It is definitely about a mother who lost her child, but to me it is also about justice. No one should walk away from a crime like that unscathed."

Anna's gaze was very direct. "You and I are on the same page."

"We are."

"So you'll pursue it?"

"Do you even have to ask?"

"No." Her smile was spontaneous, and he felt that flicker of appreciation for who she was and a sense of understanding that maybe had been missing in his previous relationships.

He found it intriguing.

"Can I talk to Mrs. Dunn?" he asked. "Not everyone wants to speak with the police."

Anna nodded. "We can go together. She knows me, and she's sharp as a tack, as my own grandmother would say. She's just really past the age to care for such a young child.

But I pushed to have it approved because it was so important to her and, quite frankly, she'll do her best, I know it."

"Just let me know when and if the creek don't rise, I'll be there."

Her mouth twitched. "You do that on purpose, the country boy thing."

"Sometimes." He grinned.

* * *

He was way too attractive, and her aversion to another involved relationship aside, Anna just felt it might be happening anyway.

Chris was more complex than he let on, which made him interesting from a psychological point of view. Her ex-husband, for instance, had absolutely no problem letting you know he was an intelligent man and would handle any situation with efficiency and obtain the result he wanted. Not overconfident, but confident because it was the truth.

Detective Bailey achieved the same goal but in an understated way. You knew it. He just didn't put it out there.

Anna regarded him over the table. "I suspect you do it to make people underestimate you."

"Does it work?" He simply looked unrepentant and took a drink from his beer bottle.

She couldn't help but laugh. "It might, I don't know. I think I know you a little better than most people."

"Speaking of which, stay the night?"

"I'd like to if I'm invited."

"Always. The moppet has informed me you are welcome at any time. She's a fan."

"Trey and Stephanie are having a baby." Why she felt the need to say that out loud to him, she didn't know, but she did.

He didn't say anything right away, but after a moment or two, his comment was: "I guess I can't say I'm surprised. Does it bother you?"

"It must or I wouldn't have said anything." She was trying to work it out and maybe just needed to talk to someone reasonable, and Chris was nothing if not level-headed. She played with the stem of her wine glass, wondering why she'd discuss this with her current lover, but had apparently made the decision he might have some insight that would help. "Why would I even care? It's over."

"At the risk of putting a romantic view to it that might cast a dim light on my masculinity, I believe in your mind you know that, but emotionally you haven't quite come to terms with it yet."

"I've had quite a bit of time to face that my ex-husband is in love with someone else."

"That doesn't mean you've quite accepted it yet."

It was a strange conversation to be having with the man you were sleeping with, but she reflected on that point. "I thought I had. This new development puts a different slant on the situation. On the one hand, I'm happy for them both because I know for a fact each of them wants a family. On the other, it is an affirmation that my ex-husband and best friend have an intimate relationship."

"I don't think you have to be a detective to have figured that one out, Anna." His tone was dry, but his eyes held a certain guarded empathy. "I have no desire to know what Sara is doing with her life. Our complete distance is my greatest safeguard against any regret I might have at not trying harder to make her happy, but I do feel a resignation over it being for the best."

"But if you found out she was pregnant with another man's child?"

"I don't know. That's my point. Ignorance is my friend. Then I don't have to find out how I'd feel about it. You don't have that luxury being such good friends with Stephanie."

He was right, of course. Anna knew he was a straight shooter — in more ways than one, she thought ironically — he saw things with an analytical assessment and was able to sieve out the facts.

"I don't like that her concern over my possible unhappiness affects her desire to talk to me about it, but it *is* awkward."

"My opinion is that hanging on to your friendship with Ms. St. James is worth the effort to get past their romantic interest in each other. I like her. For that matter, I like Trey Austin as well. Relationships are just plain difficult. Carter and I have a love–hate thing going on, trust me. We are nothing alike, but we have to make it work, and a bumpy road has been smoothed so it is passable with some effort from both of us."

It was probably the most in-depth conversation they'd ever had, and despite the topic, she was enjoying it. "I don't know him well, but you are different, that's evident enough."

Chris grimaced. "Yeah, he's the respectable guy in the suit and I look like an extra in a Wild West movie. He never does anything impulsive and I'm guilty of that all the time."

"As I recall it, he got shot too, last fall."

"I got shot because I was talking to a district attorney aka Stephanie on the phone in my backyard and not anticipating it, even though I knew there was someone out there killing people. He got shot because he was trying to be polite and reasonable face to face to someone who was neither polite nor reasonable. I apparently took a less restrained position and, in the course of events, shot her. My point is made, right?"

"It is. I agree he's nothing like you, but I suspect he's also a very good police officer."

"That is not in dispute, and thanks for the also."

"Look at the cold case already. How did you do that so quickly?"

"Um, let's see?" His eyes were direct. "*You* brought it to my attention. If you think we look for things to do, you'd be mistaken. Most of the time, we're buried. If this case gets solved, you can pat yourself on the back. I'm not promising anything, but I am interested in talking to Mrs. Dunn."

"I think she'll be interested in talking to you too, because I believe she's disillusioned with the lack of progress in her daughter's case."

"I am, too." He looked contemplative. "Intuition tells me she just might know something she doesn't realize she knows."

"And you ask the right questions. Why do you think I wanted you?" She collected their plates and went into the kitchen, and he followed her, arms circling her waist as she rinsed the dishes.

His mouth was warm and teasing against her neck. "Leave it. If you really do want me, here I am."

The sex was great — there was no denying he was damn good at it, and she needed that closeness right now. She turned in his embrace. "The dishes can wait."

"They can."

His mouth found hers and at that moment, his phone rang.

Of course it did.

She said against his lips, "Go ahead. Get it."

CHAPTER FIFTEEN

The killer considered reporting the body in an anonymous call.
Really?
Were the police so inept or the public so unaware?
Maybe the fault lay with the location. Yes, a roadside, but not one well visited, and there was no doubt the victim was really not high profile.
Which had been the main intent all long.
Maybe it was a bad idea, and it would be better to just wait it out.

* * *

The shoe was there on the porch.

He stopped dead, one foot on the top step. It had been set right by the front door, and it had to have been put there between the time he'd driven Samantha to work and the time he returned.

Mick's first thought was she could attest it hadn't been there when they left.

His second thought was that she couldn't swear he didn't have it all along and put it there on his arrival back home.

"Dammit," he muttered, furious and conflicted as to what to do next. It was not a match for the one tossed through Sam's broken window, which the police had confirmed belonged to his sister. He'd had all the locks changed, and it didn't appear anyone had broken in. It really was not a crime to leave a shoe on someone's porch — other than trespassing, he supposed. Why did he have the distinct and disturbing feeling that this shoe was related to a crime in some way and, though he wanted to deny it, another message from the killer? Though he just wasn't sure what that message might be. A call to Detectives Bailey and Carter would not make his already disordered life any better.

If it was evidence in some way, how could he *not* call? Someone had deliberately killed his sister.

Still . . . fuck.

There was no doubt in his mind someone was taunting him and, as infuriating as it might be, making him someone of interest to the police.

He texted Bailey, who was just plain closer in age and less formal than his partner, so it was more comfortable to be able to send a message in the tone of his current mood and reaction.

Another shoe. This time left on my front porch. What the hell is going on?

He got an immediate text back. *Don't touch it.*

I haven't and I won't.

He took that advice and went around to the back door and dug out his new keys. The snow had melted overnight as the weather adjusted back to more moderate temperatures, and the sun had peeked out from behind the clouds.

Mick still entered cautiously. The house was new to him, and for all he knew, despite the inspection and now the brand-new locks, there was a way he was unaware of to get in.

Quiet.

He'd take that.

For one thing, he needed to work, and now that he had access to wireless other than on his phone, he could actually contact the staff he'd hired for the company, not to mention be available for his clients.

There was still furniture in various rooms placed haphazardly, boxes piled around, and he needed to check in with his parents.

And now this added a dimension he didn't quite understand.

Someone was paying unwanted calls he could live without.

What it meant was unclear.

Neither of his parents answered the phone. That did not make him happy at all, but he left a message rather than just getting in his car and going to the farm, because he was fairly sure he was going to have company soon.

Sure enough, a car rolled up about an hour after his text — he saw it from the front window in the loft where he was still setting up his office, putting away essential things he needed day-to-day so they were handy and stacking boxes that could wait. There was no question his life was on hold.

He went downstairs and shrugged into his coat, then went around from the back in time to see them putting the shoe into an evidence bag. "So that means something to you," he said by way of greeting.

The older one, Carter, replied, "Thank you for notifying us. If you wouldn't mind, we'd like to look around and then might have a few questions."

It sounded less than wonderful, but he was resigned to it, and if he could help — though he had no idea how he could — he would. "I thought about not calling. Sam gave me some insight to the conversation you had with her. I can't imagine killing anyone, much less my own sister. I didn't even know that other poor girl."

"When we begin an investigation, everyone is a suspect." Carter was unapologetic.

It made sense, Mick supposed, but still. "I saw that shoe and, given the other unwelcome delivery, figured it was the same person, so I used the back door. It wasn't there, for the record, when I took Samantha to work this morning, so it happened during the time it took me to drive into town and drop her off and then drive back."

"Did you notice any cars near the entrance to your driveway or parked anywhere where they could see you leave?"

He shook his head. "I can't say I did, but then again, I wasn't looking for anyone either. Just come in when you are ready and ask away."

Bailey, his collar up against the chill, nodded. "Will do."

Mick could count on it. That didn't need to be said. They were going to question him, and he didn't even blame them, but the problem was he had no explanation.

He needed another cup of coffee, to try to call his parents again or get in his car and go over there if they didn't answer, to schedule a remote meeting with his staff, to do about a dozen other things with the house . . .

About fifteen minutes later with a perfunctory knock, they both came in, tracking a little mud from the melting snow which told him they'd walked around the house, and when they apologized, he just shook his head. "A welcome mat is the least of my problems at this moment, so I haven't gotten around to that yet."

Bailey seemed bland. "I don't have one either, so no judgment here."

"That was a different type of shoe than the one left at Samantha's house that belonged to Amanda. I have no idea what is going on."

To his surprise, Carter actually answered the question he knew better than to ask since they didn't seem to be inclined to give out information. "Second victim's."

"I was afraid of that." He took in a steadying breath. "I'm getting surveillance cameras. I shouldn't need them here in the country without any close neighbors, but apparently I do."

Bailey leaned on the kitchen counter, his expression thoughtful. "Why you? That's the real question. We know you are asking it as well."

They were also asking themselves if he was playing them, deflecting the investigation by pretending to be a victim. Fair enough, he'd be suspicious too.

Should he mention Shawn and Samantha's perception of him? Mick wasn't sure he should because he knew these two men would look into it. They'd pay attention, and he just wasn't positive he saw things in the same light. Maybe she had some valid points, but then again, it was just possible she simply didn't like Shawn Whitman.

Reluctantly, he said, "Samantha has a theory I am not sure has any validity, and there's no proof at all except her opinion that this person is capable of resentment toward me."

"Enough to murder people and try to taunt you over it?" Bailey sounded predictably interested, but also there was an edge of skepticism.

"She thinks so. If it is possible, I never really saw it and I've known him for years. We're friends. He knew my sister and she definitely shot him down when it came to a relationship — but that was years ago."

* * *

Motive.

Interesting. Maybe even double motive.

Chris always looked for it, and Carter always discounted it.

"Would your sister have gotten voluntarily into a car with him?" That was Carter, focused on opportunity.

Reynolds thought about it. "I don't know she'd have any reason to distrust him. According to Sam, she just thought his interest in her was motivated by something other than true attraction and so Amanda declined a relationship. I can't imagine why she'd travel from Nashville to here with him for any reason."

"So no, you don't think so?"

Mick Reynolds just raked his hand through his hair. "I think if there was a good enough reason, she wouldn't necessarily be afraid of it. I just can't imagine what the reason would be. Please be aware since my sister and Samantha were very close friends, apparently there were discussions I was unaware of about this individual."

"Can we have his name?"

Unless he might be a really good actor as Carter had pointed out, he was obviously reluctant to give it. "It's probably a waste of your time."

"It's called a lead," Chris prompted him. "We follow them all the time and sometimes they take us where we need to go, and sometimes it is a dead end. Don't worry, we aren't going to point a finger in your direction. We don't disclose much, as you may have noticed. We are investigating the murder of someone he knows, and I assume he lives here, or Ms. Davidson wouldn't think of him."

"His father owns an insurance agency in Willamette. He's an agent there. I think he manages it last I heard."

The Roadside Killer, newly christened by the local media with that name, might be an insurance agent? That was quite a spin on things. Reynolds correctly read his expression, because he said, "Picture rich kid supported by dad's lucrative business. I doubt he sells insurance. He has an office and talks a lot on his cell. It was an established business when we were in grade school."

"Name?"

"Whitman. Shawn actually is his first name. I always called him Whit."

It was said with such reticence that he knew it cost the man giving the information. Chris said, "You don't think he's capable of anything like this."

"The problem is I wish I could say no without equivocation."

That was pretty honest.

Even more interesting.

When they were back in the car, Carter's only remark was said in a thoughtful tone. "I have a healthy respect for women's intuition."

"I was thinking another visit to talk to Ms. Davidson wouldn't be a bad idea." Chris's impression was that she was an intelligent young woman, not to mention her striking looks, with her glossy auburn hair and those long-lashed green eyes. He'd hardly call Reynolds a lucky man considering recent events, but in that respect, he seemed to be one if she was spending her nights in his bed.

"He seemed unconvinced, but Reynolds isn't unconvinced enough to just not say anything. I'd like to hear her reasons." Carter drove conservatively, like he did everything. Unless, to give him credit, there was an emergency situation — then he could break traffic laws with the best of them. "I also want confirmation that shoe wasn't there, but I assume we're going to get it. Where it was placed, you'd have to step over it if you used the front door."

"Unfortunately, that doesn't mean Reynolds himself couldn't have placed it there before he called us."

"No, but why do I get the feeling you believe his version of what happened?"

"Don't you?"

"I admit I think he's the catalyst, not the culprit." Carter sounded introspective. "At the risk of sounding like you, I can't stomach the idea he would do something like that to his sister and his parents. Those people have to be suffering. I know there are people out there like Ted Bundy who fooled everyone, but in my opinion, they are few and far between."

Chris looked out at the bare trees but did notice some more crocus blooming in a patch at the side of the road as they went past. A nice promise of spring. "I'd like to think so."

"Or we have a drifter on our hands who has decided this county is convenient for dumping bodies. Neither victim lived here."

Chris didn't think so. "This is tied in some way to Reynolds. Unless he's trying to deflect, why this bullshit with the shoes and him? I think whoever killed those two women want us to suspect him. His return to the area and two murders, including his own sister? That's not a coincidence."

"John Newsome? Where is he? As far as I'm concerned, right now he's suspect number one."

"But he hasn't used a credit card or made a phone call. He still hasn't reported to his boss, and that is very out of character. No one has heard from him."

Carter's expression was grim and resigned. "Wise move if he is on the run."

It was possible panic had set in if he was the guilty party, but Chris didn't think so. The killer was cold-blooded, driven by anger or some sort of sense of purpose they didn't yet understand, and from talking to Amanda's friend, he didn't get that she had any sense of that from John Newsome.

"I think after we talk to Ms. Davidson, we should dive deeper and see if *anyone* has heard from him. Either way, we need to find him."

CHAPTER SIXTEEN

Waiting was a game.

It wasn't like the killer wasn't an expert on balancing normal and irrational impulses. There was certain logic in all actions, whether or not most people could comprehend the reasoning behind it. Nonconformity was considered crossing boundaries set by people with no imagination.

One way to look at it was this — if you could gaze at a painting and recognize it as a Van Gogh, it was art.

If you could look at a murder victim and realize that it had a signature of its own, that was also art.

T. S. Eliot once wrote, "There will be a time to murder and create.*"*

What an astute man.

* * *

The receptionist was a nice young woman who did a wonderful job of greeting clients and making appointments. During tax season she was just as overworked as anyone in the firm, but at the moment she looked intrigued at the reappearance of two detectives asking for a few minutes of Samantha's time.

"Those two officers to see you again."

She was glad Mick had warned her it might happen since she was buried in work and January through April were very busy months to say the least. Luckily, most of her clients were established, so she just plugged in new information, but tax laws always shifted, and she had to keep out a keen eye for those changes. "Send them in."

"I will." Bonnie left, and then a few moments later Detectives Carter and Bailey stepped into her office.

"Gentlemen." She pointed at chairs in front of her desk and pressed save on her computer. "What are we discussing today? Mick told me you might come by with some questions and unpleasant pictures."

It was Carter who answered her. "We've actually identified the victim. Did you know a young woman named Natalie Fields?"

She shook her head. "The name doesn't resonate with me."

"Tell us about the shoe." That was Bailey, the young one with the more relaxed air, like he just really wanted to talk to you instead of a formal interrogation.

"The one someone put through my window? Haven't we already?"

"No. Different one."

No doubt about it, she was confused. "I don't understand."

"I think it answers my question."

She had to say, "I'm not quite following."

"The second victim. Her shoe showed up on Mr. Reynolds's porch this morning."

"Mick's?" Her reaction was undeniably disbelief.

"Yes, so tell us about this friend of his you think might be suspicious."

"He said something? I'm surprised." She was. He hadn't taken her seriously as far as she could tell.

"He wasn't really all that eager to do so, but he mentioned it." Carter was always diplomatic. "Quite frankly, we found it of interest. What about Shawn Whitman makes you think he could have harmed Amanda Reynolds?"

She really wasn't going to pull any punches with this. If he'd said something, at least he'd listened.

Samantha took a moment to try to figure out how to put it forth in just a factual way, not letting too much emotion cloud the delivery. "I don't have any proof at all except that I know that if Shawn Whitman, for all his pretense of friendship, could get to Mick in any way possible, he would. There's a jealous rivalry going on there that is undeniable — at least it is to me — and I know you are just taking my word for it, but Amanda agreed with me. He is the proverbial snake in the grass. Mick has never seen it."

Detective Bailey seemed to consider it. "He's maybe seen it enough he mentioned it, but he didn't want to."

Bluntly, she shot back, "Would you? Would you want to think a good friend of yours was that deceptive?"

"No, I wouldn't. However, it does not make you necessarily capable of murder." Bailey did look interested though. "Give me something solid because I'm listening."

She didn't want to go this far, and she was torn, considering the question of when a secret was no longer confidential. When the person who told it to you was dead? Maybe.

"Amanda told me he tried to sexually assault her our senior year in high school. He was home from college, and he stopped by the house to see Mick, but he was out helping his dad on the farm and her mother was at some meeting for the church. She said Shawn gave her the full court press and the word 'no' didn't seem to register. There was a physical struggle she would have lost, but luckily Mick and his dad pulled up in that old truck. Shawn let her go and acted as if everything was just fine and she rushed up to her room and literally locked the door."

"Did she tell her brother this happened?" Detective Carter looked disturbed, and it made her wonder if maybe he had daughters, because he was probably about her father's age.

"No. She didn't even tell *me* until years later when I mentioned in an offhand way that I wasn't a very big fan of Shawn Whitman. I told her it was because when I first started dating Mick, he kept coming on to me. Then she explained what happened with a firm warning to never be alone with him." She added in a tight voice, "I'd already come to that conclusion all on my own."

Bailey looked like he was thinking it over. "I see. So, I agree that there probably was animosity between Amanda Reynolds and Shawn Whitman because of that incident, but it also raises the question of why she'd ever get in a car with him and take off her coat."

"Not voluntarily. She wouldn't, but obviously he had a gun, Detective."

"Whoever killed her most certainly did, that is true. Is there some specific reason that Whitman would target Michael Reynolds in such a malicious way?"

"Envy." She had no doubt. "I've seen it. Mick was more popular in school, got better grades — things like being valedictorian and the star athlete at almost any sport he tried, and in general just making it look like life effortlessly goes his way. In truth, I think he's always worked at it, and it is an illusion, or maybe delusion is a better word, it all just falls into his lap. A normal person wouldn't react with such spite, but I've seen Shawn in action. I believe he's capable of it."

Any man capable of a possible rape had a pathological mindset in her opinion, and it was disturbing.

They rose to leave. "Thank you for the information."

She wasn't positive how that had gone or if she'd been convincing or not, but they seemed to have listened.

* * *

At least his parents were home.

The white farmhouse, so familiar, with tall trees in the background, brown and gray now in the fading winter. Soon it would all be lush and green, and there would be brilliant flowers in the beds around the big porch.

Both car and truck were there, and when he got out and went up the steps, his mother opened the door before he reached it. She'd finally called him back, and he was immensely relieved to say the least. At this time, he didn't trust the world.

"I'm so glad you're here." She hugged him fiercely, which was an improvement from the almost catatonic-like state the last time he'd seen her.

"Anytime, Mom. I live close enough now all you have to do is call or text me and I'll be right here."

The attempt at being reassuring made tears well and her mouth tremble and he understood, but if there was a right thing to say, he obviously didn't know what it was, so he merely touched her shoulder. "Should we go into the kitchen?"

She nodded and he felt helpless, which he didn't like at all, because he should be able to do *something*, but he sure as hell was at a loss as to what it might be.

He learned what a few moments later when she poured him a cup of coffee, which was fine even though it was three in the afternoon. He'd prefer a beer, but he had to pick Samantha up at five, so something non-alcoholic was a better choice anyway.

"I have something to give you. That's why I wanted you to come over." She reached into the pocket of her sweater and took out a small box and set it in front of him. "Ask Samantha to marry you. I talked to her mother and know you are at the very least sleeping together because she wasn't at her house these past nights."

That was true, but this came out of left field. Normally his conservative mother would never have said anything remotely that personal.

There was no doubt that people handled grief in varying ways, just like they handled anything else. Under any other circumstances he would point out he was a grown man at twenty-eight years old, he and Samantha hadn't really been together since college, and that would be rushing things. So instead, he searched for a diplomatic way to explain it was possible they were reacting to this sudden tragic event in an irrational way.

In the end, he just pointed at the box. "What is this?"

"My grandmother's ring. You can have the diamond reset if you want before you give it to her, but I think it is lovely like it is and will suit how classically beautiful Samantha is."

He wasn't going to argue that but had a feeling someone with a degree in how to dissect the human psyche would tell him his maternal parent was desperately looking to replace her suddenly absent daughter.

Samantha was certainly a logical choice, but they had very separate lives still, and the reason they had fallen back into each other's arms was hardly ideal.

So he merely said, "Thank you."

"You've always loved her."

Life-changing decisions weren't exactly prudent at the moment. "Samantha and I have a history."

His mother looked at him with a poignant expression on her face. "I want grandchildren, and now you are my only hope. I need a baby to hold in my arms."

Whatever he expected, it wasn't quite that. He sat there in the quiet kitchen, the checkered curtains at the windows, the polished floors and traditional maple cupboards, and had no idea how to respond. This was not a conversation he ever expected to have.

"When the timing is right, of course I want a family." That was hardly adequate, but then again, he wasn't sure how he felt about anything at the moment.

Considering the discussion he and Samantha had had recently, for all he knew, maybe she was already pregnant. While he considered himself to usually be responsible, he hadn't been more than once now, and it really just took one time.

To his relief, his father came in then, walking through the back door, stopping to take off his boots. "Mick. I saw your car. Thanks for coming over."

That his father would thank him for a visit was telling. "Of course."

"How's the house?" He went to get a cup of coffee.

God, they were all trying to be normal, and it took effort.

"Coming along. Everything is delivered, I'm just sorting through it and Samantha has been helping. My interior design skills are pretty minimal."

"Maybe you take after me. I like a recliner and a good television." His father's smile was a ghost of the usual easy grin. "The rest is just frills."

He needed to be there for his parents, and what he saw was an avoidance of the topic at hand. So, he took an inward deep breath and was very frank. "There has been a second murder that mirrors what happened to Amanda. Someone left that victim's shoe on my porch this morning. It's looking like all of this involves me somehow. Don't ask me how, because I don't know. But someone seems to want to tell me something and I don't have any idea what it is. I guess I'm saying just be aware. Lock your doors, please."

He still held fast to the decision to not tell them about his sister's wallet and the rest of the contents of her purse being left in his new house.

"It's tied to you? How can that be?" His mother looked mystified.

He was too. "All I can say is that the detectives handling this seem to agree. It's not the first time I've been paid a visit. Samantha has caught a glimpse of an unpleasant experience too. That's why she's staying with me. I don't want her alone."

"Oh." She looked disappointed. "So you two aren't . . . well . . . I was mistaken?"

His personal life wasn't a subject he really wanted to discuss with his mother of all people, but he admitted wryly, "No, you weren't mistaken."

"Both of you come stay here. I'll sit on my front porch with my shotgun." His father's expression was tight. "If that bastard comes near here, I will definitely take care of some unsettled business between us. I wouldn't mind being the arm of the Lord if vengeance belongs to him."

This conversation was why he didn't really want to reveal any of this to his parents.

"You can do that if you wish, but I'm now well aware something is going on. I'm having security cameras installed so we should be fine and perhaps catch whoever is doing this. Not to mention the detectives from the sheriff's department seem interested and competent. I just thought you should be told about the problem."

CHAPTER SEVENTEEN

The moon was just a wafer framed by the skeletal arms of the leafless trees.

The killer walked along the perimeter of the property, glad that because of the cool temperatures there were no snakes this time of year. Even if a person was used to them being around, stepping on a copperhead in the dark was not a good time.

However, this particular mission was a pleasure.

The motive for this was questionable, but all of it was.

Was it love or hate?

Hard to say. That line had been hard to define for years now. But it was time to figure it out.

* * *

Anna considered Chris across the table, and she was positive she looked puzzled, because she was. "What exactly are you asking me?"

"If you wanted cream cheese for your bagel. Personally, just butter for me."

He was pretty funny when he managed to think about something besides his job. She corrected him. "No, right before that."

"Oh, yeah, that. Can you ask Mrs. Dunn if she will talk to me candidly about her murdered niece and daughter when I meet with her?"

"I can ask." Anna looked at him uncertainly. "Phrased exactly that way?"

"You want this case solved, right?" His blue eyes were direct and held her gaze.

"I do."

He finished his bagel in record time and did what he always did and left her hanging when he rose. "I've got to go. Let me know what she says."

Candidly? After he left, she thought about that word choice. So he knew something else about the case and chose to keep it to himself, which actually didn't surprise her. The more she got to know him, the more she understood he processed facts in a very linear fashion and no doubt it made him an effectual investigator, and every question he asked had some meaning to him that was not necessarily clear to anyone else.

So she would ask the question how he wanted it asked.

In the meantime, there was something she needed to do.

She called her ex-husband, a little surprised when he answered. Most of the office meetings were first thing in the morning, so she'd counted on being able to leave a message.

"Anna."

"Uh, hi. Good morning."

"Same to you." He paused, no doubt understandably curious. "What's up?"

She really needed to do this for herself. "I'm sure you know I had a drink with Steph. I thought I should say congratulations about the baby."

Silence. Then he said, "Thank you."

The one thing she refused to ask was if they were getting married. It wouldn't surprise her, but if she wanted to preserve her friendship with Stephanie, and she did, there were some fences to repair with Trey then as well. Her anger over their failed relationship had prompted some less-than-gracious

139

behavior on her part, and while she thought she was justified, it had gained her nothing. To his credit, he'd remained unfailingly polite even during the divorce process, and so she owed him civility if nothing else.

She expounded. "I hear the surprise in your voice. It isn't like I've ever wanted you to not be happy."

"I wish you happiness as well, you know that."

It was stilted but at least a conversation. She even said goodbye, which was quite a leap because she frequently, when they did have to speak to each other, did not offer that courtesy. Either she turned and walked away, or just hung up.

A step in the right direction? Maybe.

Next, she called Mrs. Dunn and asked verbatim Chris's question.

The response surprised her.

"Honey, of course I'll talk to him, but I know nothing about any niece. I'm not saying I don't have one, but my younger brother walked out the door of our house at sixteen years of age because he and my father did not get along, and that was it. None of us ever heard from him again. I do have a sister who has passed, but she had two boys."

That was curious. She was sure Chris had said both wives of the murdered couples with similar stories were first cousins, but it also accounted for why the family didn't make the connection. How he did was a mystery. "I'm sure he'll be very interested in whatever you can tell him."

After the call ended, she did text Chris. *Mrs. D said yes, she would certainly talk to you but knows nothing about the niece. There's a story there, but I am not a detective, so I'll let you handle it.*

* * *

The body wasn't pretty since it had taken this much time to find it.

As a rest stop, the pull-off was just that. No facilities, just a trash can, a single rustic picnic table, and a map in a glass case mounted on a pedestal stand that displayed all the rural roads and county highways.

Five shots, missing shoe.

"Same killer." Carter was matter-of-fact. "You called it."

There was no thrill of triumph in that. Chris contemplated the scene, standing back because he wanted no part of a decomposing body. "The ID is missing. Same thing, but I'm going to say our perpetrator might have killed him first. What do you think?"

"Before Amanda Reynolds? The victim fits Newsome's description for size and weight anyway."

"Yeah, it's him. Given the location and circumstances, I would make the assumption too. He stopped checking in with work about the same time her body was discovered."

"I don't draw conclusions."

They all did. They weren't supposed to, but every officer did it. Chris looked around. The area was wooded, secluded, and during this time of year no one would pull off to eat at an outdoor table. It was no wonder the corpse had been there undetected for so long. If it wasn't for some diligent county employee who decided it was worth it to check for trash pickup on the off-chance anyone had stopped, the body would have gone undetected much longer.

As it was, animals had disturbed the crime scene, so it was not pristine and the clothing was in disarray, but it was telling he wasn't wearing a coat either. Out loud, Chris mused, looking at the naked trees. "He abducted them both at the same time. Brought them here and shot Newsome?"

Carter, of course, wore a nice wool dress coat. In comparison Chris had on a leather jacket that was a little worn, but he considered it broken in.

Carter acquiesced, "I think that is a logical theory."

No, something felt off.

"Then he left him here, drove off with her, and stopped and shot her dead where we found her. Why? Why not kill her here too? The timeline suggests they were taken the same night, but it had to be separately. She had her purse. She went willingly. If someone is abducting you, you don't stop to get your purse."

"Or he could order you at gunpoint to bring it along." Carter was thinking it over, standing there with his hands in his pockets.

"Possible, but why? If you don't want the body to be identified easily, just leave the bag wherever you abducted them from. No, she trusted this person."

"I'm following your line of thought. What about Newsome?"

"I'm guessing he was eating his sandwich and someone knocked on his door and he had a gun shoved into his ribs and was forced into their vehicle when he opened it. The medical examiner's report will tell us volumes, because I'm doubting he didn't fight back. Whoever did this is not going to walk away."

"Not if we have any say in it."

It was their one similarity. Carter, for all his formality, held the same view of their job: justice was their purpose.

"What is the connection with Natalie Fields? Newsome was maybe dating Amanda Reynolds, so they have a tie, but why Fields?"

"We could have a random serial on our hands, but if this is Newsome, I doubt that now. It looked to me like he was abducted from his home too." This was going to hit the media. It meant he'd probably be seeing FBI Agent Wright again, but she'd come to their office instead of the other way around. Once there was a hint of a serial, then federal law enforcement tended to get involved. Chris said with sincerity, "I'm already feeling sorry for Lawrence. What sheriff has two serial cases in his county within the span of a year?"

"The official in Los Angeles maybe, but there's a definite population disparity." Carter looked around. "I know this spot must be pretty in the summer, but it's desolate this time of year. No wonder he wasn't found before now."

He was right. Naked trees crowded together, a rusting trash can and that single weathered table . . . no, not inviting for a restful winter stop. Not to mention the body half-dragged into the woods with torn clothing and a-not so-appealing appearance overall.

"The dead guy doesn't contribute to the ambiance." It wasn't sarcasm, it was the truth.

Loren arrived fifteen minutes later, but luckily the sun had finally peeked out from behind gray clouds and the temperature warmed to an almost balmy level considering the recent weather.

His first observation was pretty simple. "Nothing but paperwork, gentlemen. He is pronounced dead. Your crime scene guys have the field. I'm sure you have also determined the cause of death, but whether he was shot here or elsewhere, I can't tell because the scene is disturbed by what I am guessing would be coyotes."

"That would be my guess too," Chris agreed. "I'm glad I'm not a medical examiner — and that goes without saying — because I think he's been here for quite a while."

"Rigor has come and gone, so you are correct, Detective."

"The only good news for him is he's no longer our number one suspect." Carter's sense of humor was dry as dust.

They were going to have to use DNA for identification. Most of the damage was to the face and neck because they had not been covered, and no family should ever have to look at those kinds of photographs. He could have lived without the experience himself.

"As far as I'm concerned, Lawrence can contact the family." Chris was sincere. "Officially he's in charge of the investigation and under normal circumstances we would do it, but the identification would require a family member to give DNA, and if it were me, I'd ask why. Then an explanation of why an in-person identification wasn't possible might just give me nightmares."

"You are far too sensitive, Detective Bailey." Loren raised his brows. "At any rate, we'll take the body, and the rest of the process belongs to you as usual. I'm rather hoping for no more calls to a remote county thoroughfare in the near future."

"We are working on it."

He departed a few minutes later with his grisly burden and the necessary pictures as they waited for the crime scene techs to arrive to process the scene. If it hadn't snowed recently, they might be able to tell themselves, but it had and it would be helpful to know if he'd been shot at this given spot or maybe transported from somewhere else and dumped, so samples had to be taken.

They did have DNA from that stray cigarette butt, but it hadn't raised a flag in the system. At least if they found a suspect they could maybe confirm or discard them as the possible killer now, so that was something.

Not much. Not with three victims. Ballistics should be able to confirm if it was the same gun.

If it was, and they got a match and recovered the weapon from his person or residence, then they had the killer.

There were lots of variables in that equation.

"So we're going to at least interview Whitman, right?" With Carter he was never sure how he might want to handle it and he argued if he didn't agree, but he usually asked in deference to his greater experience.

"I'm on the fence with that. We have nothing except Ms. Davidson's suspicions."

"They were pretty compelling. Whoever is responsible for three deaths now has an issue with Mick Reynolds including trying to force a sexual encounter with his sister and that would be Whitman."

"I know." Carter looked about as perturbed as he ever did.

"How about Agent Wright?"

Carter turned away, his expression a little remote. There was a story there, but Chris wasn't about to ask. "What about her?"

"Let's see if she can find a field agent for surveillance on Mick Reynolds. Our department is too small, and they are better trained at undercover. I expect, unless I'm really wrong and he isn't telling the truth, he's going to get another delivery once this body being found makes the news."

Carter thought it over. "If she'll help us, that's not a bad idea."

"She's willing to help me on a cold case that goes back a long time. A current case where whoever is doing this is picking off people and dumping bodies? Yeah, I think she will maybe give us someone. She knows we aren't used to this level of homicides on a usual basis and has agents who know exactly how to do this."

"Our deputies know how to sniff out a meth lab like bloodhounds, but invisible observation is not in their provenance. If you think it will fly, you can ask."

He thought about it. "I'll give it a try."

CHAPTER EIGHTEEN

There was at first the element of surprise.

Then came a tipping point when the game changed. Suddenly your opponent woke up and realized you were serious, and your aim was dead on, and they were in your sights.

Was it triumph?

Maybe. There was a certain thrill they finally knew the score.

It could be that had gotten him the most satisfaction.

The killer had wondered about it now and then but put off the analysis.

He'd engaged in open warfare, and his enemy suddenly knew it.

* * *

If it wasn't for his unsettled mind, life would be good.

New house, beautiful woman naked in his arms at night, the company coming along and making money . . .

Mick understood his mother's need to desperately look toward some future joy rather than live in this moment, but he could live without the expectation he was going to make any sudden decisions right now. Amanda's unexpected and violent death precluded any happiness.

The ring was very pretty in an antique setting and the diamond certainly more impressive than the one in the ring he'd held on to all these years, but his reunion with Samantha was tenuous at best given why it had happened.

He got out of his car and walked across the parking lot so he could wait by the doors because he didn't want her outside alone for as long as it took to walk to his vehicle.

Five minutes later she came out in a hurry, carrying a box, and he straightened away from the brick wall. "Whoa, Ms. Hurricane. Can I carry your books as I walk you home?"

"Yes, thank you. Sorry I'm late. It's tax season." She handed over the box. "There's some midnight oil with my name on it."

"No problem. It has turned into a decent afternoon, so waiting was a chance to breathe in some fresh air."

"My house or yours?"

"I found my wine glasses and also stopped and bought more of the beverage in question."

She laughed. "That settles it, then. What am I cooking?"

"We're having chili."

"Hmm, with wine?"

"Sure. Why not?"

She sent him a dubious sidelong glance. "Out of a can?"

"You think I can't make chili?"

"I find it highly unlikely you found the time."

He relented. "My mother made it, so you're safe. No can was involved."

"I'll make cornbread, then. Let's stop by my house so I can change, and I'll grab the stuff for that."

There was no doubt cornbread was out of the realm of his culinary experience, so he didn't argue that one. He'd never made chili either but was convinced he could if handed the recipe and the incentive of having Samantha sit across the table from him, but it had been much easier to just accept his mother's generous offering.

He wasn't about to mention the ring again, or rings now, actually. Either one of them. Yes, they were rediscovering their romantic feelings for each other, or at least the sexual attraction, but he wasn't ready to do much more than cautiously see if other than in bed, they still *liked* each other. At this time in their lives, it was hardly holding hands in the hallway in high school or walking across campus together in college. It was time for both of them to make life decisions, and that really did mean ones that might change everything.

Decisions like sleeping together without even using protection of any kind. She'd mentioned it, he'd said they should stop and purchase some protection, and they had done that, but actually use it, no. It was very out of character for both of them, and part of him wondered if they weren't leaving it to fate.

He'd have to sort it out later because at that moment his phone beeped — it showed on the screen of his car's wireless connection, and it was Detective Bailey.

"Is it bad when a detective calls you?" He asked it conversationally, but he was hardly unaware of his visceral reaction.

Next to him, Samantha's lovely eyes were wide. "I . . . I don't know. Answer it?"

That was probably a decent suggestion. He hit a button. "Detective."

"It'll be on the news anyway, so I thought I'd let you know we've had a development. Keep your eyes open. Is Ms. Davidson with you?"

"Yes."

"We think this person might abduct people from their homes. So, tread carefully since there has been evidence of interest in you."

"I'm aware." His tone was grim. "Unfortunately. A development? Like what?"

"Just letting you know we are really looking."

End of call.

Samantha was still, her profile outlined by the muted light. "That was practically talkative for him."

"He was as informative as ever."

"I think his belief is that he was not put on this earth to impart information, just to receive it."

He disagreed. "His belief is I will be a suspect until he can confirm someone else is the guilty party. If something were to happen to you, he'd hang me. Either way, that call was to protect you, and you know what, I approve of that one hundred percent."

It was difficult to accept anyone thought he could be capable of killing his own sister or some young woman he'd never even met, but he found it difficult to believe anyone else would do it either, so the "everyone is a suspect" aspect made sense to him.

"Mick—"

"He was warning me, and he was *warning* me. That's all I'm saying."

"They can't really think you are involved."

He turned onto the side street toward her house. "Yes, they can. They can't afford not to consider it. I *am* involved in some way. But I can tell you it isn't clear to me either. I finally told my parents this afternoon about the incident at your house, and at mine."

* * *

It wasn't as if she was blind to his dilemma.

"What did they say?" Samantha would not have wanted to tell them either.

"I don't really think they knew what to say. Neither do I."

"I gave the detectives my opinion."

He shot her a quick sidelong look. "Did they listen?"

"I think the young blond one did." She was sure Bailey had, in fact, but it was clear they had their hands full if there was another death. How to tie it all together would probably be a challenge. She could decipher the random haphazard bookkeeping of busy farmers and advise them on how to invest their money, but she was hardly an expert on police work.

"On this same topic, I believe our mothers have had a discussion about our current sleeping arrangements." Mick's tone was dry. "The county sheriff's department is not the only one monitoring our activities."

"If you think my family hasn't said something to me, you'd be sadly mistaken." She thought about James and his impromptu visit to her office. "My brother even stopped by to say something to me about it. He was more worried about how I was handling what happened to Amanda but also had to point out he didn't feel I'd moved on particularly after you."

It took a moment, but then he asked, "True?"

It was hard to tell if it was a good idea to admit it or not, but she'd been the one to suggest bed, not couch, so he probably knew it anyway. "Let's just say you are the only man I've ever slept with."

He parked the car in her driveway and turned to look at her, and his expression was hard to read. "It had been six years."

"I guess I just haven't met anyone else like you."

"I doubt this is good timing for this discussion on an emotional level for either of us, but I haven't met anyone else like you either. Shall we just go in so you can change and get what you need for the cornbread and just hope no one has dropped off anything?"

She understood his point about how they were both traveling a rocky path when it came to emotion at the moment, so he was right there to stop the dialogue.

Her throat tightened. She nodded and opened her door.

All was thankfully quiet and normal in the house, no windows broken, but Mick insisted on looking around and followed her even into her bedroom, where admittedly he'd been before. She changed and he watched with a lifted brow and deliberate appreciation, which was a welcome hint of humor in a less than funny situation.

"Like you haven't seen all of me before." It was an observation based on fact.

He folded his arms and leaned against the doorway in a negligent pose. "I'm happy to say that's true. Quite a nice view. I'm riveted every single time."

* * *

After she pulled a soft sweater over her head, she shook out her hair. "The show is over. I assume we'll find out how riveted later, but in the meantime let me get the ingredients and my grandmother's recipe together."

He moved aside to let her through the doorway. "I'll be more than happy to express my enthusiasm over how beautiful I think you are later, but I'd like to be back at my house and under lock and key, where if someone was trying to break in, I could react accordingly."

"Rifle in hand."

"I'm not a huge advocate for carrying a gun, but please argue that our circumstances aren't different than they are for most people."

Targeted by someone who had decided to shoot people in a similar manner was probable cause for being wary, so she was hardly going to argue. His sister was dead. Someone was shadowing him with the intent of reminding him of it.

"I don't disagree."

"Let's go, then."

If nothing else his house offered at least an advantage of being able to hear someone come and go in a vehicle unless they did it on foot in the chill winter weather. Quiet and in the woods, there was no other recourse.

More remote, but more secure.

"Do you have baking powder?" She asked it innocently enough as she went down the staircase.

"What?"

"At the house. Baking powder? Used for cornbread?"

"Sam, I barely know if I have a pan. I only recently discovered napkins and those wine glasses were quite a find, remember?"

She glanced over her shoulder. "You do realize teasing you offsets the reality, right?"

"I know." His tone softened. "Keep doing it. I could use the distraction. But I am going to have to vote no on the baking powder."

He had the most amazing eyes. Such a vivid color and she still remembered so clearly the first time she'd ever seen him. Great-looking guy with unforgettable eyes, not to mention that mesmerizing smile. They'd basically grown up together, learning life lessons about how it all worked, not just between male and female but milestones like leaving home and taking on responsibility for your future, making weighty decisions, and finding independence.

She was in love with him again.

Or still.

It was up for argument. A second head-over-heels tumble? Or simply picking up where they'd left off? It was hard to say. James had been correct. She'd never gotten past it, so it could be either one.

She gathered what she needed, and they went out to his car, but his phone rang before they could even get in and when he glanced at it, he looked up at her in grim contemplation. "Guess who."

"Not Detective Bailey again, I hope."

"Nope." He shook his head. "I'm going to have to take this."

"Who is it?"

"Shawn."

CHAPTER NINETEEN

Sometimes decisions were made for you.

It had happened before.

What constituted a reflexive action and a conscious choice when all the repercussions were weighed and measured was an inner debate the killer had yet to determine.

It came down to a simple equation. At what point did the darker side every single human being had, whether they wanted to admit it or not, begin to prevail?

Hate, envy, malice aforethought, the desire to remove an obstacle so thoroughly it never stood in your way again . . .

On paper, it sounded bad.

In reality, it was satisfying

And necessary. What did they know?

* * *

The question was multi-faceted when it came to the response.

Chris had to admit he wasn't quite sure if it was a good idea, or a bad one, for Reynolds to grab a drink with someone who was presumably a childhood friend but might have killed his sister, not to mention two other people.

Was the invitation just a gesture of sympathy and good will, or a desire to find out if there was a suspect?

Good question. If he hadn't heard the story of why Whitman might have enmity toward both brother and sister, he might dismiss it as just an old friend wanting to get together.

"Where is Ms. Davidson going to be?" he asked, thinking it over. "Not alone. That's not just a suggestion. Whoever is doing this, she would be the next likely target if it really is aimed at you."

"I've taken that into consideration. Until this is resolved, we're inseparable unless she's at work."

It was hard to fault his biting, determined tone. The loss of his sister and the manner that it happened was bad enough that his protective stance was understandable.

"I think that is a wise decision. Keep us informed on when you plan to meet with him. Mr. Whitman is definitely a person of interest to us because he has some history with your sister. Tell me something, does he smoke cigarettes?"

"He used to now and then in college when he drank. I don't know if he does now because I really haven't seen him in a long time since I just moved back. Why?"

"Please tell me when and where you plan to have this drink. It really might help us with this investigation. I'll make sure she's safe."

If they could just get some DNA, it would be definitive whether Whitman was a viable suspect or not. It would prove nothing except circumstantial evidence, but it could certainly steer them toward the direction needed to deepen the case. If he discarded that cigarette close to the second body, they could have him knowing the first victim and in proximity to the second.

All it really would take is a sip from a glass in a restaurant and two detectives asking to be able to collect a sample before it was taken away to be washed.

"I will if you'll arrange to have someone watch Samantha. I don't know if I agree with her suspicions or not, but what if he wants for me to leave her alone at an appointed time? Me at the bar by myself and her vulnerable?"

"We are certainly thinking along the same lines."

Reynolds audibly exhaled. "I'll call him back and let you know."

"If you see Detective Carter or myself at the bar or restaurant, do not acknowledge us, please."

Chris hung up and called Carter, who was out of the office. "We might have a break. It's thin, but I think it's all we've got."

When he explained, his partner's response was predictable. "I'll keep an eye on Ms. Davidson. I'd stand out like a sore thumb in some bar geared toward your generation. Balding, middle-aged guy in a suit? I don't think so. You'd fit right in."

The only problem was the wait staff was more likely to believe Carter was a detective and hand over the glass without argument. "Let's see where the meeting is and make a decision then."

"Keep me up to speed."

Doreen sauntered up to his desk. "Here you go, cowboy. The ballistic reports you've been waiting for just came. Also, you have a federal agent who just arrived to see you. Aren't you special today?"

He laughed, because the truth was Doreen really was worth her weight in gold — which was not inconsiderable — to the operation of the sheriff's department, and he appreciated her efforts to make everything run smoothly. "You've instilled in me the belief I am special all the time," he replied, trying for an earnest look.

"Smartass. I'll send him over."

Since it was about ten steps to his desk, that wasn't far. He was a young man — maybe a few years older — and he had a clean-cut look but was also casual in khakis and a golf shirt, with brown hair, light-blue eyes and easy manner. "Detective Bailey? I'm Hamilton Norris with the FBI."

He rose and they shook hands. "Have a seat."

"Agent Wright thinks a lot of you and sent me to do a detail. Fill me in?"

It was nice to hear, and this solved the dilemma. They didn't have to choose which one of them followed Reynolds, and an FBI agent would easily be able to obtain DNA.

So he outlined the case. "Three murders. Two women, one man — we can connect two of them but have no idea how the third one ties in — yet there is a similar style going on. Five shots each, and he or she takes one shoe from the victims."

"Trophy?"

"The killer doesn't keep it. Whoever it is has bestowed two of them on the first victim's brother, Michael Reynolds — we are waiting on the third — and so that is who we really need you to follow."

Norris looked interested. "Is he a suspect?"

"I don't think so, but it is a possibility. His main problem is no one was watching so no one can confirm he didn't do it. We just don't have the manpower, and the truth is, in this area if you are a deputy, someone is going to recognize you because you probably went to high school together. Surveillance is not possible without them coming up and asking how your kid is doing on the soccer team."

"Well, that isn't Nashville, but I can see that around here. Anything else? I've looked over the file."

"Reynolds's sister was killed first, then another woman — Natalie Fields — whom he apparently doesn't know was also dumped along a farm lane, so it's hard to establish an alibi, and then his sister's boyfriend's body just turned up at a wayside, but he hasn't been given that latter information. He knows there's a third victim but not who it is. If you can, watch him, and watch anyone else watching him. Not a huge task maybe, but you will be labeled a stranger around these parts."

"I can blend in."

Maybe he could, maybe he couldn't. He seemed competent and they needed the help. Chris rubbed his jaw.

"Reynolds has a meeting with our only real other suspect tomorrow. He's going to send me the time and place."

"Is there a chance he's leading us?" Norris's eyes were keen and his gaze speculative.

"I'd doubt that in general. I get criticized for this, but I have the *feeling* he's not who we are hunting. My gut says no. He's worried about his girlfriend, and I agree we should be too, because whatever is happening, he's involved somehow."

"Interesting case."

That was true enough. "He has no idea about any other law enforcement being involved, so I bet I'll get a call if he notices you more than once." Chris regarded him steadily. "If I'm wrong or even if I'm right, just keep in mind that Reynolds is a smart man. If he perceives you as a danger, he might react. If he isn't the threat, he's being threatened."

"I'm aware." Norris rose and handed him a card. "My number. I already have yours thanks to Agent Wright. Call me if there is anything I should know, and I will return the favor."

"You already are doing us a favor." Chris meant it.

"You can thank Wright." He paused and added with an inquiring look, "I understand you might be joining us."

Since he wasn't sure what had been said, Chris merely shrugged. He'd guess Agent Norris probably knew this anyway. "I'd made it through most of the hiring process until there was a fatal shooting last fall. I think that issue might be a stumbling block. I guess we will see."

"The review found you free and clear, right?"

He knew.

Chris's reply was succinct. "It did."

Norris nodded. "Well then, maybe we'll be working together again after this case."

* * *

Anna had no idea why there would be a man's shoe just sitting randomly in the driveway, but it certainly didn't belong to Chris since he wore boots as his usual footwear. She hadn't looked, but if she had to guess, he didn't even have a pair of slippers or tennis shoes.

A leather loafer certainly seemed out of character. She looked at it curiously because it was nice enough, but her hands were full since she'd brought along a homemade Greek casserole for dinner and stopped for baklava at a local bakery, and Chris was already home, so she left it there. It wasn't until a good hour later after they'd eaten that she even remembered it.

His reaction to her casual comment about a shoe sitting next to his truck was unexpected. He set aside his glass and stared at her in clear consternation. "What kind of shoe? Men's?"

"Uh . . . yes."

"Really?" His chair scraped back. "I'll be right back."

She picked up her glass of wine — a nice pinot noir — and waited, wondering what she'd said that sparked such a radical reaction.

When he came back, he gave her a direct look. "I'm sorry, but he knows where I live. I have to make a phone call."

Who knew what?

He was out of the kitchen again before she could ask the question, his phone against his ear, and when he came back a few minutes later, all he did was take his seat and pick up his bottle of beer and look at her as if nothing had happened.

Anna had a lot of flaws in varying degrees, but a failure to speak her mind wasn't one of them. "What is going on?"

He looked noncommittal. "That shoe could be part of an investigation. I just needed to let the powers that be know someone dropped it off."

She stared at him. "Like who?"

"I called the FBI. Dinner was really good, by the way. I never thought I was a fan of eggplant, but I liked it."

"The FBI?"

He wasn't going to say more and he was unapologetic for it too. "You broadened my horizons on a culinary level. Moussaka is pretty darned tasty."

She was never sure if she should laugh or cry over some of their conversations. Of course, she knew all about privacy laws and how they applied to social work, but she had to admit, he took close-mouthed to a whole new level.

"By the way, you'll be staying the night."

It wasn't like she hadn't anticipated she would, but she still never expected a decree.

Chris read her expression correctly. "I want you to anyway, don't get me wrong, but this particular killer is vindictive. The shoe was a message and I got it loud and clear. He knows where I live and breathe. That means he probably knows about you."

"He?"

"Women are bloodthirsty too, but I assume, with the given evidence, it is a male."

"Why?"

"The bodies were moved in the second and third cases. That takes strength."

That was a logical deduction. She'd be hard-pressed to move a human being that was, literally, dead weight. She looked at him curiously. "Vindictive?"

"Dropping off personal items taken from the victims to a family member. To me that indicates a sadistic sort of taunting. In my case, I think it's a dare. How do you interpret it?"

There was no denying it was interesting behavior. "It seems to me you have a narcissistic killer who wants to draw attention to his crimes as a personal show of power."

Chris propped his elbows on the table and regarded her thoughtfully. "That sounds pretty accurate to me, but I'm not the psychologist."

She corrected him inelegantly. "Like hell you aren't. You practice it all the time, you just don't have a degree in it. In your job you constantly deal with the result of unacceptable human behavior and have to dissect *why* someone would do a thing like that, to find out *who* might do it. You label it motive, but it really is a psychological conclusion."

His mouth quirked in wry amusement. "I suppose that's true, but I can tell you if Carter were sitting here with us, he'd argue motive is a waste of time. Opportunity is his main investigative tactic."

"I would postulate the different approach lends well to teamwork." They certainly were very different men in her opinion.

"Postulate is a fairly high-falutin' word in this neck of the woods, ma'am." He did his best country boy imitation, which was fairly even-keeled in her opinion for a man who had had a dead man's shoe dropped off in his driveway. Then again, he dealt with the reality of the darker side on a daily basis.

She did too, to a certain extent. Broken families, neglect and abuse, bewildered children, poverty, teenaged pregnancies . . .

There was nothing like working the front lines. Besides chemistry in bed, they had that in common at least. She raised a brow. "But you know what it means, so the backwoods routine doesn't work."

"And here I thought you found it charming." He grinned, but it quickly faded. "I wish I understood why this particular perpetrator is taking so many chances, because let's face it, he is. Is it really a sense of arrogance that he's smarter than we are? Most criminals eventually lose that battle and as technology moves forward, we are even getting better at it."

"I took a criminology class in college, and according to that professor, it's a high you can get addicted to just like a narcotic. Power is an aphrodisiac, and taking someone's life away from them is the ultimate power."

"I believe I agree. I can't say I've worked many serial cases, but those are unique animals."

"You've worked a few high-profile ones. Just recently."

He looked at her. "I'd like to reverse that trend."

She said softly, "I'll stay."

CHAPTER TWENTY

A real plan would have been better.

The question was how sustainable the current impulse and execution would be in the long run.

His nemesis knew what he was but not yet who he was. That was the real battle, when push came to shove, when they recognized each other fully.

It was inevitable: one day they would.

* * *

He walked into Kelly's with mixed feelings.

Mick still remembered the day he had gone in there legally for the first time because he was of age to buy alcohol and Shawn was with him. They bought each other a drink and toasted the moment.

Was there a reason he chose this place?

Same age, same class, same background growing up, they were just two old friends getting together.

Like now? He wasn't sure. Samantha's suspicions had certainly carried enough conviction that he considered the possibility she was right, and his conversation with Detective

Bailey told him that man also weighed her opinion as a consideration.

Shawn was already there and had chosen one of the tall tables near the bar, a beer in front of him, his dark hair impeccably styled, wearing what was obviously work attire of tailored slacks and a nice button-up shirt. He didn't look like someone who would murder in cold blood, but then again, was there a uniform?

"Rey. It's good to see you. Been a while."

Perfunctory handshake and a slap on the shoulder. Nothing off-key. He took a seat across and nodded. "Yeah, you too."

"Kind of a rough homecoming."

So he did want to bring the subject up immediately. Was that unusual or just a statement from a concerned friend? He wasn't sure. "I couldn't agree more."

A server cruised by, observed only one beer on the table, and stopped. Mick ordered a lager and gave a good attempt at a congenial smile. There was no question he was on edge, but at least that was to be expected.

"I can only imagine how you feel. When was the last time you talked to her?"

At that moment he anticipated this would be the least relaxing drink he'd ever had in his life. How the hell did he interpret that comment and question? Was it a slash of the blade or true sympathy?

"I'm not sure because I'm numb over the whole thing. My faith in the goodness of people has been shaken," he said after a moment, his tone deliberate.

"Life certainly isn't predictable." Shawn shook his head in either sincere — or false — agreement. "There are some unexpected curves in the road."

If this was a game, he wasn't going to play it. "Most certainly no one deserves what happened to Amanda."

"Given her profession, maybe she stepped on the wrong toes."

That had occurred to Mick as well, but the way it was said so dispassionately took him aback.

So he decided on no comment. "Now, catch me up, what's happening with you lately?"

A shrug. "The agency is busy, so I have plenty to do. Love life is a little lackluster, but so it goes in a backwater. I imagine Chicago was a bit livelier."

He absolutely could not go from his sister's death to details about his personal life. "It is a big city. I'm looking forward to the quiet here."

"Or you were."

Luckily his drink arrived then so he didn't need to respond. He wasn't sure how to handle such ambiguous comments. Instead, he took a sip of beer and a deep breath. Maybe Samantha was right, the underlying truth was Shawn actually didn't like him very much under the facade, but it didn't mean he would murder Amanda.

Or anyone else.

That second shoe left on his doorstep had belonged to a victim, unknown to him.

He'd tried to dissect that gesture with no success, except if the man sitting across from him had done it just to implicate him, maybe it did make sense.

So he took a drink and told the truth. "No one thinks something like that will ever happen to them."

"No." Shawn looked reflective, relaxed in his chair, his fingers smoothing the side of his glass. An act or not? Hard to say. "Let's change the subject. How's Sam?" His smile was instant and convincing. "We have a lot of mutual friends. I've already heard you are seeing each other again."

Some raucous laughter, music playing — he thought it was maybe Vince Gill — the smell of alcohol and fried food faded into the background. It seemed to be an innocent question. While the truth was they did have some friends in common, Mick hadn't really been in touch with many of them, given what had happened at such a rapid pace since his move home.

It wasn't the question. It was the look in his eyes.

Was there a hardness there or was it Mick's imagination? A glint of dislike that couldn't be completely hidden or just the usual challenge. For so many years they'd participated in what he'd always viewed as friendly competition.

"She's in the same state of disbelief as the rest of us but otherwise extremely busy because it is tax season."

"But she finds time for you apparently. Is she why you came back?"

"I came back home essentially, but she could well be part of it. That remains to be seen. Normal doesn't apply right now."

His old friend nodded and agreed. "Yeah, there's some definite tension in the air around these parts." He lifted his beer to his mouth and took a solid drink and set down the bottle. "You've heard there's a third victim?"

Maybe that was the new development. Bailey hadn't mentioned what it was, but then again, he wasn't exactly a fount of information. "No. Who was it?"

"John someone, I didn't catch the last name. I don't think he was from around here. Nashville maybe. I wonder if there's a connection between him and Amanda."

It was that statement that did it. They were playing a game and he'd never been given the rules. He'd dealt with boardrooms and arrogant assholes who thought they had the upper hand, but this was so deeply personal he was at a loss as to how to react. Sam was right. Either he was just gloating over the fact it ever happened because Amanda had at one time rejected him and he was still angry about it, or he was the one that committed those three murders.

Either way, it was a definitive moment.

It could be taken as innocent enough, but he no longer thought so. It was tempting to go across the table, ending the conversation in a very satisfying way, but unless he could actually prove something, he'd probably just end up in jail for battery.

Instead, he responded with calm. "If law enforcement can make a connection, I'm sure they will."

* * *

Samantha had no idea she still had a client waiting after hours, but given the season, she was not surprised either.

That changed when he came into her office.

Nice-looking older man, well-dressed, reserved demeanor, but not a client.

Detective Carter. "I'm here to make sure you make it home safely. Not my usual detail, but this is not a simple case, Ms. Davidson."

She looked at him in dismay. "What's happened?"

"There's been a development that has us concerned."

A development? That word again. What did that mean?

It was an answer but also a non-answer. She gave him a level look. "At least tell me if Mick is okay?"

"To the best of my knowledge, he is."

That was a relief anyway. "Let me save this and I'll get my coat and keys. The receptionist wants to wrap this up too and go home."

For her at the moment that meant Mick's house, which was isolated in the woods by that little lake, no neighbors. Maybe she should go to her house in town first and wait for him to pick her up there.

He was at that moment sitting there with Shawn, sharing a drink, and she did wonder how that was going. It was clear he didn't totally disparage her take on the situation, but neither did he fully buy into it. That uncertainty spoke volumes to her anyway. He didn't wish to believe it but thought it was possible.

Maybe that was his signature calling card. Michael Reynolds was a decent person and expected it from others.

She texted him. *I'm going to my house. Let me know any evening plans.*

He immediately texted back. *Is Bailey with you?*

Carter.

OK. Good. I'll be by soon.

What exactly was going on?

She found out a half an hour later when Mick relieved Carter of his duty by pulling into the driveway. The detective departed with a nod, and she went and climbed into the car, saying by way of greeting, "What is going on?"

"There's been a third murder." Mick's expression was tight as he waited for her to fasten her seatbelt and put the car in reverse. "Shawn told me about it."

"How'd we not know?" She hurried to buckle in.

"The police are watching me, not talking to me."

"Then how did *he* know?"

He backed out onto the street. "Isn't that a good question. If that information has been made public, I haven't heard it. He claims he has a friend who knows someone who works for the sheriff's department that told him. It was a vague statement."

"Another young woman?"

"The victim? No, according to him, someone named John. He couldn't remember the last name but knew he was from Nashville. He actually said to me he wondered if this man — who was apparently murdered — might have known Amanda."

She stared at him. "*What?*"

He glanced over. "Yeah. It really was not a subtle conversation. Whether he killed her or not, he was not sorry about my sister's death and he made it pretty clear. I think I might be permanently over the drink-with-an-old-friend scenario."

"Does Bailey know?"

"He knows a lot more than we do, I can promise you that."

She agreed he probably did, and it was a good thing. "That's his job."

He didn't say anything for a moment but turned onto the road that headed out of town. "There was a guy at the bar, and he was not watching us deliberately. He was listening to our conversation if I had to call it."

"How could you possibly come to that conclusion?"

"I think his expression was about like mine."

"Are you serious? That is what you are basing it on?"

"Yes, I'm serious. And I guess I'm basing it on how carefully he seemed to be uninterested in us but just had the feeling that we were why he was there."

She blew out a short breath. "Well, if Carter hadn't walked into my office this evening to announce he was escorting me home, I might doubt you more."

"I doubt myself enough for the both of us at this point. I had a conversation with my mother yesterday I didn't see coming that perhaps someday I'll tell you about, but now is not the time."

She understood his feeling that life was suddenly so out of balance it was hard to adjust. She felt the same way.

"We're old friends." She said it softly.

He glanced at her, his features defined by the faint light from the dashboard. It was already fully dark. "What?"

"I hope you will reconsider the being over the drink-with-an-old-friend attitude. I'm thinking fondly of a glass of Chardonnay, but not alone."

At least that drew a short, spontaneous laugh. "You will always be the exception to every rule I have as far as I can tell. Let's make it two glasses. I'll be the bartender."

"I'll be the cook, then." Since he was barely moved in, she knew the grocery store was his last priority and she'd visited her own refrigerator and found some chicken breasts, arugula, bottled dressing, and grabbed two potatoes from the pantry. She was hardly a chef but, as a busy professional, she could throw dinner together on the fly.

"I hadn't really even thought about food," he said somberly.

"That's not a surprise."

"Tragedy happens to people all the time. I keep telling myself that and I listen, but I don't know if that realization helps all that much."

He was working it out, and so was she. If someone was following Mick, that was probably good rather than the opposite. "I have the feeling that this door will close fairly soon."

"Slam in Shawn's face, you mean?" Mick sounded angry but still uncertain. "I don't know if his attitude was indifference or an indication he might be guilty. I wasn't sure how to react. One thing I do know is that I sure as hell won't let him near you."

She thought about Amanda's description of Shawn's aggressive behavior. "You can be sure neither will I. At least they no longer suspect you apparently."

His brows went up just a little. "Oh, what makes you think that?"

She shot him a disbelieving look. "Detective Carter bothered to come to my office and see me safely into your hands."

He slowed for several deer crossing the road, their silhouettes framed in the headlights. "I think that maybe they were making a point to let me know if anything happened to you, I'd be under a microscope like no other since you were delivered into my care safe and sound."

She hadn't thought of it that way.

CHAPTER TWENTY-ONE

Walking on that shaky branch had been done before and it had held, but who knew this time.

There was no connection, so they couldn't make sense of it. The killer was fairly sure playing a wildcard would work, but then again, it was spinning a roulette wheel. They'd identified the second victim very fast. That was unexpected.

But then again, this was a gamble.

Three cards in and he had the upper hand.

* * *

"Oh yes, it was quite a memorable conversation. I'm trying to decide still who was trying to bait the other more, but they were definitely doing a tango. Reynolds probably deserves a medal for not going for it." Norris looked like he was really reliving the confrontation. "He was being pushed."

The sheriff's office was quiet this morning, all the deputies out, only Chris and Carter in Lawrence's office. Doreen was at her desk, but she always was as far as he could tell. If he found out she slept there overnight, he would not faint with surprise.

"So you think Samantha Davidson is correct." Chris didn't say it as a question.

"I think there is tension there and maybe her theory holds water. I have the bottle bagged and ready for the lab to run the DNA." Norris looked serious. "It was a strange conversation to me. If they are friends, it didn't seem like that sort of interaction."

"If Whitman is a match for that cigarette, then we have a foundation for a case."

Carter argued, always the voice of reason. "We have to have something more to connect him to Natalie Fields."

"What if she's a random? I'm worried about that with the DNA match too. He stopped and picked up a fresh one tossed out a window to throw us off?" Chris was capable of defending his stance.

"That smart?" Norris looked interested.

"He could be. I know for a fact that Reynolds is that smart and Whitman thinks he's a contender for the title."

"So we aren't sure."

"So far, we have no proof." Carter took a sip from his coffee cup.

Chris didn't necessarily agree, which was not unusual. "You tell me. I'd say Reynolds would be more likely to be able to fool us with that trick, but Whitman is more my guess because of the vindictive behavior afterward, and unless Samantha Davidson is lying to us, he tried to sexually assault our first victim."

Norris looked like he was undecided. "It could be she was steering suspicion away from Reynolds because they most definitely stayed the night together in the same bedroom, so there is involvement there. Lucky him. However, I thought he was genuinely thrown by how Whitman acted at the bar. I've done surveillance before and I don't think he was pretending the surprise."

Chris had to agree that Samantha Davidson was a very attractive young woman and he'd thought the same thing, and he was also in agreement they had a similar impression of Mick Reynolds. "I don't see any motive for killing his sister, much less some woman that, as far as we are aware, he didn't know. And he didn't know John's last name, which I believe because neither did his parents. I highly doubt they'd lie to us."

"And he took the time to find it out for us." Carter was surprisingly in agreement now and then.

"So Whitman is the main target?"

He was learning about how the feds worked. As a county detective they had only cases, no targets. "I think main suspect for now, but here is my question. Why was Amanda Reynolds so secretive about John Newsome anyway?"

He was now thinking out loud, a few wheels spinning, wishing he had something better to drink than the less-than-perfect coffee Sheriff Lawrence insisted would make a man out of anyone, it was so strong. It might peel the paint off a car, but it wouldn't ensure your masculinity.

"Hold on, wait a minute." Chris scratched his forehead, thinking hard, looking for it. "We are not seeing this clearly. There's a link . . . I can sense it. Three identical killings and we can link two of them, but the only thing I know about the unrelated one is her social worker thought she was clean."

Carter was astute. "Drugs?"

"Could be. This particular part of our fair state has an unsavory reputation for having some problem with that."

Norris wasn't slow either. "Amanda Reynolds worked as a forensic accountant for the state, and she knows Whitman, who works for his father's firm."

"I think I'm starting to get the impression Amanda wasn't actually seeing Mr. John Newsome and that is why her family didn't know anything about him. What if they were working together to bring Whitman down? She certainly had an unpleasant history with him."

"So much for a calm little county." Norris looked perturbed. "So your theory is that she decides to get some retribution by having him investigated because there is a hint of impropriety in the books, stumbles over a link to a drug ring of some sort, and so he kills her and the investigator she hired?"

Chris was having trouble digesting this too. "Let's not dismiss that someone is dead who was a former user, who could maybe point a finger."

"Now we have a thread."

Carter was the veteran and good at this. He was the person to listen to and so Chris contemplated it. "What we're thinking is that maybe Amanda had a clue that the business wasn't up and up, and decided to personally look into it since she was not a fan of Whitman in the first place, and got a whiff of something off? So she hired Newsome and they both ended up dead? That explains a lot to me."

"We have zero proof that ever happened, but if she paid him, there's a paper trail."

Norris shook his head. "She was a *forensic* accountant. We deal with them on a regular basis. They can spot things a field agent could never find. No, she didn't work for the federal government but for the state, yet she had the tools she needed if she thought something was going on. I wouldn't leave a hint of a clue if dealing with illegal drugs. The word ruthless doesn't even describe the dealers."

"They don't pull their punches, true enough," Chris admitted. "We deal with it more than we care to around these parts."

It was undeniable, there were some cases where they were sure the disappearances or deaths were disputes over profits or losses from an extremely toxic and illegal industry they could barely keep under moderate control. The DEA helped all they could, but they were outnumbered — and outgunned, half the time.

"I guess we'll see if the DNA test gives us anything." Carter's demeanor was as reserved as ever but his expression thoughtful. "This slant on it makes me look at these three murders differently than before. Maybe those deliveries of personal items of the victims aren't so much malicious as they are a warning to just not pursue it too much or there will be retaliation."

Not good news if that was true. "If you're right, I guess I've already gotten my first warning to back off."

* * *

Anna got there first, and Mrs. Dunn answered the door with an anxious smile. "Hello, honey. Is something wrong?"

The older lady was dressed in a wool suit and shoes with a low heel probably in deference for meeting with a detective, a formality that when she met Chris Bailey would probably be dismissed as an unnecessary effort.

Anna smiled in reassurance. "I just talked to the school, and everything is going very well. I'm just here as a friend for you while you talk to Detective Bailey. He's very nice, and I think you will like him."

She knew she did, so it was easy to be sincere.

"Come in and we'll wait for him." They walked into the living room, which was tidy and well-kept and doubtfully ever used given the immaculate surroundings. It was reassuring to see that such things were still on the radar and standards maintained because managing even a small household while caring for a young child got away from a lot of people, much less someone who was eighty years old. According to the school principal, her great-granddaughter seemed stable and adjusted.

Well done, Helen.

Chris was on time, she'd give him that. Maybe he had a grandmother with a strict adherence to timetables. She'd have to ask someday. He'd mentioned his brother but otherwise didn't talk much about himself. Could be he was just male and reticent, or private enough he didn't share. She'd met his mom but only by accident.

They were still on a journey, traveling the same road cautiously. Absolutely fine with her. She'd rushed in once. Never again.

He pulled in and he'd brought his partner with him, though she hadn't quite expected that, both of them getting out of the black car. Carter had absolutely no interest in pursuing federal law enforcement that she knew. This cold case would be a waste of his time.

Or maybe not.

To Anna's surprise, Carter greeted her client by her first name. "Miss Helen. How are you?"

Mrs. Dunn nodded. "Officer Carter? You look so much like your father I'm never sure which one of you I'm talking to."

"I'm here with Detective Bailey since he's going over the old case. We work together."

In contrast, as usual, Chris looked like he was about to climb on a bronc at a rodeo. His hair was tousled, boots on the worn side and, as far as she could tell, he didn't mind at all that he didn't look like a detective, he just cared if he was a good one.

It was unfortunately part of what made him so attractive.

He waited politely until Mrs. Dunn took a chair, gave Anna a brief greeting that hinted at no indication they had ever shared a bed, and looked dubiously at the sofa draped in a hand-knitted afghan before he sat down.

Then — interesting to her from a psychological viewpoint — he took charge. Carter was older, clearly had more experience, but he just let Chris talk.

"So," he said in the slow way he had of thinking out loud, "can you explain to me what happened years ago that left you in a position where you didn't even realize you had a niece, much less that she and her husband were murdered in the very same way as your own daughter and son-in-law?"

Helen basically recited just what she'd told Anna, only her tightly clasped hands showing her tension. Then she said, "You think this is tied to my brother Clarence, don't you?"

As usual, Chris walked around the direct question. "It definitely seems it was his daughter killed in a similar manner in Kentucky."

There was a hesitation, but Mrs. Dunn asked, "Is Clarence still alive?"

Chris did look reluctant to answer, but he did. "No, ma'am. He died a few years ago. He was a mechanic by trade and belonged to a union. I was only able to trace the connection between your daughter and him by the similar nature of the crime, and then on a hunch I checked into what your maiden name was. It matched the father of the young woman in the other murders. I believe the reason why no one thought to do that before was the murders were in different states, and years apart. Birth records showed you were siblings."

"I think you are one clever young man." Helen Dunn looked moved. She cleared her throat. "So, you have answered already a few important questions for me. Thank you for putting so much effort into it."

Anna couldn't agree more, but there were more questions still hanging out there. One of them was how he found time to even look into this with the shooting cases, but she was just grateful he had. She had to ask the loaded question. "So why in different states, why cousins, and why years apart?"

He didn't answer her; he looked at Helen. "Your brother married a woman who already had a child. The stepson seems to definitely have walked a crooked path. He was in and out of jail, and I assume you didn't realize your daughter had started to communicate with your brother's daughter. I can't provide enough evidence as of now to prove it, but the three years between the crimes coincides with three years the stepson spent incarcerated for several violations of the law."

"Good heavens." Helen's hand went to her throat.

"He knew your daughter was married to a doctor. They would, to the reckoning of most people, have money and other valuables. I've looked over his record, and you should be grateful he spared your granddaughter. He also spared his stepsister's children."

"And was intelligent enough to use different states for both crimes." Detective Carter was as ever analytic. "It all is circumstantial, and he is nowhere to be found. I'm going to guess Mexico or maybe even Canada. We have extradition with both, but we have to trace him, and he disappeared years ago. He never did pay taxes, so we can't trace that."

"No, he's closer than you think. I know where he is." Chris didn't sleep much at night, so he'd really looked.

"What?" Carter stared at him in open exasperation. "Do you mind sharing information like that with me?"

"We don't have enough right now to charge him, but we will."

CHAPTER TWENTY-TWO

There was a certain beauty to the plan, in this case location, location, location.

The cemetery was along a road leading to virtually nowhere. When they'd built at a considerable cost a new highway with double lanes, this country road had become beneath the notice of travelers. The county maintained the pavement, such as it was, with patches for the deep potholes, and it was mowed in the summers along the shoulder so the vegetation didn't take over.

The body would be discovered eventually.

Let the game continue.

* * *

The painting looked stunning above the river rock fireplace, not hung but just perched on the walnut mantel, resting against the wall, a perfect size suited to the room.

The Young Lovers. It had been signed and titled on the back.

"Where did you find it?" Mick studied it and admired the simplistic style. It wasn't precisely what he would label primitive art, but maybe southern impressionism if there was such a categorization. Soft edges and blended colors.

Two people in a small rowboat on a lake, the girl wearing a feminine straw hat with a long pink ribbon, the young man shirtless and grinning, holding up a fish on a line, the oars trailing in the water as the sun set just above the trees, giving the bucolic scene a scarlet glow.

It was just the right touch.

"My grandmother gave it to me years ago when they moved into town. It used to hang in her dining room, and I think my great-aunt bought it for her at an art exhibition in Knoxville." Samantha looked pleased, standing back and looking at it with her hands on her — in his opinion — very nicely shaped hips. "My house doesn't have the right place for it, but here it fits."

So do you.

Not in the right place for that conversation, but he had his mother to thank for lodging it in his head in the first place. "I really like it there. Are you sure you want to give it to me?"

She gave him a look that question deserved. "Yes, or I wouldn't have done it."

"Then thank you." He meant it sincerely, because it suited the house and the surroundings, and their relationship as well. They had certainly been young lovers, holding hands in the high school hallway, sharing a locker, front porch goodnight kisses that lingered on, then moved on to college nights sharing a dorm room single bed, whispers in the dark . . .

He kissed her then, just a light pressure of his mouth on hers because he was grateful she was there to share his evenings, not just his bed. A different sort of communication. Six years had given him a perspective of what he wanted. The passion still existed but was tempered by a realization that her company in his life was what he'd missed the most.

Her hand came up to rest on his shoulder, the other one at his waist. It might have turned into a very pleasurable afternoon if her phone hadn't started ringing.

She murmured against his mouth, "Sorry. Let me look."

"Sure." He let her go — with some reluctance — and turned around to open an unpacked box in the corner he hoped was the final one. Rain streaked the tall windows.

"That was Sandy's number, but no one said anything." Samantha looked pale suddenly. "I think someone was there, but . . ."

"An accidental pocket dial?"

"Maybe. I would think so, but I did give the detective her number and so she's involved in all this."

He had to agree with that. Uneasy was his reaction. He straightened. "Call back. If she answers, all is well."

Sam's fine brows drew together, and she hit a button. "Good idea."

She waited and stared at her phone after a minute or so. "That's weird. Someone answered but didn't say anything."

The truth was he didn't like it either. He walked back into the kitchen and wished he felt fine with having whiskey at this time of day. "I don't like it, but it could be nothing."

"I could swear I could hear someone breathing like I was in a horror flick."

He shook his head, leaning against the counter. "I'd call Bailey, but first of all, it could just be nothing, and second of all, it seems like I'm implicated at every turn and I'm not going to play into that. Let's ignore it."

"What if something has happened to her?"

"Sam, if I knew what to do, I'd do it. If someone other than her has her phone . . ." He trailed off, not even sure what to say.

They looked at each other.

Finally, he said in resignation, "I guess you should call Bailey and at least report it. If Shawn hadn't acted so off, I wouldn't be on edge, but I am. I agree, since she doesn't usually call you, it was strange."

Would he dismiss it if people weren't being killed in some ritualistic fashion? Maybe. He'd call the detective himself, but he'd made a few too many of those calls lately and had the uncomfortable feeling he had too much of the attention of the local police as it stood. Not to mention, he hadn't gotten the phone call, she had.

"I think I will just tell him what happened. Let him decide if it is worthy of alarm or not."

"That sounds like a reasonable course of action."

If he was a detective — and he had no desire to pursue that occupation — he would not want to be bothered with every small fact, but he wouldn't be happy if parties involved failed to mention something that might help.

"I'll try her again in a few minutes." She set down her cell on the counter and managed an impersonation of a smile as the rain hammered suddenly at the window. "I think it is supposed to be like this all afternoon. Just listen to it come down."

"At least it isn't snow."

"True enough."

He wouldn't have minded spending this inclement afternoon with her in bed in the most enjoyable way possible while listening to the whisper of the rain. That is, if life were the slightest bit normal, but it just wasn't. So he went over and took a beer out of the refrigerator instead and twisted off the cap. "How about you?"

Samantha's brows went up a fraction but then she said, "Good idea. I may take you up on that. Shades of college. Remember breakfast club?"

"Seven thirty in the morning on football Saturdays and all the bars opened. How could I forget? And it is four in the afternoon."

"You just won me over. I'll take one and then try Sandy again."

* * *

No answer.

The cold beer tasted pretty good, but it didn't help much with the call to Detective Bailey, who did answer.

She was worried she was wasting his time, but then again more worried she wasn't.

"This is Samantha Davidson. Ah, well, I have no idea if this means anything at all, but Sandy, the one whose number I gave you because she was friends with Amanda Reynolds, tried to call me," She paused. "Or someone did from her phone. They didn't say anything, but they were there. I've tried calling back three times. I can't get a response."

"I . . . see."

"I'm maybe wasting your time."

"Ms. Davidson, considering she knows two people connected to three similar murders, I'll look into this."

"Shawn Whitman was the one who told Mick about the third murder."

"We're aware."

When the call ended, she gazed at Mick, not exactly defiant but questioning. "Am I wrong?"

"I wish I could definitively say yes," he said with evident regret.

"One of the seven sins. Envy."

"I don't know about that part of it."

"Honey, women are jealous of each other all the time." She gave that statement her best southern twang and swirled her hand in a theatrical circle. Then she added in a normal voice because it was a serious topic, "It happens with men too."

"I know you believe that."

"I do. Why else would it be one of the seven sins? And I think Amanda died because of it. Not because of you, so stop right there, but because of *him*. You want an ordered world, and it isn't one."

"I want a world that makes sense to me." The set of his shoulders was taut, and she knew he meant it.

"You aren't in his shoes."

"Jesus, Samantha, what does that mean?"

"Have you ever read *A Separate Peace*?"

He'd already thought of it. She could see it on his face. "Knowles. Yes. I've read it."

A part of her understood his resistance to go along with her theory, but she also thought she was right, and while in the classic work the antagonist wasn't a serial killer, this wasn't a fiction novel.

She crossed her arms over her chest. "Mick, he's an adversary, not a friend."

"We've been over this. I don't disagree. I'm not convinced either."

"I'm thinking Detective Bailey may solve your indecision."

"Has it occurred to you this might be about *you*?"

"What?" She blinked.

He considered her. "Men usually are at odds over two things. A show of power or women. You are beautiful, I don't think that point is arguable."

She considered him back, the wide shoulders and confident air, those unforgettable eyes . . .

It was a very nice compliment.

"We see it differently. Since this is an ongoing discussion, I'll point out the flaw in your argument. He doesn't want me as much as he wants what you have."

"Do I have you?"

Equally nice comeback.

She wasn't sixteen any longer. "It depends on how much you want me."

If there was nothing else to be said for Mick Reynolds, it was that he had an easy charm. "If you can't tell, I guess I'm not doing things right."

"Oh, you do most things just fine."

"Just fine?"

She put her hand on his chest, her palm against solid flesh and bone. His hand came up to cover hers. "I think you know the answer. Better than fine, how's that."

His fingers tightened. "What are we doing?"

"I don't know exactly."

"I don't either. That can't be good."

They weren't using birth control and she knew he wanted to ask why, but when it came down to the decision, it was his choice as well and they weren't talking about it.

For two intelligent adults, they were acting as if leaving it up to fate was a reasonable course to follow. It was her turn to comment. She gazed at him. "I think we've both made a decision that might be life-changing and never talked about it."

"With each other."

"Right. Should we?"

"Talk?" He actually laughed, but it was quiet. "I don't think so. I believe we are on the same page and have had that conversation but not in words."

He could be right. The communication had been there, but more content needed to be addressed.

"I don't think I ever fell out of love with you. I tried."

"You tried?" His brows drew together. "I don't even know how to take that."

"Why be romantically involved with a man who lives in a big city several states away?"

"Maybe come join him?" He said it in soft challenge.

This issue probably needed to be addressed at some time. though whether this was the right moment was unclear to her. "I had to finish college, for myself and my parents who paid for every penny of my education but couldn't afford out-of-state tuition."

"You stopped answering my calls."

"I'd heard you'd started dating someone."

"I believe I was trying to get over you also, but only because you seemed out of reach."

She didn't want to know how many women he might have slept with in those six years they were apart, not because she thought he was indiscriminate, but because if she found him so attractive, she assumed other women did as well. Actually, she knew they did. Plenty of opportunities in a city like Chicago.

"Nightlife, sophisticated settings, the corporate world. I imagine—"

"No, you're wrong because I can tell from the tone of this discussion what you are thinking." He caught her waist, interrupting and looking at her directly, their faces inches apart. "That's not how this Tennessee boy lives his life. Why do you think I moved back?"

No other lovers? She didn't believe it or expect it. On the other hand, she wasn't going to ask for specifics. She touched his cheek. "You came home."

"I think you might have been a part of that."

When he lowered his mouth to hers, she thought dinner might be postponed for quite some time.

It was.

CHAPTER TWENTY-THREE

What an unexpected evolution.

The impatience had been replaced by anticipation.

Interesting. At least to the killer.

It had started with a simple compelling motivation, but now it was all different.

* * *

It was clear Sandra Lea Rolla was missing.

Social media had helped him track down her profile page so he could figure out where she worked since she wasn't answering her cell phone and didn't return his calls. Samantha Davidson didn't know the name of the law firm she was attached to, but he found out. They occasionally hired private investigators for certain cases.

There was the connection he needed to Newsome.

They were pursuing something, and it was a deadly inquiry.

It was a familiar refrain to hear she didn't show up for work and hadn't for two days. A pattern, a determined killer, and unless she was aware of the danger and had decided to hide, another possible victim connected to the same case.

Chris hoped she was alive and well, but so far, all the victims had in common were a lonely farewell on a country road, so that was where they needed to look for her.

Not a small task in this corner of the world. Winding two-lane highways, lots of crowded woods, creeks, and then the big rivers. If you wanted remote, you could find it.

Carter echoed that sentiment. "Waste of our time."

Bailey wasn't sure that was true. "Lawrence is losing his cool over this. I don't blame him."

His partner shot him a sardonic glance, driving with his usual competence. "Losing his cool? Were your parents even born in the seventies?"

"They were born in the sixties, and for your edification, we still use 'Damn the torpedoes, full speed ahead,' and that is way older."

"Admiral Farragut and I can't remember the last time I used that quote, but do go ahead. Where?"

"If I were the killer, someplace close to where Reynolds lives. He's the trigger."

"As much as I like to find you wrong, I think you are probably right. I am not really ready to walk those remote lanes and skirt the streams."

Chris couldn't help it; he had to grimace in acknowledgment. "You need to dress more like me."

"So I can tramp around to search for discarded bodies? I'll let you do it."

"Let's just hope that isn't what we are doing."

"You know I agree with that."

"I don't think this is the same as the other ones." He was thinking out loud. Moodily he contemplated the vista of drab trees, though there was a promising hint of green here and there. "If Whitman is guilty and our theory holds, he had clear motive for the first three killings, especially Amanda Reynolds — there was a conflict between them and she was looking for a way to get to him. But none for this one."

"None we can see. We don't know Sandra Rolla is a victim. Let me point out she is a paralegal and a friend of one of the victims. Maybe the killer is afraid she's heard his name mentioned or somehow knows what is going on. She hooked Amanda Reynolds up with a private investigator."

Always the voice of reason, Carter was right. Chris was operating on the assumption that a normally responsible person came to work each day or at least called to say there was a reason for a necessary absence, and she was tied to two other murders.

They at least needed to ask Reynolds if they could look around.

What happened next might make or break the case. The real question was if they found her, was it because he was canny enough to keep perpetrating that theory someone wanted to frame him?

Intelligent, yes. But was he their quarry? He was unconvinced.

If they found anything even close to the property, he'd be inclined to agree with a suggestion they bring Reynolds in for questioning.

He answered the door with a less-than-welcoming and inquiring look on his face, and who could blame him. "Detectives?"

"Do you mind if we take a look around?" Carter did have a way of making unpleasant requests in a civil way.

"I don't think so, but given everything, can I ask why?"

"It has to do with an ongoing investigation."

Michael Reynolds stood in his doorway and gave what was probably an appropriate answer. "I hope so. That's not my question. Feel free, but tell me you have a legitimate reason for asking in the first place."

"We do."

He evidently knew a stone wall when he met one. "Go ahead."

They walked away, and Carter said with his usual pragmatic approach, "If you have some sort of plan, I wouldn't mind hearing it. I'm trained to investigate crimes that have actually been committed."

"Aren't we doing that? She's part of the equation."

"Or else just dodging five bullets that she thinks might be coming her way?"

A grim possible reality, but after walking all around the small lake and the barren woods, they found nothing out of the ordinary other than a deer skull probably from the fall when a hunter had dressed his kill on the property and left the remains for the scavengers. Six-point buck with antlers still attached. So maybe shot out of season?

Not a surprise. People around these parts did sometimes hunt for food.

Not everyone was Reynolds, who could afford this kind of place, but there was no one dead in the woods that they could see besides one young deer.

Back to a zero.

Not that he wanted to find a victim, but he was worried she was out there.

They went back to the house and were greeted with a keen-eyed inquiring look from the suspect and were invited inside. Good, they had, as usual, a few questions. This visit was quite inconclusive so far.

The living room had turned out nicely. There was even a fire going in the stone hearth, the warmth nice in the cool of the afternoon. Leather couch, big square coffee table, all very masculine, but there was a vase of spring flowers that obviously came from a florist on a side table, and Chris imagined Ms. Davidson was responsible for that. He kind of missed the old recliner, but there was a plaid chair, and he chose that.

Carter was direct. "Thank you for the cooperation."

"Do you think for a moment I wouldn't do anything to help you solve my sister's murder?"

It wasn't like he blamed Reynolds for the reaction, as they had just searched his property and that was a borderline accusation of possible guilt. "We always try to determine the truth. That is our job." Chris thought it was a diplomatic response.

"And I appreciate that, but why here?"

"I'm sure you understand why. You're connected to the cases in some way."

"Oh shit." Reynolds ran his hand through his hair. "Something *else* has happened?"

Carter was his usual composed self. "When Ms. Davidson gave you the number for your sister's friend, did you give that information to anyone else besides Detective Bailey?"

"No." Quick and decisive. He shook his head. "The minute Sam gave that number to me, I called you. I'm not an investigator. You two are."

* * *

Dissection happened on a table he didn't care to sit at, but sometimes Chris had to pull up a chair.

Lawrence was unhappy and he never hid that well. "What in heckfire is happening?"

"She's connected to the three other murders and is missing." Carter was somber but his tone even. "We're looking."

The sheriff was a good lawman. He took that in and did a short summary. "So you did an assessment and your theory of where you might find her didn't work out. What is your next move?"

It was a very valid question. Chris was sure the sheriff was catching heat for three murders in such a short period of time and no clear arrest in sight. "I think our perp is growing more subtle and he is engaging us in a different way. No roadside involved. He is challenging us to find her."

"Lord, son, you have a complicated way of looking at things at times." Sheriff Lawrence shook his head and was as straightforward as ever. "Given I think that is valuable insight if I was a damned psychologist — and we all know I'm not one — you didn't answer my question."

Guilty as charged there. Chris had really been thinking about it to the exclusion of almost anything else. He'd slept maybe three hours the night before. Alone too. Anna had left a message she had other plans for dinner.

He hadn't asked about those plans. Maybe he should have? There was a very good chance he was better at police work than he was at managing his personal life. That had occurred to him more than once.

At the moment he needed to respond to his boss. "This is tied to Reynolds, so I want to talk to his father."

Carter just gave him a skeptical look. "His father? The one with the murdered daughter? You don't think he'd approach us if he could help?"

"I absolutely believe he'd help if pointed in the right direction."

"And what direction would that be?" Lawrence asked it with true interest. He was much more like Carter and uninterested in why a certain person did something, but more in solving the crime and moving on to the next problem.

"First of all, I want to ask if his daughter mentioned she was looking into Whitman to him and what she had to go on. I can see why she might not to her brother, but to her dad? She might. He's also a third-generation farmer. He knows this county probably even better than we do and we're from here too. He knew his daughter, he knows his son, and I think if something has happened to Sandra Rolla, she's been left here in this county. All the others have."

"So he'd have an educated guess where?"

"I'm thinking so. Am I hoping they find her alive and well in Nashville before then, yes, but I don't know that will happen. I don't like at all that Natalie Fields was a former user and addict. Is that the connection? If Whitman uses the agency to launder money for drug dealers around here, maybe Fields made some kind of connection. She could have been the one to give Amanda Reynolds the ammunition to go after Whitman."

"Lord, I don't need another drug problem around these parts."

"I think it would be more accurate to say her death might be attached to a problem you already have, but it was caused by something else like a vendetta."

Lawrence blew out a short breath. "Bailey, don't talk in circles. I don't have time for it."

"All I'm saying is these murders were personal and maybe tied in, but this county's drug problem is not the real tinder that lit the fire."

"What did?"

"Reynolds."

They were in Sheriff Lawrence's office, and he was behind his desk, in his old chair he refused to replace because he claimed it was broken-in, which squeaked as he leaned forward and put his elbows on the mound of paperwork in front of him. "I'm going to be clear here. Tell me how. You haven't even brought him in for questioning and three people are dead. A fourth person is missing."

"He's just the locomotive that is driving the train." Chris spoke carefully, not entirely sure how to express his thoughts. "The baggage car is the problem. He doesn't even know it is there, but it follows him just the same. He doesn't have the answer. If he did, he'd tell us."

"I'm willing to believe Ms. Davidson." Carter offered that up. "I think Norris might agree. That friendly drink wasn't so friendly, and her story about how Whitman treated Amanda Reynolds sets off alarm bells. She doesn't seem to me to be the type to make that up."

Lawrence always listened to Carter, which was fine. "How do we bring Whitman in?"

That was a good question. Chris had been asking himself just that thing. "Let's talk to Ray Reynolds, see what he has to say, and go from there as we wait for the DNA results. If it is a match, we're done."

"You'll still have slim pickin's in the solid evidence department, son."

"I think Stephanie St. James will weigh the case and the history and listen to me. I know her pretty well."

"In the meantime," Carter provided, "we are trying to decide if we should interview Mr. Whitman. We don't really have a solid reason besides that he knew the first victim, but it might be worth it to let him know he's on the radar of local law enforcement."

The sheriff frowned. "Or make him harder to pin down because he will settle back and reconnoiter. Your call, but I know I don't want more murders on my watch."

Chris couldn't agree more, but it was a tough call. "I think we should let him still believe he's not been brought to our attention. He's made some risky moves and we have Norris now out there as well. He's undercover and keeping an eye on things with Reynolds."

"*If* Whitman is your man and Reynolds is his focus." Lawrence was as pragmatic as they came. "Let's just hope we find Ms. Rolla alive and kicking."

Chris had a real worry they wouldn't. The circle was too tight. All the players were falling off the stage one by one, and he recognized whoever was responsible for these deaths in such a methodical way was simply eliminating any witnesses. He said, "Let's go talk to Ray. It's worth a try."

CHAPTER TWENTY-FOUR

There were lonely places and then there were desolate spaces devoid of any humanity.
    Very different.
    Abandonment is a travesty.
    Apparently also an opportunity.

* * *

The lake was peaceful and the temperature in the upper forties, so Mick could drop in a line while only wearing a lightweight jacket.

It was one hell of a better way to spend a few minutes after a morning meeting than sitting at a desk in a building in a bustling city with people constantly coming to his office and interrupting him with questions or reading the barrage of emails. Not to mention the hum of congested traffic in the background. This meeting had been remote, quick and positive, and so far the staff he'd hired seemed to be efficient and as happy as he was, so motivated to work from a home base. He'd learned a lot about how to run a corporation from his time in Chicago — and how not to run one as well — so maybe it had been worth those six years.

Perfect.

Well, not quite.

He'd lost time with Samantha and had to weigh that in, but they seemed to be making it up now. It was definitely different, a new exploration, the rediscovery more interesting than their initial relationship. Man and woman, not boy and girl.

The arrival of the van with the two technicians to install the security system put an end to his fishing and introspection. It hadn't proved to be anything but therapeutic in any case, with the slight breeze and the sway of the branches on the trees. No bites this particular morning.

He'd decided, with a new cynical view of the world despite the bucolic setting, to opt for a high-end system and not rely on a country-boy upbringing of unlocked doors and friendly neighbors.

"Cameras front and back and one by the garage too."

"Door sensors?"

"For sure."

He was still talking to them when his father pulled up in his well-used truck. He got out and glanced at the logo on the service vehicle and lifted his brows. "Good idea, Mick."

"Yeah. I'm going to be here most of the time, but still, recent events are on my mind."

His father had a tendency to not pull punches. "Let's talk."

"Have at it," he told the techs, gesturing at the house. "We'll just take a short walk, but if you have a question, I'll be within earshot." His dad handled a farm and the day was nice enough, so a stroll outside would be fine with him and there was something obviously on his mind.

They walked back down to the lake, hands in pockets.

"What else has happened? Something has. The two detectives came to visit me. Asked me a bunch of interesting questions." His father sounded perplexed and unhappy, which was understandable.

That would be Carter and Bailey. Mick looked at the glimmering water. "I'd ask what they told you, but I'm guessing very little. There have been three murders now similar to what happened to Amanda. I know they are trying to figure out if there is a common thread."

"Three?" His father frowned. "Natalie Fields. They asked if she was Amanda's friend. I've never met her if she was a friend, so my answer was I have no idea. But then they started asking me about remote locations in this county. I also got a few pointed inquiries about Shawn Whitman. What is that about, Mick?"

How to answer? He had no idea except with the truth, though this was a grieving parent, and he wasn't positive that was a good idea. He weighed his answer. "I don't know exactly what happened since Amanda never said anything to me about it, but Samantha seems to believe that he's really not a good guy. She said something about it to the detectives."

They stopped by the edge of the water.

"Yeah." His father's profile was austere and remote. His hair was going from blond to gray but in a distinguished transition, and it was ruffled by the light breeze. "He was your friend, so I didn't think too much about it. I got the impression your sister agreed with Samantha because she said something to your mother about him asking her out and she'd turned him down flat. That was years ago, but when they started asking questions, I remembered it."

His father might be a rural Tennessee boy, but so was he, and he thought they were both pretty practical but also insightful. Mick bent over and picked up a rock to toss it in the water. "I'm just wondering if there's more to this investigation than we can see from what we know."

His father's expression was troubled. "If I had to call it, I'd say you're right there."

"You come up with anything with the remote location suggestion?" The breeze was late February cool, but the sun was warm as they stood there just looking out over the water.

"I did. A few of them. That old logging trail by the state park that belongs now to the DNR. Three Notch Road. It floods so much it is always in rough shape. Since they built the new highway, no one really uses it. There's Waverly Road and no one uses it either since that church burned down, and if you want deserted, that is a no man's destination. There are certainly Reynolds buried there."

"I think they are casting around in all directions for something, but I have no idea what it is."

"You know, years ago a young woman was found dead there in the church cemetery. Maybe twenty years or so ago. You were a kid. I'm trying to recall more details."

No, he didn't know that. He stared at his father. "Really?"

His cheeks ruddy, because despite the sun it was still cold, his father shook his head. "I doubt it means anything anyway, but I know I thought it was a convenient choice for someone to put a body. Those graves don't get visited often. She was there for a while before she was found, so when they asked me, I just remembered it."

Bailey and Carter would get specifics. Of that he was certain.

He wondered if Shawn knew about that old tragic discovery in a deserted graveyard.

"They will pick up that ball and run with it." He really had no idea what was happening on the sidelines, but he did know the players were in the game.

"Someone killed my child." His father's voice broke, and that was not his usual self-possessed persona. "I am counting on those two officers to find them and at least hold that person accountable."

Mick felt exactly the same way for more reasons than justice being served. He was afraid for just about everyone he knew at this point. "Who is with Mom?"

* * *

Samantha finished with her last appointment and closed out the file, glancing up to see the receptionist was in the doorway. "Yes, Bonnie?"

"Client to see you. I didn't realize you had another appointment, and I have to pick up my daughter." The young woman looked apologetic.

She didn't have another appointment. Not unless another CPA had to cancel with one of theirs, but she'd need their file, so it seemed unlikely they'd refer them without saying something or asking her to stay late.

Sam felt a frisson of dismay that she knew who it might be. "Who else is still here?"

"Um, Greta. She's going to lock up."

Wonderful. A sixty-year-old woman on the slender side with a penchant for listening to jazz in her office with headphones while working late.

Not much protection there.

She glanced at her phone to check the time. Mick was due to pick her up. She didn't like this at all. "I'll come out to talk to this person. Please note I don't have another appointment and remember what he looks like."

Bonnie blinked. "Okay."

She got up after shutting down her computer and fully expected to find Shawn Whitman waiting in the reception area, and she wasn't disappointed. It wasn't like they hadn't seen each other now and then just in the course of coming from the same place with mutual acquaintances, but it was hardly usual for him to stop by her office.

In fact, it had never happened before.

Dark hair, nice features, good build, he was not an unattractive man, but that insincere smile and the coldness in his eyes were familiar.

"Sorry I just dropped in, but I was passing by and saw your office parking lot was pretty empty and thought I'd take a chance you'd still be here. I'm sure Mick told you we had a drink the other night. Nice to see him again, and I guess you are back together."

He was telling her in a very definite way he knew Mick was taking her back and forth to work and that perhaps he should be careful.

She'd been pretty sure before but at this moment felt a literal chill.

"We're seeing each other." She didn't know what else to say and kept it low key. "Yes, he told me you met up."

Nice to see you? Hell no.

Bonnie might only have a high school education, but she was bright and personable and handled the job with the phones and greeting clients efficiently and evidently. Right now she could sense the tension, and despite declaring she needed to leave, she lingered behind the desk, arranging paperwork and appearing seemingly busy, which was hardly an act in tax season.

If she hadn't been there, Samantha would have been even more nervous and she was on edge enough. What was the point of this?

"Just wanted to say hi. Nice to have him back, right?"

"It is." She summoned a smile.

"It's about time for him to pick you up."

To her relief, he turned and left. Immediately as the door closed, Bonnie said, "I'm sorry, but that was just weird."

"Yes." Sam couldn't help but agree grimly.

"Is that man stalking you or something?"

"Actually, I think he's stalking my boyfriend. Thanks for staying a few more minutes."

"What?" Her blue eyes were wide. "That's double weird. No problem about waiting, but are you going to be okay now if I leave?"

"Mick will be here soon to pick me up," she reassured her, and at that moment he walked through the door.

"Was that Whitman pulling out of the parking lot?" He looked both concerned and relieved to see her standing there. "He came here?"

"He just dropped by." She said it blithely, but it wasn't how she felt about it. That impromptu visit was disturbing, and they could discuss it later, but for now, she wanted to get out of the office. "I'm ready if you are."

"I'm out of here too." Bonnie hurried out the door and they followed, and yes, the parking lot was nearly deserted. Mick pressed a button to start the car and politely opened the passenger door. Sam slid in, grateful to be leaving.

He went around and got in, his face set. "I understand you not wanting to discuss it in front of anyone else, but what the hell did he have to say that he'd come to see you at your office?"

It was a legitimate question. "He just indicated without saying it outright that he knew we were spending time together and that he knew you were bringing me back and forth to work."

Silence. He pulled out of the parking lot and didn't speak for a few minutes. "I don't like this game because I don't understand it."

The evening was deepening, the nice afternoon changing to indigo skies with the encroaching dusk. Sam looked out the window and murmured, "Of course you don't. Logic doesn't apply, and you believe everyone should be reasonable and operate under a set of rules."

"The idea you were even face-to-face with him for a few minutes sends me into a near panic just in case he really is dangerous."

"Bonnie was there. I made sure she didn't show him into my office and leave us alone. When she came and told me I had another appointment and I knew I didn't, I thought immediately of him. I'm aware."

His smile was humorless. "Yes, I believe you pointed him out to me as a possibility and I admit it shakes my faith in my ability to read human beings and judge their character correctly, especially after that drink the other night. Looking at him from a different angle has explained a few questions I wasn't cognizant I even had."

"Like?"

"I knew he cheated on tests in high school, but just to see if he could get away with it. He bragged about it and thought it was funny. Does that make him a sociopath? I'm starting to wonder."

"It definitely makes me question his moral values. Would you do it?"

"No, but we aren't the same person. His dad would laugh it off. Mine would be livid if I did something like that. Why not just spend the time to study? That was how I was raised."

She knew he was telling the truth. Michael Reynolds wouldn't ever consider getting by on anything but his personal merits. If she was certain of anything, he would never cheat. He wasn't a paragon by any means with plenty of the normal human failings, but a decent, intelligent human being who held himself to a certain standard. He wouldn't find it amusing to get away with something underhanded. He simply wouldn't consider it in the first place.

"I think maybe that you and Whitman aren't the same person is the source of the problem."

CHAPTER TWENTY-FIVE

It was not for the faint of heart.

Luckily, he'd left that behind a long time ago.

The killer wasn't shy about death. He'd been ten when his mother died, and remembered blood everywhere, eyes open.

Not the finest moment of his life.

So the setting didn't bother him too much. It was fitting.

* * *

They found the body easily enough.

The headstones were speckled with lichen like a malevolent disease, some of them drunkenly tilted, all of them worn so the names and dates were not even legible in some cases, many of them from before the Civil War. Most were shaded by some venerable pines that had been there as long as the graves they guarded.

Winding Lane Cemetery. No irony there.

They were on the path that went through the oldest part of the graveyard and was probably overgrown in the summer but this time of year was simply lined with dead grass, which was appropriate to the location. She was sprawled face down in a graceless pose, one arm bent under her, brunette hair shielding her face.

Carter shook his head. "You have to be kidding me. What a charming setting."

"Not so much." Chris didn't consider himself superstitious or even someone who particularly believed in the occult, but he would not want to traverse this particular piece of real estate on a moonlit night. Now was bad enough. "That said, I doubt this section is visited by anyone except maybe some history buffs. Generations have come and gone since these folks were put in the ground. Good hiding spot, and if they knew about the previous murder, a clever choice."

"You do realize either Whitman or Reynolds could know of it." Carter skirted a pile of last year's fallen leaves as they looked around on a less-than-perfect search for any obvious evidence. "They were children then, so they didn't commit that crime, but we know at least Reynolds's father remembers it."

"So Whitman's could as well. Their sons are the same age. It could probably be true for both of them."

They were still waiting for Loren, and Chris could only imagine what he'd have to say about this fourth visit. Some dry remark, no doubt, but that didn't mean he didn't care about the victims; he did, or he wouldn't ever bother with such an inconvenient job.

He didn't disappoint when he arrived and got out of his vehicle. "Ah, Halloween in February, I see. The two of you should have worn caps and cloaks and each have a magnifying glass as you lurk among tombstones."

"We are working on it," Carter informed him without rancor, because the man had a point. There was an active killer. "It looks like the same pattern."

"I'll do my part." Loren pulled on his gloves, stethoscope around his neck, not that it was necessary. He went on, briskly professional as usual. "Any idea who she is?"

"We do." Chris was able to say that at least. "Unfortunately, part of the same case."

"I believe I agree with the unfortunate part. Let me take a look."

It didn't take him long.

When he departed with his unfortunate passenger, Carter said somberly, "We have a problem. I mean I *knew* we had a problem, but not like this."

"No." Chris wasn't a fan of the desolate location. "He's definitely local. At first, I thought maybe not, but he is. Not everyone would be aware of this place and the history."

"I agree." Carter looked grim, but the morbid setting would make anyone that way.

"There's a tie." Chris looked at the crooked gravestones and shook his head. "There has to be. He's taunting us to find it. She was missing a shoe again. What is up with that?"

"Just something to indicate it has a meaning for him that is personal, and we won't be able to figure it out? I don't know. You are the one that wants to be a profiler. Let's go."

There was no point in them staying, and truthfully, Chris was worried about Anna. There seemed to be a systematic circle of elimination, and if that was Sandy Rolla that had just been put in a body bag, and he was sure they'd just found her, Anna was connected to one of the other victims in Natalie Fields.

And tied to him as an investigating officer.

He called her the minute they were back in the car, aware Carter could hear every word, relieved she answered. "Tonight?"

No greeting. That was smooth, but he wasn't feeling all that charming at the moment.

Luckily, she was flexible to his sometimes abstracted behavior and odd hours. "We can. Busy day. It might be hamburgers." She paused. "Everything okay?"

"Hamburgers are fine. I can even cook those, believe it or not."

"What's wrong?"

"Your place? I'll bring the burgers and grill them."

"You are not going to tell me. Fine, my place."

"It's a date, then."

When he hung up, his partner said in a calm voice, "I'd be worried about her too. So far everyone who has given us information has been threatened in some way, and Ms. Hernandez identified the second victim."

He'd never told Carter he was involved with Anna, but then again, Chris hadn't really talked about Sara either. However, Carter was a competent investigator and an observant person, and that he'd figured it out wasn't exactly a surprise. "How worried?"

"Four people are dead. I think that says it all as we drive away from yet another crime scene encounter with Loren. I think Ms. Davidson could be right, or we might be dealing with an unknown entity, but let's face it: Reynolds is somehow a key player."

That his father had speculated correctly on where they found the body didn't help him, and neither did the possibility he knew the story about the woman found there years ago.

"Yes, and I think he knows it full well and is as unsure as to why as we are, or that is my impression."

"Unless he knows full well."

Chris shook his head. "No. We're missing something. Looking at this through a different viewpoint I'm not in disagreement that his arrival back here spiraled off a series of events we all find disturbing, but keep in mind, Samantha Davidson also had connections to all the victims except Natalie. Is this about her?"

"I thought she said no to the jealous boyfriend question."

It wasn't like he hadn't been dissecting this situation to the extent he lost even more sleep than usual, which was saying something. "What if she doesn't even know he exists?"

Carter shot him a quick sidelong look. "Secret admirer syndrome?"

"Think about it. She's . . . memorable is a good word. I refuse to use hot because I'm not sixteen any longer, but it applies."

"I frequently disagree with you, but I do give you that. The question is who."

"Well, Whitman is the obvious choice."

"He is, and he has a history with Amanda Reynolds."

That was true enough. Thinking out loud was a habit he couldn't break. "I can't connect him to Fields, and how would he know anything about Sandy Rolla? Let's not forget Amanda Reynolds would not have gotten into a car with him."

"Unless forced at gunpoint."

That was possible, of course.

Still the feeling lingered they were missing something.

* * *

Anna made a salad with chopped vegetables and arugula and a simple parmesan dressing after putting on some classical music. The kitchen table was set for two because apparently this was going to be a casual meal.

Chris had sounded on edge when he called, but he frequently was that way and she suspected she was guilty of it too. They both had challenging jobs in different ways, but hers stayed with her constantly and she knew his did too.

That had been a problem with Trey also. Some of the dedication to their relationship was sacrificed to another passion, and it was a mutual flaw.

Day by day was her plan. With caution over becoming too involved, though she had to admit she was happy he'd called. Chris Bailey was definitely an interesting addition to her life.

He arrived with his little dog, a grocery bag and a six-pack of beer. "I'm a little late, sorry but, this hasn't been an easy day."

"I agree." She pointed at the counter. "Note the glass of wine, but I probably would have had that anyway. Care to tell me your tale of woe?"

"No." He relented then and said, "I don't want to ruin the entire evening. We can talk about it later. Let's not upset the moppet."

She took the hint. He needed a little downtime, and she was on board with that. "Let's not. I won't ask how your day went, and don't ask about mine either."

"There's a deal I'll accept."

"I didn't even know detectives negotiated."

He took out a package from the bag and smiled, which he didn't do often enough. "Only occasionally, and I will deny that I ever admitted that in court if called to testify."

"I'll never tell."

"I know you won't. Now, about these burgers . . . do you want yours raw or burned? I only have two speeds."

How come she knew she'd be the cook? But she didn't mind and was amused. "Let me take care of it with medium."

"I was kind of hoping for that, to be honest." He set the buns on the counter. "I'm able, just not that good at it. I eat the end result, either way. So far, I'm still alive, but I didn't want to put you through it."

"You do have a habit of getting distracted because you are always thinking about something else."

"Not always."

The meaningful look wasn't lost on her and was flattering. They were a little past flirtation since it was physical already, but she did enjoy their evenings even before they went to bed and sexual banter was fine with her. . .

The knock on the front door was unexpected, but when she placed the pan on the stove and turned to go answer it, she was startled when Chris caught her arm. "No," he said decisively. "I'll go."

Then he drew his weapon, which of course he always carried, and she'd gotten used to that, but she certainly had never seen him with it in his hand.

"Maybe we will have to cancel the deal and talk about your day after all," she murmured.

"Stay here. Let me find out who this is." He walked purposefully out of the kitchen, and she most certainly listened to the cop voice which held a definable authority, mostly because she wasn't sure what was going on. If a shoe could make him call the FBI, who knew what was happening behind the scenes.

A shoe? Of course, he'd never explained — she knew he wouldn't and respected that silence. She didn't supply details of her cases either.

But a drawn gun did raise eyebrows and he didn't want her to answer her own door?

That was alarming, and on the phone, he'd sounded like if she had other plans, he might have insisted anyway. Natalie Fields was dead. This concern had to be connected to that in some way.

He came back in with a rueful smile. "Your neighbor brought over a piece of your mail that was in their box instead. I think I startled her answering your door."

"Brandishing a gun? I would think so."

"I wasn't brandishing. What have you been reading lately? Old westerns? It was more that a man she didn't recognize was the one who opened it."

"Who did you expect to come knocking?"

"If I knew the answer to that question, they would be under arrest." He picked up his beer and took a solid drink. "I don't know if they have any idea you identified Natalie Fields or not because I haven't quite figured out how they are getting their information."

That was quite an explanation coming from him. More than she expected. "The Roadside Killer."

"You check the news."

"I do."

"I don't know why the press glorifies these predators with nicknames." He settled into a chair, his blue eyes holding a glint of disquiet. "I know what he is, just not who he is." He added, "But he's set himself up for one hell of a fall because all four murders are premeditation, and we are serious about the death penalty in this neck of the woods. I can connect them. I just haven't found it quite yet."

The number registered with a small chill. "Four?"

"Watch the ten o'clock."

The hamburgers began sizzling as she processed that news. No wonder he had had a bad day, and no wonder he was sitting there moodily watching her cook and sipping beer.

No wonder he'd drawn his weapon before he walked to the door.

She got out a spatula, musing out loud. "This person is slipping pretty quickly out of control, maybe on a high from the first murder."

"My thoughts as well. He's covering his tracks, but he's going to find out all crimes leave evidence. If he goes to sleep tonight thinking he's done an adequate job, he is severely underestimating the bloodhounds sleeping under the porch."

Despite the fact she now understood he was there to protect her and there was nothing funny about that grim reality, she had to laugh at the analogy. "Do you think Carter would like being compared to a dog?"

His grin was wry. "Probably not, but hey, those dogs can really follow a scent. He should be flattered."

"Somehow I don't think he would be, but I see your point." She sobered. "I hope you catch this one soon. Natalie was one of the ones I was pretty sure I'd helped save and now she's gone anyway. I'm heartbroken over that."

"You did. Her foster parents were still close enough to her they were going to report her missing, which meant she had a caring family." His voice was quiet. "I know you said she was clean now and her tox screen came back that way, but she knew something or the wrong someone. You said she stopped by to see you now and then. Was she dating anyone? Did she mention it? When we contacted her foster parents, who we found thanks to your identification, they didn't know."

That was a good question, but he was skilled at asking those.

She picked up her glass of wine and considered it, gazing at him over the rim. "I'm trying to remember if she said something like that. Usually, we talked about school and how she'd gotten a part-time job but nothing really about her personal life. I wasn't the big sister she never had or anything other than an authority figure with some control over her life for quite some time. We are the gatekeepers and a place to turn if it becomes necessary."

Chris looked reflective. "I guess in essence we have the same job. We try to make the world a safer place."

She took a sip of wine. "I'll drink to that."

"Where was the part-time job? Did she say?"

In her experience so far, he never asked pointless questions, so she thought back. "At an insurance agency, I believe."

His eyebrows lifted a fraction. "Is that so?"

Her interest sharpened. "That means something?"

"It just might."

CHAPTER TWENTY-SIX

There was a scythe of a moon, the water glimmered, and it was almost absolutely silent.

Cold night.

The killer wasn't positive of his purpose for this visit except he was restless, wondering, uncertain . . . he couldn't quite define it.

Living on the edge of a precipice was both a thrill of danger and a stimulation.

The house was dark. They were in bed, then, no doubt together, and he hoped Reynolds had enjoyed himself because that joy ride was about over.

How to finish this was the problem.

* * *

Early morning.

Gray light slanting in and Samantha breathing softly next to him, her disheveled silky hair spilled across the pillow.

He wasn't sure if his mother giving him that ring had been a sign or not. Even he wasn't completely sure if she was why he'd come back. Mick had wanted her to finish college and move to Chicago — but she hadn't done what he expected.

His fault maybe for never asking her. Arrogance on his part? Oh yes, it could be. He crossed his arms behind his head and thought it all over. The confidence he'd once had that his ordered existence was under control was shaken right now and that wasn't in question.

He slipped out of bed and went to make coffee, pulling on jeans and a sweatshirt before he went quietly down the stairs.

The light to the security system glowed reassuringly as he walked into the kitchen. The coffee maker was a fancy contraption — his father's words, not his — that his mother had bought him for Christmas that could make a pot or a single cup of the user's choice. He chose to make a pot since he had not only a houseguest but a lot of work to do. Moving had been time-consuming, and there was no doubt the events that had unraveled after his arrival back home had taken toll on his schedule and productivity.

Understandably so.

How his parents managed to get up to face the day showed a very profound type of courage. They had each other, and luckily for him, he had Samantha.

When she wandered downstairs an hour later, at least he'd checked his email from the day before. Her hair was deliciously tousled, and she wore only his shirt from the night before, which showed a satisfying amount of long, shapely, bare leg. "Coffee . . . thank you."

"You're welcome." He poured her a cup and handed it over, and asked abruptly, "What are you not telling me about Shawn and my sister? There's something more to the story, and that has become obvious to me. Looking back, she seemed really uncomfortable around him. My dad noticed it too. He said something to me about it."

She took a sip of her coffee and then sighed. "I promised her I wouldn't say anything about it to you. I told the detectives."

He stared at her. "But you won't tell *me*?"

"Do you want me to break my word?"

"I don't believe she's here to know if you did or not."

"I'd know."

He was well aware she possessed a stubborn streak. Six years of distance proved that. "While I admire your integrity, at least tell me if he hurt her or if he just scared her."

"The latter. I think you arrived just in time."

Instantly he knew right when it had happened and recalled Amanda's white-faced retreat. "I believe I remember that afternoon. I knew something was wrong, just not exactly what. I'd have torn him into a million small pieces."

"Maybe that's why she never told you."

"I might still." He meant it with bitter sincerity. "No wonder he acted so strange when we shared our 'friendly' drink. Either he was the one who killed her, or he was afraid I thought he was."

"I think it is only too possible it is the former, as you know." She rested her elbows on the table, her mug held cupped in both hands, her expression pensive. "That incident proves he's not a nice guy with high moral standards, but why would he kill her, or anyone else?"

"I believe there is a lot more to this than we know."

"I agree. That said, why would anyone else try to torment — and I know that is a dramatic word — either of us by making such macabre deliveries?"

"I acknowledge whoever it is seems to be paying attention to our lives."

"That seems to be true of more than this individual if our mothers are discussing us spending our nights together."

"Yeah, well, they can discuss our relationship all they want, but he's the one that has me lying awake at night." He meant it. "He is another entity altogether."

"What are we going to do?"

He wasn't sure what she was asking exactly. "Can you define the question?"

Samantha was quick on the uptake. "About him. Our mothers are just a side note at this point, and yours is fragile right now . . . I can't imagine. I'm saying you can't continue to drive me to work and then take the time to come pick me up. It is inconvenient for you and for me."

He looked at her. "Sam, it's inconvenient to be dead. I can work around this, but I can't work around worrying about you walking safely into your office building. Indulge me. Please."

"This person is after *you*."

"I didn't know Natalie Fields at all. Why kill her if it is about me?"

She did acquiesce after a moment. "Good point. I'm trying to make sense out of something that doesn't to me."

"You aren't alone there." He stated it with feeling.

Then he told her, dancing the fine line between truth and a desire to not alarm. "We had a visitor last night, and he was obviously paying attention because he wouldn't come close enough to the house to make his film career debut."

* * *

"What?" Samantha stared at him.

It was simple enough. "I couldn't sleep and walked over to the window, and there was someone standing at the edge of the woods. I saw him fairly clearly because of the moonlight. Not his face, he was too far away, but I got a general idea of his height and weight."

"Shawn?"

"No. I don't think it was him."

It wasn't like she didn't want to be proven right particularly, but the response was disconcerting.

"I really don't want to think about a stranger in the woods, Mick."

"It didn't give me a warm fuzzy feeling either. It was obvious he was staying far enough away to avoid the security cameras, so he knew they were there."

"You're sure?"

How he managed to pull off looking like a Hollywood actor with a graze of a morning beard and uncombed hair

213

she didn't know, but Michael Reynolds could easily be the classic heartthrob in just jeans and an old hoodie that had a U of T logo on the front.

His profile was remote as he looked out the glass doors onto the deck facing the lake. "I don't know if I am sure of anything right now, but wrong height and bigger build if you can trust a middle-of-the-night scrutiny from a window."

She thought it over. "I believe you have good powers of observation and you do know Shawn. Okay then, who else?"

"I believe I'm counting on the police to figure that out. Though I don't know if reporting I saw a man in the woods looking at my house will do any good or just make them more convinced I'm trying to pin all this on someone else."

It was a quandary. "I think you should tell them," she said finally. "Full disclosure of all information that could help them. You had nothing to do with all that's happening, so give them everything."

"That sounds reasonable, but I know I'm under surveillance already. I've told you that. I'm not sure I want them to know I've figured it out, because I want him to keep doing it. He's good, I'll give whoever this undercover guy is due credit, but I still noticed him in the bar and if he was wearing a bulky coat, it could have been him in the woods, but I don't think he was tall enough."

"Let's hope it was."

The alternative was unsettling.

It wasn't that she wasn't aware the danger was out there, but she preferred that maybe the shadows also held the promise of help.

Apparently, Mick had the same attitude. "I have to admit it is not exactly wonderful to realize someone is lurking outside your home for some reason, whether it is because they have ill intent or because they suspect *you* might have ill intent."

The stark truth in that statement was sobering. "If it helps at all, I gave you a very good character reference."

His smile was faint. "Thank you. I assume since you are willing to fall asleep next to me and maybe even have my child, you do hold me in some regard."

"You can be so old-fashioned sometimes. Whatever happened to 'let me get you knocked up'?"

"I don't look at it that way."

She knew he didn't. "I don't either. It was a poor joke."

"Since we are on the subject, I am old-fashioned."

"Please, Mick, I know who you are."

"I thought maybe I should let you know where I stand on the subject."

For a man who was quite gifted in tender and passionate moments, he couldn't articulate it easily, and since he was proficient in everything else, she found it an endearing flaw.

"We can address that if it happens, but in the meantime, are you going to call Detective Bailey?"

"Yes, I guess I will." He looked resigned. "Hopefully whoever is watching me saw the man too or else I'll be reporting another unconfirmed event they will look at with a jaundiced eye."

"Or jaded eye?"

"Either one. Are we splitting grammatical hairs over a cup of coffee?"

"I'd rather argue the finer points of casual sayings than think about whoever might be out there."

"Maybe with binoculars, watching us have our said coffee and admiring your bare legs. I'm still driving you to work and picking you up until this is resolved in some way."

It didn't sound like an argument she was going to win from the firm tone of his voice, and since it seemed like they were suddenly living together anyway, she let it go. If it made him feel better, then that was exactly what she wanted. "Fine."

He did look relieved. "I know that sounded like an order and not a request, but while I appreciate your colleague seeing you to your car, I'd rather be right there, especially after Shawn just dropping in that way."

"Well, I highly doubt I'd ask him again because Jack handles all the financial for the Whitman Insurance Agency. If he saw Shawn lurking around my car, he'd probably just go over and shake his hand."

"Your firm handles their financial business?"

Samantha wasn't sure why he was so surprised. "We do for a lot of small family enterprises in quite a large area. That's why Bonnie thought Shawn was legitimately there to see me at the office. Occasionally we see each other's clients if there is a time conflict, but Jack would have asked me and sent the file, so I knew that wasn't it."

"Has he ever asked you to handle anything for their firm?"

The expression on his face gave her pause. "Jack? Actually, no. Why?"

"I don't know. I keep looking for connections and I have no idea of what significance it could be, if any, but there's another one. He knows you and he knows Shawn. Did he know Amanda?"

"The same profession? I suppose he might have, but do I know every accountant in this state? No. I don't. He's a little older than me, so also older than her."

Just thinking about it brought on a pang of now all-too-familiar sorrow. All those years as friends haunted her and she could only imagine how Mick felt.

As if he was thinking along a similar vein, he said, "I met you because of her."

"I can say the same thing."

"My parents are putting off the memorial service until the case is solved." His voice was somber.

"They need time to absorb what happened." She knew she did.

"My dad asked if I could go pack up her apartment. I can see why he doesn't want to be the one to do it and why he doesn't want to have my mother have to do it, so if you have the time, maybe we could do it together? I'm not looking forward to it, so I understand if you decline. If I had a choice, I would."

It wasn't like Mick was vulnerable very often, but he looked that way at this moment, his eyes shadowed, the set of his mouth a fine line.

"Of course I'll go. Be forewarned, I might cry a time or two, but we can handle it together."

"That sounds like a plan."

Just the tone of his voice told her there was a double meaning in his reply, but now was not the time.

She silently agreed.

CHAPTER TWENTY-SEVEN

Plan in place.

Two birds and one stone.

It would end it all, or hopefully so. Maybe one wildcard left, but he knew he could take care of it if necessary.

In too deep. It wasn't an option to back away now.

* * *

"The DNA from Whitman doesn't match the results from the cigarette."

Well, shit. Chris didn't say it out loud, but he sure thought it.

Norris looked unsurprised and pragmatic. "You know as well as I do sometimes evidence doesn't pan out and we have to dig deeper. Four dead, either the same perp or a copycat, but all we need is a solid suspect. I'm with you that the cigarette would have been a fast solution to that particular death and tied it to the others, but that isn't what happened. It doesn't mean it wasn't Whitman, it just means that wasn't his cigarette by that body."

"True." Chris rubbed his jaw. "If I can persuade Lawrence, do you think maybe having a deputy watching Reynolds instead would free you up to keep track of Whitman?"

Norris leaned back in the single chair Chris had across his desk and laughed ruefully. "I have the distinct impression he made me. If you have a deputy that can fool Reynolds, I'd be surprised, not to mention from what I've seen, everyone around here knows everybody. I think you are the one that pointed that out to me. No, he'd be a choirboy if one of yours was trailing along behind him because he'd know they were there. Not that I'm saying your department isn't efficient, but I'd guess it would be a worthless waste of limited manpower."

"So just switch to Whitman?" Chris was feeling around for this, the last murder telling him it wasn't some outsider, it was personal, and the killer had a purpose. "How did he know I'd talked to Sandy Rolla? It was Reynolds that gave me her number via Samantha Davidson, he knew, but if he isn't the one, who else would know?"

Norris looked thoughtful. Like Chris, he wasn't suit and tie, but maybe at best casual business, pullover shirt and tan slacks, nondescript and in the background. "There's money involved in this. A lot of accountants are on our radar. I agree there's something personal with Reynolds and Whitman, but is it distracting us?"

"I've been thinking about that too." He had been. Ask the moppet, who endured his vocal speculation in the middle of the night with patience and a flop of her tail. "The circle is very small, so someone is protecting themselves by eliminating anyone who can point a finger, but they all know each other."

Norris agreed. "I agree. Either sexual or monetary in cases like this one."

"This might be about both." He was starting to finally maybe get a handle on this. A glimmer of light at best, but there was dawn on the horizon. "A forensic accountant with the state finds something amiss with either a tax record or employment filing and personally hires a private investigator to be able to nail the company because she has a genuine dislike for someone who works there. And with good reason, because attempted sexual assault is probably vendetta worthy."

"So Whitman is the target? I'm here to help, but it is your investigation."

"He was Amanda Reynolds's target as far as I can tell, and he does have a possible connection to Natalie Fields. I'm trying to decide how to handle getting that information. I think Lawrence will approve of asking for a court order, but I'd rather look into it quietly. Tax records have to show it if she worked for the Whitman Agency."

"That sounds like a good place to start. In the meantime, I'll—"

Chris interrupted, which he would normally never do, not to a federal agent or even anyone else because he'd been raised by a southern mother to be more polite than that, but in this case, it was warranted. "Hold up. If you were about to say follow Reynolds, he just walked through the door. He's talking to Doreen and she's pointing him in my direction."

"Well, shit. I'm certainly made now. How often do main suspects come visit you anyway, Bailey?"

"It's an unusual occurrence. I'd just stay for the conversation if I were you, so I don't have to fill you in later. He has something to say, or he wouldn't have bothered to come see me."

"I think it is too late for me to depart discreetly anyway."

Carter wasn't at his desk, so Chris got up and pulled his chair over next to Norris and offered Reynolds a nod. "Have a seat. I assume you are here for a reason."

Michael Reynolds took one look at Norris and raised his brows. "Were you following me or Whitman? I'm hoping you'll say me."

"You're *hoping* I'll say you?" There wasn't a blink of an eye at the clear recognition, but then again, he'd been the one to say he thought Reynolds had noticed the surveillance in the first place. "I'm Norris, FBI."

That had an impact. "FBI?" Reynolds took a moment but recovered. "Okay, good. Three people are dead and one of them is my sister. By the way, the reason I'm here is to tell Detective Bailey that you aren't the only one following me."

As had been pointed out, this was his investigation. "All right," Chris said, "tell me."

He looked at Norris in assessment. "Someone was watching the house last night. Even in the dark I could tell it wasn't you. He's taller, a bigger guy in general. He somehow knew I had a security system put in because he stayed out of the range of the cameras. What the purpose was I'm not sure, since he didn't even come near the house. However, it was pretty damn disconcerting to see someone walking the edge of the property in the dark."

"Did Ms. Davidson see him as well?"

He shook his head. "I know this sounds quite similar as to when the window in her house was broken, but she was asleep this time as well."

This whole series of murders really might be tied to her, Chris had decided. She was in it somehow unbeknownst to her because he highly doubted she was involved voluntarily. He inquired as neutrally as possible, "In your bed?"

Reynolds gave him the look that asking that personal question deserved. Even Norris's brow furrowed. "I'm sorry, but what does that have to do with anything? We're consenting adults. You've met her, would you make her sleep on the couch?"

He wanted to challenge him to help with this case. The guy was smart, well-educated and successful, and he had a vested interest in unraveling his sister's murder. No doubt it stung to be under suspicion when he was grieving.

Their expressions changed from critical to thoughtful as he made his point. "She's the only one that connects the dots to all of the victims so far. You return and pick up where you left off in college on a sexual basis and this all starts to snowball?"

"If you are looking for a name of someone besides Whitman who could be unhappy about that, I don't have even a suggestion, so talk to her. Samantha is perfectly capable of speaking for herself, and frankly, she'd prefer it. Yes, I moved back, but there's a six-year gap there."

He could follow the train of thought.

* * *

Just because she'd told him there was no one else serious — and Mick believed her because in all the time they'd known each other she'd never lied to him as far as he knew and it had been voluntary information anyway — that didn't mean someone she viewed casually looked at her the same way.

There was no doubt *he* didn't.

Mick thought out loud. "Look, Sam didn't know the second victim, so how could that possibly connect her?"

"She told us Whitman pressed her for a romantic relationship. Whitman knew your sister."

"Whitman also knew the second victim?"

"I don't know that for sure." Bailey just looked bland.

It was said pleasantly enough but firmly. There was a lingering sense that *I'm not sharing that, especially not with a possible suspect* was included in there, just not stated out loud. Mick had to accept with bitter cynicism that the timing was not in his favor, nor was it that someone involved in the murders seemed to be targeting him.

"My sister seems to have had a legitimate grudge against Shawn Whitman." He said it slowly. "Sam won't tell me exactly what caused it but acknowledges something did. I believe I know exactly when it happened because I was out helping my father on the farm, and when we went back to the house, he was almost overly cordial, but she was pale and ran up to her room. My mother was out, so when he'd gotten there, she and Shawn were alone for a while."

"We are aware."

He wasn't going to lie to a detective and an FBI agent. "I think Samantha is afraid I might decide to confront him about it, and it is tempting as hell to do so. But I can't see what good it would do."

Norris interjected, "I think he might be concerned about it too. I heard that conversation between you and him."

"Amanda never said anything to me. According to Samantha, she didn't say anything to her for quite a while either."

"Could it have been Whitman that you saw last night?" Bailey asked, his gaze sharply inquiring.

That question he could answer decisively. "No. I know him. I have for a long time. Played sports with him, went to college with him, obviously we know each other. Wrong height and wrong build. It was dark, but I can tell you that much. That's why I'm here. Do I still think he's a decent guy? No, I don't, not after what happened with my sister and Samantha. If it was him, I'd have gone out in a minute to confront him, but whoever is doing this doesn't seem to have a problem killing people. I'm not bad with a rifle, but I'm not exactly Wyatt Earp. But who else would just stand in the cold woods in February and watch my house?"

"Good question. I'm curious as well who would be out there."

If you are telling the truth. That hung in the room, but Mick had expected it.

"Samantha got a visit from Shawn Whitman at her office, and luckily the receptionist was still there. Bonnie didn't think too much of it because one of the other of the firm's accountants handles Whitman's finances for the insurance agency, but Shawn did lie about having an appointment with Samantha. It was evidently a very strange exchange that made her really uncomfortable, and he made it clear he knew where she spent her nights. That seemed to be the entire point of it. Even if he wasn't the man watching the house last night, I think he has some sort of involvement."

Something in what he just said made an impact. Bailey looked at Agent Norris, and they seemed to share some sort of silent communication.

He was, of course, not informed on what the revelation might be, so he stood. "I just thought you should know if it

223

helps at all. I want this over on many levels. Now I get to go empty my sister's apartment."

It was true he was headed to Nashville and not looking forward to that experience either except picking up Samantha. He knew she didn't have the time to do this, so he appreciated that she'd somehow arranged to make room in her schedule to help him.

It would take more than one trip to get it done, and he had no idea what his parents wanted to do with her belongings and furniture, but this mission was just to collect personal items and then a moving company could do the rest.

Like turning the last page of a book you didn't want to end.

* * *

Chris watched as Mick Reynolds left and then turned to Norris. "Thoughts?"

"I think you have your link."

"Yeah. Maybe. I'm starting to think there's something bigger here. I'm trying to tie the common thread and I think he just handed it to me, but it isn't illuminating the sky exactly."

"He doesn't know about the fourth murder."

"We haven't made it public yet." Chris had to point it out.

"No, I meant he doesn't know because he's not the one." Norris said it matter-of-factly. "If he was, he would never have walked in here unless he's trying to play an interesting game. I just don't think he'd risk it; he's too intelligent. Nice house, beautiful girlfriend, walking away from a high-paying job for a company of his own that seems to have potential? No."

"I really never have thought he was the one. But he lit the match somehow."

"Through Samantha Davidson."

"Let's go talk to her again tomorrow."

CHAPTER TWENTY-EIGHT

The dogs were sniffing around.

He knew they were there, the hunters with the scent of his blood tracking him through the woods.

Poetic analogies aside, all he needed was one more kill before he faded into the shadows.

The rest were necessary, but this one would be a pleasure.

* * *

Samantha forfeited her lunch time between clients to talk to them, one a familiar figure now, and the other one an unknown. Mid-thirties and nice-looking, the man who introduced himself as Agent Norris had a keen, assessing gaze, and she instantly reevaluated her opinion he could pass for a mild-mannered high school math teacher.

FBI certainly caught her attention.

They both sat down in front of her desk at her invitation, and neither one smiled.

Not a good sign.

"There's been a new development, so we have a few more questions." Detective Bailey had a deceptively relaxed appearance always, but the underlying intensity was there.

"I will do my best to help if I can. Amanda was my closest friend."

Samantha did not care to spend her evening in the now unoccupied apartment again, but she certainly knew she wasn't going to let Mick do it alone. Personal belongings were the sum of a life and they had put them in generic boxes and yes, she'd cried over a few pictures and the cheerleading uniform Amanda had held on to from when they both were on the squad. Memories crowded and she did her best to hide it but doubted she succeeded. The trip home had been very subdued.

"Closest female friend." Bailey didn't smile to soften the correction. "I realize this is personal but might be important. It seems to me her brother is your closest friend. Again. During that six-year gap in your relationship, who did you see or have any involvement with that might resent his return? This all seems connected to you, and whoever is committing these murders certainly seems to have it in for Michael Reynolds."

She didn't disagree with that about Mick and was relieved if the viewpoint wasn't that he was the one responsible, but she really didn't have much of an answer.

All connected to her?

It was disconcerting to say the least.

Still, she thought back. "The two years after he left for Chicago, I was finishing my degree. I moved back here and got this job, and yes, I went on a few dates here and there, but nothing serious. I completely avoided Shawn Whitman because, not to sound like my grandmother, I just don't believe he's a good person. You are already aware of that."

"But the agency his family owns is managed here?"

What does that have to do with anything?

She answered readily enough. "Not by me. I declined to pick them up as a client. Jack Rhodes handles their financials."

"I understand Shawn Whitman came to see you recently."

That information certainly came from Mick, because other than Bonnie, no one else knew. "He did. There was no point to it except he wanted me to know he knew where

I was staying overnight." She looked at them both one at a time very deliberately before she said, "Shawn Whitman is not obsessed with me. He's focused on Mick. Always has been. I'm hardly a therapist, and I don't think it is homosexual, but something drives it and he can't seem to let it go."

"I'm more wondering if someone else is obsessed with *you*. Have you mentioned how Michael Reynolds had a security system put in to anyone?"

What kind of a question was that? She sat back and stared at Bailey — she really wasn't following. "How is that important? He just bought a house. Many people put in a security system."

"Whoever was watching the house was careful to avoid it, and since it seems likely it was the person who broke in once before, they knew something had changed. Usually by the time they are close enough to spot the mounted cameras, you've already caught them on video."

That was a valid point.

He added, "It seems to me whoever it was out there in the cold woods was just looking at the house, maybe thinking about you staying the night with another man?"

There was no doubt she was not a psychologist and doubted Detective Bailey was one either officially, but he'd thought it over. It took her aback and a moment to answer. "If that is true, I really don't know who it would be."

"According to Michael Reynolds it was a tall man with a bulky build, but his vision was impaired by the darkness and the fact the person was standing at the edge of the woods."

It was difficult to not suddenly have a flash of memory, and the world suddenly came into a vivid focus that was unwanted, one that she'd prefer to reject as absurd. She took a moment. A long one.

"I did mention the security system to someone here at work because he asks every evening if he should walk me to my car. He did that before Mick insisted on driving me and picking me up. It can't mean anything, but he is a tall, big man."

It was ridiculous, but . . . there was a connection.

"Can we have a name?" Agent Norris seemed to have correctly interpreted her expression.

"It can't be me. I absolutely have never done more than go out to lunch with him a few times and that was business. He's a married man." She added with flat emphasis, "No affair, not even a chance. I would never even dream of doing anything like that. He has a nice wife and three kids."

"He might dream of it though." Bailey sounded pragmatic and resigned to the realities of life, which given his profession wasn't a surprise, his blue eyes direct. "Many a married man has crossed that line or at least wanted to do so, kids or not. Can you please tell us who it is?"

"Jack Rhodes."

"The man you just told us handles the Whitman account?"

She nodded unhappily. Jack was a nice man, or so she'd always thought. Often preoccupied, but they were all busy. Pleasant, and yes, he did stop by her office frequently, but she just thought he was being friendly.

"He's never been inappropriate," she said reluctantly, "but he does ask a lot of questions. About my evening plans, and so forth. I will admit in retrospect he seemed to know about Mick coming back to Tennessee without me saying anything. All he said casually was that he'd heard my old boyfriend was moving back. I don't believe I'd told anyone at the office. Mick didn't even tell me, Amanda did. But he'd told Shawn Whitman because they occasionally communicated over the years."

"That's interesting."

Of course, Bailey wouldn't tell her why he found it interesting, but she had to agree in a very uneasy way. "Why on earth would they share that information? Shawn might care, but I can't see why he'd tell his accountant."

"A good question. Thank you for the cooperation."

When they left, the first thing she did was call Mick. "Do you know what is going on? An FBI agent and Detective Bailey just left my office."

"Part of it might be my fault. They asked me some questions I thought I could answer, but to be fair, if they are about you, I said I thought you'd prefer to answer them yourself."

That was true. He was willing to let her make her own decisions without input, though six years ago they probably should have had a discussion. That certainly was the proverbial water under the bridge, and for all she knew they were better off learning a few life lessons on their own before rekindling the relationship older and wiser, as James had put it.

"They asked with some unsettling implications. Could you come a little early? I think I'll have Bonnie reschedule my last appointment."

She was thinking along the lines that she didn't want him to leave his house at a predictable time.

Two hours later she decided she really was distracted.

It was uncomfortable to have questions now about someone she saw nearly every single day.

How *did* Jack know Mick had quit his job and was going to move back? Even before her session with Bailey and Agent Norris, she had wondered about that comment. Sitting there at her desk, she looked blankly at her computer screen, not seeing the display, but still thinking with concentration. Since she trusted Shawn not at all, there was a sense of something going on behind the scenes.

Why the hell would they talk about her personal life?

Unless they were more associated than just client and accountant?

She called Mick back. "Can you come now? We need to talk. I'll work from home."

* * *

Home.

Mick liked the sound of it when she used it in reference to his house.

229

She looked professional — but also stunning — in some sort of soft ivory wool dress with a belt around her slender waist, her vibrant coloring a nice foil for the neutral shade, though he was hardly a fashion expert, but he knew if he liked something when he saw it.

"You're beautiful." He said it softly as she turned from setting her computer case on the kitchen counter and he took her coat. "I know you've heard it before, but since I failed so miserably when we were together in the 'I love you' department, I was wondering if I'd ever told you that."

"Thank you for the compliment, and yes, you did fine in that regard. Let's hope you are the only one that thinks so."

"Sweetheart, everyone thinks so, and I assume that remark refers to some of Bailey's questions."

She leaned against the counter, arms folded across her chest, her usually smooth brow furrowed. "They certainly raised some questions for me. What if that *was* Jack Rhodes last night? Emotionally, I think that's ridiculous, but I remember being surprised when he mentioned you moving back here because I hadn't said anything, not even to my mother. You hadn't told me your plans. Amanda was the one who told me. How would he know unless it was from Shawn? I can't see it being a topic of conversation."

"I believe you are of interest to both men."

She didn't like the idea of that at all from her expression. He'd been thinking about it too.

Her voice was tight. "And while I highly doubt Amanda would get into a car with Shawn Whitman, she might trust a colleague of mine that is a married man, father of three, and works in our office if he came up with a plausible story of why she needed to go with him."

"Especially if she wanted his input as an accountant looking into possible money laundering or something equally suspicious concerning one of his clients. 'Let's meet and discuss, but I have a late appointment.'" His voice was grim. "I can see it. Force her into the car and drive her to the middle of nowhere and get rid of the threat."

"I hate this," she muttered. "I like Jack, and we're just speculating. Is it too early for a glass of wine?"

"A visit from the FBI negates the time-of-day factor. I'll pour you one."

Her laugh was hardly because of humor. "Or detectives, and that's been a more-than-once event."

"There you go. It's a wine-worthy occasion." He'd finally found his countertop rack for holding a few bottles that he'd bought in Chicago when he first moved there. It was art deco and suited the house, so he'd put it out, and he selected a bottle of merlot and deftly uncorked the bottle.

"What are we going to do?"

He got out a crystal glass — at least his kitchen was finally getting organized, so he knew where one was — poured and went over to hand it to her. The answer was simple enough. "Spend a lot of time together."

The brush of her fingers as she accepted the wine even managed to be sexy, as did her resigned smile. "I admit I don't object to that and that's nice of you. I can do a lot of work remotely, but I'm not sure how to avoid the office for certain clients who really want to talk to me face-to-face, and I don't know how to explain my sudden need for working out of office more than usual."

He could see her dilemma, but she needed to see his as well. "I agree it is better that your associate not notice you are suddenly absent and avoiding him until Bailey, Carter and Norris can get a handle on this, but on the other side of the coin, I can't work either worrying about you constantly. See it from my point of view."

"Mick—"

He cut off any possible objection. "Until otherwise informed, if there is any chance Jack Rhodes or Shawn Whitman are involved, I hope you like my company."

She just looked at him and took a sip of wine. "I think you know I do."

It needed to be said, so he did it. "Sam, I should have asked you to marry me when I bought that ring my last year in college. Obviously, that was my intention. We were just so young, and life was changing so fast. I pretty much dropped the ball and regretted it for a long time."

She sighed and set down her glass. "You don't own all of it. I wasn't willing to budge an inch about moving away from here, and you worked pretty hard to get to a position where you could get a high-powered job. I think we both made some mistakes along the way. We didn't want the same things and refused to compromise. I've come to the conclusion that marriage involves a lot of that, which is logical because it is two people going on a journey together."

There was no doubt she was right on that point. "I didn't like the big city life at all, or really the corporate world. I did well enough and there was some satisfaction in that, but I moved back here."

"I should have maybe given it at least a try so I could be with that farm boy from Tennessee."

"You're stuck with him now until further notice."

"Duly noted."

He went to the refrigerator and got out a beer. Might as well, since it was apparently cocktail hour even if the conversation hardly lent itself to a festive bent. He twisted the cap off the bottle. "It has to be money. Amanda figured it out, was trying to prove it and nail Shawn, and your friend Jack was, as the accountant for the firm, in on it."

"I'm thinking along the same lines if Jack is involved. He has a lot to lose. Wife, family, job . . . if the insurance firm was running a sideline business and hiding it, he's a smart man and would figure it out."

"And Shawn is a smart guy too, so he'd maybe offer a cut."

They just looked at each other. Samantha nodded. "Greed is a powerful force. I think I make a decent living, but I'm not supporting five people either. I have clients that try to avoid taxes and I have to rein them in because I spot the discrepancy. Some of them understand it isn't worth it to break tax laws, and some of them try to shrug it off as something they can get away with."

"But I assume the clients you are speaking about obtain their money legally. If you don't," he spoke slowly, thinking out loud, "there's no choice but to not report the income."

"Yes. If whoever is paying you reports it in a 1099 or as payroll, you have to. You really don't want the federal government coming after you if it all doesn't match up. Money under the table is a different story."

"You are the accountant. How could my sister get tipped off there was something off?"

"Taxes, I'd guess. If they were spending or banking more money than they reported, she'd be able to figure that out easily enough. Bank transfers to other countries as well, especially if the companies receiving the money exist just on paper, but someone might have tipped her off to that. I'm guessing the latter. Contrary to what most people think, tax returns are not a matter of public record."

"Maybe that is the connection to Natalie Fields in some way."

"If only we had Amanda's phone to see if there was communication."

"There's a reason he took it."

"Bailey could get the tower records. Not the actual conversations but who she called."

"That might be worth looking into."

"I bet they already have."

CHAPTER TWENTY-NINE

There was great advantage to being underestimated.

The resulting shadows were camouflage that allowed the killer to move silently without notice, always present but not noted. Off the beaten path.

However, the world was taking him seriously now.

He'd watched the news. Infamy had never been his goal. Perversely he was enjoying it.

* * *

February dark. Nothing like it.

Moonlit trees and bare branches.

Chris was very ready for spring and not enjoying the chill breeze, but this was a fishing expedition. He was casting, moving through the woods, waiting to see if anything would rise to the surface.

At least he had a suspect. Well, maybe two. He wasn't a forensic accountant but had what he thought were pretty good instincts, and there was a lot of motive out there. The connections were there between Whitman and Rhodes, between Whitman and Amanda Reynolds, between Rhodes and Samantha Davidson. There was a circle, and after some considerable help from Agent Norris, he finally was able to connect Natalie Fields to the insurance agency.

Next to him, Norris also stood in the shadows, "Let's see if he shows up."

"Rhodes drives a black sedan. I'm telling you, that was what convinced me Reynolds might be right. That first murder, I do think he was speeding away from the crime. I have a completely impartial witness who saw a car just like that right after the murder."

"He's moved to number one, but he's got an agenda we don't quite understand."

"No, we don't." Chris just glanced over at him.

Partners right now, watching the house with Reynolds and the lovely Ms. Davidson inside, Carter keeping an eye on Anna in town. "You get my back and I'll watch yours. This guy is dangerous."

"Oh yeah. Four people dead, he has something going on."

As for whispers in the dark, this wasn't what he wanted, but if it was necessary, he'd be cold and crouched behind an old woodshed near the spot where there was a clear view of the downstairs window of the master bedroom and the surrounding woods. At least it was too cold to have to worry about ticks or snakes, to take a philosophical view on it. The bright side.

So they waited.

Other than that brief conversation, they didn't talk. When it was so quiet, voices carried, especially near water.

When the bedroom light went out, there was no doubt that Chris was envious of the idea of warmth, a soft mattress and a receptive woman. Especially if he was wrong about all of this and Reynolds was enjoying all of that, and he was cold and hunkered on the dark woods and guarding the house of a murderer.

Then Norris touched his shoulder and, thanks to the moon, when he pointed, Chris caught the silhouette.

A figure at the edge of the line of trees, just standing there.

Reynolds was not lying.

Tall man, different build, it wasn't Whitman from his description, and if it was, Norris would recognize him because he'd been in that bar.

But Rhodes? Possibly.

If they detained him right now and he was carrying a weapon that proved to be the gun used in the murders, it was over.

If he wasn't, the most they could do was detain him for twenty-four hours for questioning, and the only penalty he'd pay is a slap on the wrist for trespassing. It would give him a chance, the moment he was released, to dispose of the gun. Chris wasn't even sure they had enough to take him in for questioning. So far, he was just standing there looking at that window and had done nothing. Even if his reason for such irrational behavior was a secret longing for Samantha Davidson, there was no law against that except your own conscience as a married man. He still couldn't see the benefit in killing both Amanda Reynolds and John Newsome, or for that matter Natalie Fields for just working as a secretary for an insurance firm.

Unless he was cooking their books for them to cover up illegal business dealings and Amanda had figured it out with John's help. Maybe Natalie had noticed as well.

No way to connect him to Sandy Rolla.

Damn.

Norris looked at him and he shook his head. Unless he did something more illegal than stand and stare at a window, he wasn't going to tip him off he was even a suspect. They had a lot more against Reynolds than they did him.

At this point anyway.

Until he took something from the pocket of his coat and, still standing far enough back to be out of range of the cameras, threw it in an arc toward the porch and, when it landed with a thud, turned and sprinted up the driveway.

"Go follow him, see if you can make his car," he told Norris as they both sprang up. "Sure as hell hope that isn't an explosive device, but I'll find out one way or another."

"Be careful." Norris took off like a track star and Chris hoped he followed his own advice, considering Rhodes, if it was him, might have a gun, but a federal agent was certainly a trained professional.

Cautiously he approached the porch, switching on a slim flashlight he always carried in his coat pocket.

The object was not a pipe bomb or anything close to it. A shoe.

They had him.

The front door swung open, and Reynolds stood there in jeans and nothing else, a rifle cradled in his arm. "What the hell? I heard a noise. Why are you here?"

Evidently, he was a light sleeper or on the edge, one of the two and maybe both. Chris didn't directly answer. "I think this is your lucky night. There are now two witnesses to corroborate your story of a man lurking just out of sight of the cameras that might identify him, and I suspect that shoe he tossed on your porch might belong to Sandy Rolla."

"Amanda's friend? The one that helped us with identifying Amanda's boyfriend?" He looked suitably incredulous. "Why would you think . . . oh shit, no."

"Yeah. And unless you hired some tall man to come toss her shoe at your door, someone else is responsible, not you."

"I didn't." His gaze was quite direct.

"I never thought you did."

Reynolds gave a humorless smile. "I suppose I should thank you for that, though I'm not sure why since I haven't done anything at all."

"Well, give us a break, as we have to put all the pieces of the puzzle together."

"If I am no longer public enemy number one, that's fine with me."

"I believe this person has taken your coveted spot. Keep that rifle handy and Ms. Davidson close until further notice, please. Tonight might break this case, but that depends on Agent Norris."

"Agent Norris?"

"We will be in touch."

* * *

Mick went in to find Sam in the kitchen, waiting for him, wearing a feminine version of a flannel nightshirt patterned with tiny roses. She looked about sixteen with bare feet and disheveled hair. He'd never paid attention to what she wore to bed because he usually removed it as promptly as possible, so he only saw it on the floor.

"What was it that made you jump up like that?" Her eyes were wide and inquiring.

"I heard something and I admit I'm on high alert. I wonder why."

"And?"

He could hardly fault her for the question. "I don't even want to tell you."

"Mick."

The remonstrance in the way she said his name made him reluctantly decide to give her part of the truth anyway. "There's been a fourth murder apparently and we just got another special delivery. Luckily, Bailey saw it."

She blinked. "Bailey is out there?"

"He also said something about Norris. I think this house was part of a good old-fashioned stake-out that actually paid off."

"So he knows you were in here and that man you saw outside wasn't something you invented? The fourth murder is terrible news, but that isn't."

He wasn't about to tell her it was someone she'd shared a companionable drink with not that long ago and she'd helped get the victim's number for the police. "No," he agreed, weighing it all. "Until I hear from Bailey, you definitely aren't going to work. We can drive in together and pick up any paperwork you have to have in hand. You can use my office upstairs and I'll relocate to the dining room or something."

Sam was intelligent and she could read him fairly well. Slowly, she said, "This fourth murder, we know the person, don't we?"

"Let me put it this way, Bailey's advice was pretty much to not let you out of my sight. Since I'd already come to that conclusion as you know, I'm going to follow it until he contacts me and says there's been an arrest."

"You really think it's Jack."

"He said it was a tall man. I assume that means taller than usual because I'm six-one and I'm going to guess Bailey is about my height, so a tall man to him probably means someone taller than either of us. When I saw him, he was also obviously a pretty big guy."

"It fits him, I agree. I just don't know why."

"He made a bad decision, and other people are paying for it." He added with true grim feeling, thinking about his parents and their grief, not to mention his own, "Dearly."

"You're that convinced."

"More and more. He's in bed with Shawn. If it hadn't been for that ill-fated drink and what he tried to do to Amanda, I might still doubt your theory about my supposedly good friend, but I have joined your team."

"I wish I didn't have one," she said in a quiet voice. "So I'll tell Bonnie to just collect the paperwork being dropped off for me, put it in my office and, if anything is urgent, just to call me."

"Sounds like a plan we should never have to make."

"No, we shouldn't."

They just looked at each other in mutual disbelief over recent events, and Mick finally shook his head. "I'm more than grateful you are back in my life—"

A knock on the door interrupted whatever impulsive thing he might say next.

"Stay here and stay back." It was nothing less than an order. He slipped loose the safety on his rifle. "I'm hoping this is Bailey or even Norris, but who knows."

He walked to the door. "Who is it?"

"Reynolds, don't shoot me. I'm just not in the mood."

Bailey.

That was a relief anyway. Mick opened the door to see him standing there, looking cold and unhappy. "Agent Norris is evidently in pursuit and has taken our vehicle. Mind if I wait inside while I make a few calls?"

"Oh, you are more than welcome. Maybe I can go back to bed and not worry about some serial killer lurking outside my house in the deserted woods."

The detective walked in as he stepped back, his expression definitely grim. "I don't know exactly what we're dealing with. I think someone who believes this is a way of protecting themselves. No random victims, they all know each other. There's a purpose."

"If my sister was still alive, I bet she could tell you what started all of this." There was no way to rein in his bitterness.

"Norris can confirm if it was Rhodes with a license plate number if he was able to follow fast enough. With probable cause we can tear the Whitman Agency's business records apart and comb over them with a magnifying glass."

"But right now, you don't have it."

"No."

"I might be able to give it to you." Samantha's voice was quiet, and she'd come out of the kitchen. "I have a key to the offices and access to the files in the main database. I could give it to your FBI friend, and I bet their accountants could figure out if any of the income was exported."

That did catch Bailey's attention, not to mention he thought perhaps there was an appreciative male perusal of the view. "Keep talking, because I'm listening."

CHAPTER THIRTY

Full circle.

The killer could feel the coil tightening, like a constrictor eager for the next meal.

He was about to be swallowed whole if he had to guess.

Someone had anticipated his visit.

He'd gotten a glimpse of whoever followed him at a dead run up the driveway before he sped away. Medium height, brown hair . . . no, it wasn't Reynolds even in the moonlight filtered by high filmy clouds.

Luckily, he'd had the foresight to not take his own car. Who? He wondered as he made random turns and took the most convoluted way possible home just in case he was being followed.

He'd find out tomorrow.

* * *

"I didn't catch up to him quite fast enough, and maybe it isn't who we think it is. Not a black sedan." Norris looked disgusted when he pulled back up to the house and got out of the car. He slammed the door shut with some vehemence. "These backwoods roads . . . he lost me."

Chris could sympathize. He was hoping that would work out, but it didn't, so he moved forward. "Well, I know it is getting late, but care to go on a field trip?"

Samantha came out of the house then, Reynolds right behind her. She'd changed into jeans and a long coat, her slender silhouette outlined by the porch light, her expression determined. "Let's go do this thing. At this time of year, it is possible someone is still working even at this hour, but hopefully the office will be deserted, and we can send the information." She looked at Norris. "After that, it'll be up to you folks."

He looked at Chris with understandable inquiry. "Explain?"

"In the car? This might kill two birds with one stone, as they say. I want both Rhodes and Whitman."

"Let's do it."

They pulled out of the driveway right behind Reynolds and Samantha Davidson.

"Tell me how," Norris said.

* * *

"I could maybe lose my job over this, but I don't care. Found it."

Samantha accessed the codes, and Reynolds intervened. "Let me."

She glanced up from her computer in her office, fingers over the keyboard.

He said with quiet assurance, "I'm really good at this sort of thing if I say so myself. I'll send the files and they will never know. Ask my former employer." He turned to Norris. "Give me an email address, and it will go untraced, so she won't get in trouble, but you will be able to verify it came from this office, just not identify the individual computer."

"Are you serious?" Samantha Davidson stood. "Go for it, whiz kid."

He took her chair.

And it was literally done in minutes.

"They will never know," he definitively said.

She looked at him in open amusement. "You're sure? I thought you were some kind of corporate guru who swung big deals based on marketing trends."

"I am a man of many talents."

"I can attest that is true."

Both Norris and Chris probably looked amused at the sexual innuendo. And perhaps envious.

Norris checked his phone. "Okay, files are loading. I'll send this on to the powers that be and see if we can make sense of what might be going on between Whitman and Rhodes. They can wake judges up in the middle of the night to get court orders for financial records if they really catch a whiff of something and think it is urgent enough."

The sound of the door opening in the reception area startled them all, the chime loud in the relative quiet because it was getting late, the street outside deserted and the parking lot empty.

That the light was on in her office wouldn't escape anyone.

Ms. Davidson could explain working late, but how could she explain three men who didn't belong there with her?

Chris had the feeling he knew exactly who was arriving at this time of the evening. It was one thing to work late. It was another to have a growing sense of desperation because maybe you knew you had entered into a bargain that might be in your rearview mirror and was, as you considered it, a really huge mistake.

Desperation. Defined in his dictionary as the way to solve a pressing problem by whatever means are necessary.

That's why when the knock came on the door, he and Norris instinctively stepped back. Not that concealing themselves in the room was an option, but to give themselves options.

In turn, Reynolds stepped forward, placing himself close to Ms. Davidson.

Just don't get into the line of fire.

The door opened, because that sharp knock had been perfunctory at best.

To Chris's surprise, it wasn't Rhodes. A woman, maybe mid-thirties, stood in the doorway, dressed in silky pajama pants and a coat, her expression militant. Loose brown hair, a little disheveled, she was probably attractive if it wasn't for her hostile expression. She took in the tableau. "Where is he?"

Samantha was the one that said, "Patti, what are you doing here?"

"Jack isn't home. I thought he was here." Then she added accusingly, "With you."

The implication was obvious.

"With me? No." Samantha was firm, direct and composed.

Reynolds spoke in a firm tone. "I promise you on our arrival about twenty minutes or so ago, the office was deserted. Before that, Samantha has been with me ever since I picked her up from work late afternoon."

He was ignored.

"Why does he have pictures of you on his phone? I found them the other day."

Samantha looked truly startled. "What?"

"Dozens." The woman's eyes were hard as glass.

"I only see him at work."

"Supposedly. Oh, they are innocent enough, no lingerie involved, just you at your desk, you walking to your car, you talking to the receptionist, but why does he have them?"

"I have no idea."

Chris was starting to get a sense of two dynamics at work. Frightened of how deep he'd gotten himself with whatever was going on with Whitman, Rhodes might also be obsessed with a woman he couldn't openly approach, and when Reynolds returned back home, those two problems had lit a fire that was not contained.

He decided to step in. "Mrs. Rhodes, I'm Detective Bailey with the sheriff's department. How did you get here?"

The woman seemed to notice him and Norris standing in the background for the first time, all her attention focused on Samantha Davidson so far. "What?"

He was patient but to the point. "Did you drive?"

"Well, yes, of course."

"Your car?"

Now he had her attention. "No. Jack took mine." There was a pause. "He said his was low on gas, but there was actually half a tank. He claimed he had a client meeting here since they couldn't make it at any other time. Did you say detective?"

He and Norris exchanged a look. "Ma'am, we'll be right back."

In the parking lot there was a black sedan. Norris took a picture of the license plate with his phone. "The net is closing in. He's worried enough to change cars with his wife and lie about it."

"With his *suspicious* wife." Chris couldn't help but point it out. "She knows something is up, just made the wrong guess. Not entirely wrong obviously if he is taking pictures of Samantha Davidson and leaving them on his phone, but if he knows she's opposed to ever agreeing to an affair, maybe he just wants to fantasize about it."

"And get even with Reynolds for being the one who had slept with her? Killing Amanda would nicely serve two purposes. Eliminate the threat of an investigation and deal quite a blow to the possible competition of that happening again."

"And maybe once he stepped out on that deadly road, he decided to just keep traveling?"

"Sounds more and more possible to me."

"We are drawing conclusions."

"Correct ones, I'm going to guess."

No doubt Chris had to agree. "But proof? Taking your wife's car is not against the law. Maybe she has a nicer car and he just lied about the gas situation so he could drive it instead."

"Don't sell me short, county boy. I got a picture of it. Not the plate. It was dark and he was pulling away, but the make and model are probably identifiable. If it matches hers, we can bring him in for questioning."

That was the best news he'd had since this all started.

All the case needed was a crack to widen to a fissure and turn into a crevasse. If Rhodes was responsible for all these deaths, he'd toss him in and not look back.

"Let's go find out."

"I agree."

They walked back inside to a quiet room. Mrs. Rhodes just looked bewildered now, more distraught than angry. She demanded, "Why did you go look at my car?"

"Your husband's car," Norris corrected. "Could you please tell us the make and model of *your* car?"

"Why?"

"I'm Special Agent Norris of the FBI. Mrs. Rhodes, we'd appreciate your cooperation. What kind of a car do you usually drive?"

"FBI?" Her expression went to pure alarm. "What's going on? Where's Jack if he isn't here? Has something happened to him?"

Norris was pleasant but had the same attitude toward answering questions. "If you wouldn't mind, ma'am? Your car?"

Third time was apparently the charm. "A silver Lexus SUV."

* * *

It was an odd way to view the situation considering she'd just been apparently accused of being culpable in allowing a married man to cheat on his wife, but Samantha actually felt sorry for Patti Rhodes.

She wasn't positive she knew exactly what was going on either, but she was in a better position than the stricken woman standing in her office with two law enforcement officers questioning her.

Norris just gave a brief nod and Bailey seemed to understand. He said, "I'll call Sheriff Lawrence and fill him in."

"I'll take care of the other part of it."

They walked out on their phones, and she was left again with Jack's angry and now confused wife. Thank goodness Mick was there.

Patti said in a shaken voice, "Jack is in trouble, isn't he?"

It was obvious enough his wife had known something was up or she wouldn't have checked his phone. They'd always liked each other as far as Samantha knew, so it was clearly the pictures that had sent her to the office this late at night. "I think it is possible."

"I thought for sure he was meeting you." She sank down into a chair as if she just couldn't stand any longer.

"No. Never. He hasn't even suggested it and I wouldn't ever have agreed anyway. Jack is a friend and a colleague. That's it. There's nothing sexual or romantic between us." She had to admit she didn't like the idea he'd taken pictures and she hadn't noticed it.

At all.

"Then he's involved with something else that isn't letting him sleep at night and making him impossible to talk to. He's started smoking again. You say you're friends, so do you know what it is?"

Asked directly, Samantha was at a loss. After a moment, she responded, "No. Do I suspect he has a client maybe pressuring him to do something illegal? It could be. It happens to accountants all the time. You want to be helpful and save them as much money as possible, but at what cost if they are skirting the edge of the law? I know nothing solid at all. You are hearing pure speculation on my part."

That was diplomatic, and Mick was letting her do the talking.

"So he's in trouble."

"I don't know."

Mick could sound extremely reasonable, and he finally spoke. "Mrs. Rhodes, he's lied to you, and it seems to me he's on edge from what you just told us. I'd say yes. There's a federal agent here. Your husband might have crossed some line."

There was no doubt that was possible. That was up to Bailey and Norris to determine. And murder was quite a line.

"He won't answer his phone." Patti's eyes filled with tears. "I thought it was because he might be in the middle of doing something he shouldn't, that's why I'm dressed this way. I tried going to sleep, but I just couldn't. I threw on my coat and came here to see if I could find out if I was just imagining it. It's late. Where is he?"

If Samantha had to make an educated guess, his phone was off so no one could track it. Jack wasn't quite the friendly, easy-going man she thought he was, but he most certainly was intelligent.

"I have no idea," Samantha said truthfully. "For all we know he did meet with a client here and then they went out for a drink or a cup of coffee."

Maybe with Whitman to inform him there was a problem.

Or maybe Whitman, for all her intense dislike of him, had no idea it was possible Jack was responsible for the recent string of murders. On the other hand, he'd known about the third one before it had become public. If they were walking hand-in-hand down a dark path, maybe he knew full well what was going on.

Her vote was for the latter because Mick was such a target for Whitman.

Or was he such a target because of Jack?

She and Mick watched Patti Rhodes get up and abruptly walk out the door, not saying anything else, because what was there to say? They certainly had no authority to stop her and no reason either.

Mick spoke first. "Uh, is it just me or has this been an interesting evening?"

He still stood by her desk, and she looked at him and shook her head. "Every evening with you is interesting, it seems."

"I believe I told you Rhodes might be emotionally involved with you whether you were aware of it or not."

She considered her reply. "I just never considered it. He never did anything to indicate it."

"I think his wife caught on easily enough something was up." He leaned a hip against her desk and crossed his arms across his chest. "I think most wives might wonder if a man who worked with someone like you might take an interest."

"Someone like me? What does that mean?"

"You're unforgettable. Just ask me."

"I remembered you too." Her voice softened.

"I think we've helped all we can tonight. Back to my house?"

She stood. "Please. I spend too much time here anyway."

They walked out, and she turned to lock the door as Bailey walked over. "Thank you for the help with this. I don't think I need to tell you to be careful if your plans are to return to either of your houses. It remains in question whether or not Rhodes realized Agent Norris followed him, but if he did, the whole equation could change."

She was afraid of the same thing. It seemed to her that the situation was escalating. "If it is Jack, his wife is going to confront him, and he'll know we were here at this time of night with law enforcement. And he'll know why."

"I agree that's probably what will happen. We have enough to take him in for questioning, but if Whitman is involved, I'd like for him to go down as well. The problem is we have to get Rhodes first."

CHAPTER THIRTY-ONE

The killer ironically compared the biblical commandments to just one line that would sum it all up without needing ten of them.

Thou shall not give in to temptation.

The entire thing in a nutshell, no chiseled tablet needed.

He should probably have taken his interpretation to heart on many levels and yet had ignored his own introspection. There was no doubt he was a sinner and temptation one of his downfalls.

This evening particularly.

* * *

He was sure there were two key elements to this case. The location of the bodies meant something, and the shoe fetish had significance.

With a solid suspect, Chris dug deeper.

It came down to one simple thing.

In the course of his training and the literature he'd pored over pertaining to the behavior of criminals, he'd come to expect certain observations, one of which was the possibility of a need to see the scene of the crime again to settle it all in the mind of the perpetrator.

The question was which crime and which scene.

He was really starting to wonder about the dead woman in the cemetery years ago.

Luckily, he had access to old police files, but he also had access to Doreen. He got up and went over to her desk and waited until she finished taking a call. "What can I do for you, darlin'?" she asked.

"Do you remember anything about a case some years ago where a woman's body was found in that abandoned graveyard by the church that burned down and was never rebuilt?"

"The one where you just found the latest victim?"

"That's the one. I don't even know what year it happened or the name of the victim, so finding the file might be a challenge. I tried to search our database, but it isn't in there, so it must be in the archives."

"I'll get it for you if you'll answer the phone."

"That's a deal." He took her chair as she headed for the stairs to the basement where they stored the older paper files, hoping no one would call with a question he couldn't answer. Doreen was so efficient because she knew anything and everything about the sheriff's department and how it operated. Even Lawrence went to her with questions pretty frequently. He might be sheriff, but she was the go-to. Her sister Darlene was in charge of dispatch, so between the two of them things ran smoothly.

Carter came in and looked amused to see him at Doreen's desk. "So you've been demoted, and Doreen is finally a detective. Seems fair to me."

"She's getting me a file, and we both know she can find it ten times faster than I could." He leaned back and gave a wry smile.

"I can't argue that."

"You know, I think she has a more comfortable chair than I do."

"She deserves it more than you do. What file?"

"I want to look at the case of the dead woman that was previously found in the cemetery. Maybe there's some significance even though it happened a long time ago."

"So Rhodes isn't at his office, but according to the tower, he's called Whitman three times already this morning."

"If his wife told him we were there, he has to be panicking."

"Maybe."

"It's tax season, he could explain the calls away at this point." It was an observation, no more. He thought Jack Rhodes had been panicking all along, trying to cover his tracks because he'd been helping Whitman launder money. "His wife drives a pretty expensive car and she's a school-teacher. I realize accountants make decent money, but Samantha Davidson could give us a good idea of what he actually earns."

"I think Norris and the FBI's special accountants will nail down the fraud. I just want to solve four murders."

He couldn't agree with Carter more. Let the feds handle the financial twists and turns, and they'd put the important part to bed.

"Here you go, honey." Doreen emerged from the doorway, a file in her hand. "I knew if I saw the name on it, I'd remember. Such a shame. She wasn't even thirty yet and left a child behind. They never caught whoever did it either. Work your magic, boys."

"Thanks for this." Chris accepted the file from Doreen.

As they walked back to their desks, Carter came to Chris's and sat in the chair meant for visitors. "Of course I remember that case. I didn't work it, but now that I think about it, that all sounds familiar. She was divorced and every-one was sure her ex-husband was probably the one who did it, but there was just no way to prove it."

That caught Chris's attention. "I'm going to go over this with that in mind. Why did they think that?"

"I don't know the details — that was a long time ago. No solid evidence was my impression. They didn't even bring him in."

Interesting.

"I'll let you know if we need to follow anything."

His phone beeped then with a text, and he glanced at it. "Reynolds. He wants me to call him."

"Do it." Carter went to his own desk and sat down.

He did.

"This is Bailey."

Mick Reynolds sounded subdued, but who wouldn't be in his position? "I have a question, but of course, put that way, I know you won't answer it, so I'll just tell you why I called."

"That sounds like a plan."

"You asked me if Shawn Whitman smoked cigarettes and I don't know why. While you were out of the room, Patti Rhodes mentioned her husband, in addition to not sleeping well or talking to her, was smoking again. Does that mean something to you?"

It did. "It just might," he said, fingering the report Doreen had given him.

"I just remembered it and wondered if the information was worth giving you a call."

"We appreciate it."

It was his turn to go over to Carter's desk. "That might be a worthwhile call. Jack Rhodes apparently smokes when he's anxious."

"So we need his DNA."

"If it is a match, it will seal the deal to getting a warrant for his house and his car. What we need is the murder weapon."

"We have enough to bring him in."

"After last night, yes." Chris agreed. "But we can't keep him in for more than twenty-four hours unless he is charged, and then if we can't hold him, he'll have time to get rid of the weapon. He could claim he just found the shoe lying there in the driveway and picked it up and threw it because he has a thing for Ms. Davidson and was ticked off she was staying the night with Reynolds. His wife might even support that story because she's convinced he's involved at least emotionally. *If* we can even prove in any way it was him. Let me talk to

Stephanie St. James. A district attorney should be able to give us a clear picture of what she could do with what we have."

* * *

Chris Bailey had left an interesting message on her cell. When she was able to grab a moment, Stephanie finally answered.

Yes, to the meeting and the drink. Where?

Your choice.

She chose a small bar that was near downtown, not exactly trendy but quiet and discreet, and it was doubtful that anyone would recognize a district attorney meeting with a county detective with the rural clientele.

Bailey was as usual in his casual attire — badge and shoulder holster. He ordered a beer and she asked for a glass of water. When their drinks arrived, she picked up her glass and raised her brows inquiringly.

"Four murders and we have him in our sights, but before we pull the trigger, I want to know he's going to go down without being able to run or get rid of evidence."

"This is the Roadside Killer?"

"Yes, ma'am."

"I'm listening."

He outlined the case. The dark sedan spotted speeding, the fact the first victim was investigating — possibly — a client of the killer, that Michael Reynolds inflamed the problem by returning to the area, the relationships were complicated, plenty of proof of motivation but very little physical evidence . . .

"Whitman is by all accounts a sociopath, and yes, this is speculation, but Rhodes is under his thumb. He used the man's obsession with Samantha Davidson to goad him into taking such drastic action because her former lover was coming back and Whitman knew it. The obsession I can prove: he's been taking secret pictures of her, and there's a picture of his wife's car leaving Reynold's house taken by an FBI agent to support this."

That was hardly enough, but it was some connection of the dots.

"A DNA match to that cigarette would take care of a grand jury." She mused out loud, thinking about it. "If the FBI comes through with evidence that Amanda Reynolds was correct about the Whitman Agency being a front for something illegal, that would help, but we'd have to prove Rhodes knew she was looking into it."

"If she called him from her office, then we're out of luck. Getting records from the state is unlikely. If she called from her cell, then we can pin it down even without her phone just from whatever company she used, but who knows if she called him at all. It seems to me she was doing this on her own hook with the help of a now dead private investigator who died the same way, and probably the same night. Her laptop is missing from her apartment and she wasn't doing this for the state; this was a personal project."

"I see your dilemma, Detective." As things stood, she'd be reluctant to charge just yet on first degree — which was what all these four crimes deserved — because a good defense attorney could argue most of it. "Find me proof. Either the weapon being found tied to Rhodes or DNA on the cigarette near the second victim would work for my office, but otherwise we might struggle to prosecute. Four counts of murder are not an easy sell for a professional who is a family man with no previous record."

"I'm working on it." Bailey was always extremely straightforward, she knew that from previous experience. "I think he's losing it, the house of cards is collapsing, and he's in the underpinning."

"That's more your area than mine. I don't catch them. I make sure we hold them accountable."

He nodded, thoughtful, intense as usual and focused, which made him very good at his job. "Carter wants to bring him in, but I'm dragging him back on that one. I told him to let me talk to you first. Glad I did." He paused and lifted his glass to his mouth, took a drink and then remarked, "You look good. Anna told me about the baby."

"Did she? I'm sure you noticed it anyway when I took off my coat."

"Let's hope I am able to pick up on the obvious." His mouth quirked into a smile.

"It was hard to tell if she was okay with it or not." That was pretty honest.

"I don't know if she could even answer that question, so I'm not going to do it for her."

She regarded him across the table. "Anna is one of the best people I know. I understand you are seeing each other."

He looked noncommittal. "We are."

She had to laugh and shake her head. "Life is funny sometimes. The things you don't necessarily see coming."

"True enough. Since we've established I need more to arrest Rhodes and stop him cold, can we now talk about that old case of the murdered couples?"

Back to business. That was fine with her.

"Yes, we can. What do you have for me?"

"The perp is in prison. Yet again. But he did murder four people. If there are more, I haven't found them, but there could be. He's a lifelong offender."

"How are we supposed to prosecute?"

"Oh, I have him. Two cousins, different states but same method, and he's the stepbrother of one of them. The crimes are connected, and when he was arrested years later on a different charge, he was still driving the car of the woman he killed here in Tennessee. No one connected the cases, but you had to be really looking for it."

The longer she knew this man, the more she thought under that down-to-earth country boy exterior worked a very agile mind. "And you were."

Chris Bailey exhaled. "Yeah, really. I need you to hold this person accountable for these crimes. It will mean a lot to Anna and even more to one very nice older lady."

"You have evidence?"

"Besides the car? Probably. He stole guns in the second homicides and I bet used them in subsequent robberies, which is why he's in prison right now in Ohio. Not a super smart guy, but he has committed murder and so far gotten away with it. He'll get out and do it again. Let's stop him."

She was . . . impressed. To her, Chris Bailey approached law enforcement from a unique angle. On a personal basis, he went after the offender as if he always had a stake in it, and it wasn't just a job.

"You solved a twenty-year cold case just like that?"

He regarded her with a steady gaze. "Not just like that. Mrs. Dunn lost her daughter. I found the answer for her. She deserves it. You deliver the justice. Deal?"

There was no thinking that one over. "Deal. Send me all you have."

"I'll get Rhodes's DNA or that gun for the roadside murders."

Somehow, she thought he would.

CHAPTER THIRTY-TWO

It wasn't sustainable.

This fevered pace was a balance between sanity and complete loss of control, the rollercoaster gaining momentum, the passing landscape a blur.

The killer needed to put on the brakes, but it was probably too late.

The skid was sideways toward a cliff with a deep pool at the bottom. Even if he survived the plummet, he was going to drown.

He pressed a button and tried again.

No answer.

Fuck this.

* * *

Mick didn't think he'd ever sit at a dining-room table at his laptop with a rifle propped next to him he was ready to use at any given moment. First day of March, blue skies and a positive forecast, except on a personal level.

The gun was a "just in case."

Security system, locked doors, firearm. He hoped he had it covered.

Samantha was upstairs working, and he should be working too, but it was more than a little hard to concentrate.

He was having a difficult time dealing with the realization that he'd essentially asked her to have a murderer walk her to her car. Not that he'd requested him by name or even known who he was at the time, but it made him grow cold all over. He wasn't sure Carter and Bailey completely agreed, but in his mind, Jack Rhodes was probably guilty of the murders.

And he took secretive pictures of Sam when she was unaware.

The mild-mannered accountant and the insurance agent in bed together. It sounded like a bad play, not a real-life situation, but might just explain a lot. He could see Shawn using the agency as a front for something illegal and persuading his accountant to walk a crooked line. He wouldn't think it was wrong, he'd think it was clever.

That Amanda's life was forfeit absolutely was so wrong Mick couldn't really take it in.

The sound of a car registered through the quiet of the late afternoon.

"Someone is here."

Samantha evidently heard it too. She came into the room, one of his flannel shirts with the sleeves rolled up over her wrists dwarfing her slender body paired with faded jeans and woolly socks. How that could be sexy he wasn't sure, but she managed it. All that glossy auburn hair and those exceptional eyes; he understood Rhodes's obsession, he just didn't forgive it.

"I know. Why is it I'm reluctant to go look?" He got up and picked up the gun. "I feel ridiculous doing this, but on the other hand, I think caution is the best plan. Stay here."

"Don't worry," she remarked, her voice terse.

A knock on the door made him relax at least somewhat because anyone that would announce their presence probably meant no harm. He kept it short and sweet when he got to the door. "Who?"

"Bailey."

It was the appropriate voice and inflection. He opened the door. Boots, jeans, badge, tall and blond. The real deal. "Come on in."

"Thanks."

He walked in. Mick pointed. "I'm working in the dining room. Fine with you?"

"I've a few questions, that's all."

Of course he did. As far as he could tell, Bailey was a man of questions.

Mick led the way, almost surprised to see Samantha had listened to him and was standing by the table, looking relieved at the identity of their visitor. Her smile was tremulous. "Hello, Detective."

"You are actually the one I came to see, Ms. Davidson."

"Oh?"

It was almost five o'clock and he'd gotten virtually nothing accomplished all day and yet signed on two more clients. Something had to give. Mick announced, "I'm going to have a beer in anticipation of the upcoming conversation. Anyone else?"

"Wine." Samantha's answer was short and sweet.

"One, sure, thanks." Bailey almost looked amused. "This is going to be an interesting conversation, and it's been a long day."

Almost amused.

"Interesting how?" That was Samantha as he went into the kitchen to the refrigerator. Taking out two pale ales and an already open bottle of Chardonnay, he poured her a glass and took it back out to the table.

"Jack Rhodes didn't show up at your office this morning."

"So that *was* him," Mick muttered grimly.

"Has he ever mentioned his parents to you?" Bailey looked intently at Samantha.

She frowned. "Not really. In passing only. I do know his mother died when he was fairly young, and he lived with his father. I don't get the impression they are close."

"How young?"

There was no doubt she took a moment. "Ten? That's what comes to mind. I think he mentioned he was in fifth grade. It was hardly an in-depth conversation. I think it was

Mother's Day and I mentioned I'd ordered flowers for mine. He said he wished he could for his."

"Did he say how she died?"

"No." She was definite. "I'd remember that."

Bailey looked thoughtful, taking a sip from his bottle of beer. "I think I might have a handle on it."

What the hell did that mean?

"Can I ask how Jack Rhodes's mother's death pertains to anything?" Mick was trying to follow, but that wasn't always easy with Bailey.

In return he got the usual cryptic answer. "I think it might be significant. It might even make this case."

How so? He refrained from making a futile inquiry. Bailey wouldn't explain.

"Where is he?" He felt he could ask that one.

"We are working on it. You've been helpful. Thanks." Then Bailey got up in a lithe movement. "Keep the rifle handy. We're watching his house, we're watching this property. But we can't be everywhere, and I know you've pointed out you aren't Wyatt Earp, but it seems to me there might be a sense of nothing left to lose and that is the worst kind of adversary to have. Just an observation. Don't shoot Norris, by the way."

At that moment, as if on cue, there was the sound of a single gunshot.

* * *

Winter woods, cold silence.

Chris wasn't positive it was the best decision he'd ever made, but he went up the driveway to try to decipher what was going on. Sidearm drawn, he was hoping to take his own advice and wouldn't shoot the wrong person.

That he did not need.

A shadowy figure moved to his right, and he whipped around.

Luckily, he was able to recognize Norris, though it was dusk with shadows gathering. He lowered his weapon. "What happened?"

"I don't know. It's getting dark. I didn't see anything, just heard voices and then the shot. It was pretty close by."

Rhodes *and* Whitman?

His first guess.

It wouldn't be the first time by far that two people conspired and collaborated on murder. Chris stood there in the fading light and felt the chill wind ruffle his hair and a similar chill over four murder scenes. It made so much more sense that two men could be more effective than just one murderer.

"If he has talked to his wife, Rhodes knows we are watching. At the moment I don't have enough to arrest either one of them with murder on the table."

"Maybe not, but they think either Reynolds or Davidson has information that can hang them is my guess or they wouldn't risk this. At least it is two on two, and I'm going to bet we are better shots."

"Don't be too sure. They've unfortunately been practicing." It was a cynical, terse observation.

"I wish that wasn't true."

Their voices were quiet, and they were definitely both on full alert, standing in the shadows of two large oak trees, but Chris was well aware their voices could probably still be heard. However, in an environment like this, so could any movement.

"I don't know where they are. It concerns me." Norris sounded tense.

"They don't know we're here either or it wouldn't be happening." They were both on the edge.

The crack of a shotgun and the sound of exploding glass answered that question about their location. Lit interior and the backside of the house . . . people visible inside . . .

Rhodes considered himself cornered because they had him, or almost. Whitman had a lot to lose as well — maybe the first random shot was just a diversion.

Running toward the house was not a wise decision, but they were law enforcement and there for a reason.

"Now we know. The back French doors. I'll go right, you go left."

Another shot.

Chris veered off to head toward the back at a run, going around the house, still not knowing where they were. If that really was the kind of weapon he'd just heard, he was outgunned and so was Norris.

Shit.

The uneven lighting didn't help, a twilight nightmare of darkness and dim illumination, and armed with only his Glock, he wasn't happy. Close range he was fine but from a distance, he was a target.

The only good news was as he skirted the house and looked around the corner, they couldn't see him any better than he could see them.

House utterly dark.

Power cut from within, or without? He wondered as he moved cautiously around the corner. Hopefully the shot that had shattered a window hadn't hit either of the people in the house, so Reynolds had decided to kill the lights to keep them from being targets. However, if somehow the power to the house was off grid now, the security cameras wouldn't work.

Not a perfect scenario. People stumbling around in the descending dark with guns?

He wasn't a fan, especially since he thought the anxiety bar was pretty high when it came to the opposing forces. They had to have realized Norris had been there the night before for a reason and just taking chances like this meant there was a lot at stake. He completely understood just getting up in the morning was dangerous, but if there were two men out there trying to dodge first-degree murder charges, that made it a very dicey situation.

Or were they dodging something else? Organized crime maybe? Possible and a dangerous bedmate.

No matter what Carter thought of instincts guiding investigations, Chris believed Whitman was the driving force behind this. Easing out from behind the sparse cover of a leafless bush, he circled to see if he could tell what window had been broken.

The French doors onto the back deck were the answer.

There was a gaping hole and shattered glass all over.

Was one of them already inside? Or was someone waiting in the shadows? He couldn't see anyone with a swift assessing glance around, but there were gathered trees close to the house and it would be hard to spot someone who didn't want to be seen.

It depended on how well orchestrated this was. Was it simply a mission of impulse now that the edges were crumbling? If he went up those steps, he'd be fair game, but, he decided, it was hard to hit a moving target unless you were really good and steady.

So he went for it.

A rapid ascent, moving swiftly, hoping Reynolds had had the immediate sense to barricade himself and Samantha in a room because he knew law enforcement was back up and already on site.

Glass crunching under his boots, a sense of urgency and danger . . .

"What the hell?"

Reynolds in the darkness of his kitchen, his shadowed face set, merely a figure outlined in the doorway.

"It's me." Bailey eyed the gleam of the rifle pointed right at him, but then again, he was holding his weapon extended too.

Maybe it was the lack of lighting, maybe the shock and outrage over having his home attacked, but Mick Reynolds did not lower his weapon and kept it steadily aimed in his direction. For a split second he wondered if he'd been wrong all along and maybe he was staring down the killer, but then he heard the sound — the slightest crunch of the broken glass — and knew someone had followed him up those steps and was right outside the door. He was simply in the line of fire.

Two things happened at once.

He moved left, and the timing was very much in his favor since someone fired through the shattered door and the bullet thudded into one of the cabinets. He would have been hit if he hadn't realized at that last split second.

Both he and Reynolds fired back, the sound unfortunately deafening, because discharging a weapon in a confined space — much less two at once — accomplished a definite problem with your hearing, at least in the short term.

It didn't do the door any favors either, but it was already destroyed.

No idea if anyone was hit or still a viable threat.

Someone shouted, "Hold your fire. He's down."

His ears ringing, Chris only barely heard it but edged toward the doorway, fairly sure that had been Norris.

Sprawled body, a man with a flashlight in one hand and a gun in the other kneeling next to him . . .

"Rhodes?" Chris could only barely hear himself speak.

"No." Norris shook his head and looked up at Reynolds, who had stepped out behind Chris, rifle still in hand. "Your friend Whitman."

Reynolds said with bitter emphasis, "He was no friend of mine."

CHAPTER THIRTY-THREE

It should be over.

He was ready for it, had prepared for what might be inevitable, but the way it happened didn't follow.

The killer wasn't dying.

He lay there in the wet, decaying leaves from last fall. The clammy embrace and fecund scent felt like death, but no, it wasn't. No spirits hovering — no angels and no demons.

Alone, cold to the bone, and desolate. He was bleeding, but it just wasn't enough.

He would maybe have preferred dead.

It was hard to tell as he struggled to his feet.

* * *

The situation felt like she was trapped in an action movie.

It was excruciating to not know what was happening, listen to gunfire in the background, and be locked in complete darkness. Except for her phone.

Then quiet. Minutes passed. No one came to the door of the master bedroom where she currently sat, lights off as instructed, door locked.

She thought about calling 911.

Two problems. There was at least one officer on the scene already, and an FBI agent. It might cause more confusion than help the situation. The other was that while she knew exactly where she was, it wasn't like she had Mick's actual address memorized. She could tell them how to get there, but not what was happening or give a physical location.

So she sat there on the edge of the bed until there was a faint wail of sirens in the background and then she went to unlock the door. She wasn't just going to sit there any longer. She hadn't called, but someone had.

Lights were on and she could hear voices.

The kitchen was quite a sight: broken glass, cold air pouring in through the missing door, five men standing there in subdued conversation, all of them with serious expressions. At some point help had arrived evidently as there were two young deputies in uniform . . .

But Mick was alive and, as far as she could see, unharmed.

She'd always thought the phrase "weak-kneed with relief" was an exaggeration, but she found it wasn't and braced one hand on the doorway. At that moment he glanced over and realized she was there.

"Sam?" He came over in long strides and caught her in a solid and reassuring embrace. "You okay?"

"I'm fine."

"You're trembling."

She eased free and gave him the look he deserved. "Of course I am. I could hear people shooting at each other, or I assume that was what was going on."

"Yeah, that was what was going on." He ran his hand through his hair and exhaled. "I thought I moved back here for peace and the quiet countryside." Then he looked at her very directly. "Or it might have been for you."

That declaration caused an inner tremble of another kind.

"I'm glad you came back, whatever the reason." If they didn't have an audience and if there wasn't the clear sound of rescue vehicles arriving, this might have been a very different conversation. "What's happening? Who needs an ambulance?"

"It's hard to say if anyone does."

That cryptic response wasn't helpful. "Care to explain?"

"I would if I could, but I'm not in charge here. My house might be a crime scene, but I'm not part of the conversation of how it is going to be handled."

There was something he didn't want to tell her. Perhaps there was a six-year gap between their previous relationship and the renewed one, but she did know him. Yes, boy to man he'd changed some, but intrinsically he was the same. Samantha said, "Stop trying to spare me and just tell me, please."

"You might have been right about Whitman."

"How so?"

"The ambulance is for him, but I doubt he needs it."

How it was phrased registered.

"Shawn?"

"You're the one who warned me you thought he was dangerous."

"Treacherous." The reality was chilling as she slowly corrected him. "He's . . . dead?"

"No one here is a doctor. That's why paramedics were called in." Mick sounded calm, but she doubted he was. He looked suddenly world-weary, if she had to describe it. Those notable hazel eyes were shaded, and he looked resigned rather than upset. "It's possible I'm the one who shot him. Or maybe Bailey because we both discharged our weapons pretty much at the same time. I don't know. Norris also thinks it could be him."

She was shocked, but then again, she wasn't. She'd heard it happen.

After a moment, she searched for the right words. "Mick, you didn't initiate any of this."

"That is true enough," he agreed. "Who thinks they'll ever be in this situation?"

That sentiment she could relate to because she was certainly off balance. "I don't know. Where is Jack in all of this?"

"On the run, I would guess."

At that moment the paramedics arrived, swirling lights and sirens shutting off.

"I'll let them in." Mick headed toward the front door, and she stayed back, uncertain and not sure what role, if any, she played in this drama.

Men poured in, and a young deputy met them in the hallway and directed them toward the kitchen. It seemed incongruous that she'd taken out a casserole dish earlier and it sat on the counter in all its empty glory, waiting for her to whip up her Aunt Ellida's famous escalloped chicken recipe but now probably full of broken glass.

Her evening was shattered as well as far as she could tell.

Mick came up and put his arm around her waist. "Let's just move away from this."

"Like to Antarctica?"

A faint smile touched his mouth. "I never thought it would tempt me, but that holds some appeal at the moment."

"We could wear matching parkas."

"That seals the deal right there." He urged her toward the hallway. "I think under these circumstances we should find somewhere quiet and let them come for us if that is what they need."

* * *

Mick didn't like situations he couldn't control. He owned that facet to his personality. The bustle outside hardly needed him in the mix because he'd be in the way. It was also getting cold, so he led Samantha back toward the bedroom where he'd practically dragged her because hopefully it was still warm, turning lights back on as he went.

Mick called his parents just to make sure they were safe, relieved when his father answered the phone.

"Just checking in," he said evasively. He'd explain when he could, but right now, he truly didn't know exactly what was happening.

"We're fine. Well, as fine as we can be."

It wasn't like he didn't understand. "Just stay vigilant." He paraphrased Bailey, "The police can't be everywhere. Samantha says hi. We might even stop by a little later. I'll let you know."

He basically hung up on his own father, something he would never dream of doing under normal circumstances, but normal was nowhere in sight. Samantha had sat down on the edge of the bed, and her eyes were full of shock. When she spoke, her voice was barely above a whisper, or maybe he was just still hearing-impaired from all the gunfire.

"Mick . . . why would Shawn ever do anything so utterly reckless? I mean I don't think much of him as a person, but I thought he had more self-preservation than that. Law enforcement was here."

The question was did he know that?

"You mean the gunfight at the OK Corral?" He sat down next to her. "I wonder if Rhodes even told him about last night. How much do criminals trust each other? I am not an expert on the subject, but I'd guess not very much. If I had to guess, Shawn expected it would be just the two of us here."

It chilled him. His light rifle against whatever weapon used to shatter glass and a determined assault would not be a fair fight. He'd underestimated the opponent for sure, but then again, he hadn't started this conflict.

She looked away for a moment, her expression detached, but a convulsive swallow moved the muscles in her slender throat. "So he came to kill us."

That summed up what he'd been trying to not acknowledge. He took her hand, lacing their fingers together. "I think both Shawn and Jack Rhodes got into something that promised easy money, but Shawn underestimated how much my sister despised him, and even if you won't tell me specifically what she confided in you, I have a fair idea. She was keeping an eye on him, and he didn't realize it until it was too late. They were in over their heads and decided to fix the problem."

"By murdering her." Samantha's mouth compressed and her body shifted to rest against him. "Oh God."

"Maybe once they started, they couldn't look back, but we are speculating." He put his arm around her. No doubt about it, she was tense, and he couldn't blame her. He added, "I have no idea how deep they were into what made them take such drastic action, but Bailey and Norris will find out."

"I hope you realize if they were laundering money, it was for someone else. Even if Shawn is dead and Jack running scared, those people might still perceive us as a threat even though we don't know a thing."

He agreed only to a point. "If they ever knew there was one. To be frank, I think those two thought they could just handle it and acted independently."

"Jack doesn't seem like the type who would—"

"Take clandestine pictures of you?" He didn't apologize for the interruption. "Well, to me Shawn didn't seem like someone who would shoot out the windows of my house either. Neither one seems like the type to kill people in cold blood, but someone did."

His phone pinged. He pulled it out and looked at it. "Bailey. I don't know I've ever had someone text me from within my own house before "

Samantha just shook her head. "He's a Tennessee boy and my guess is you are in a bedroom with a girl, so he politely declines to look for you."

That won her an impetuous kiss she obviously didn't see coming, her mouth warm and soft under his. "Samantha, you are every inch a woman, and we are so far past boy meets girl that we need to talk. Is that a date?"

"It is."

He was going to propose, and he knew it, and he wondered if in each male's life there was a definitive moment when you understood it was time to commit, no matter how much of a leap of faith it might be.

There was no way he could speak for every man but, in his case, he wondered if he was good enough for her. He'd do his best, but good enough? That was a question hanging in the air.

He wanted a simple life. Did she? Woods, water and the pleasure of the sunrise and sunset . . .

There was a feeling she knew it too.

"His text said 'all clear'."

"They want to talk to us." She looked resigned.

"I'm guessing." With reluctance he let her go and stood. "Let's go see what he wants. Then I suppose I'll take you out to dinner and we'll go to your place for the evening because we can hardly stay here."

Not with the gaping hole where his French doors used to be, though he'd thought about replacing them anyway with something more suited to his lifestyle, like high-efficiency sliding doors. He guessed now his insurance would pay for them, though how you explained that a potential murderer had taken them out with a shotgun was going to be a very unique conversation for both him and his agent.

"I suppose we can't," she acquiesced and took his hand, still pale but resolute. "I can hear vehicles departing, but no sirens."

He could too.

No urgency. That didn't bode well.

In his mind it was clear enough. Whitman had brought it on himself however it had turned out. Was he sorry? Mick was sorry about the whole damn mess.

She was right about one thing — he hadn't started this, but there was a one to three odds he might have ended it.

CHAPTER THIRTY-FOUR

The killer found it ironic his staunchest ally was probably his biggest liability. Accusatory, suspicious, but able to step in if it might affect her lifestyle as the fragile fabric of their existence unraveled.

So he offered the part by calling and asking for a ride and safe harbor.

She accepted the role.

The bullet had hit his chest but, as far as he knew, just gone through the fleshy part under his shoulder without penetrating anything major because he wasn't coughing up blood. Blood loss was likely his worst enemy, for he was light-headed, in pain and drifting.

His brother-in-law was a doctor, and she silently waited at the window until the arc of lights indicated someone had pulled into the driveway.

"He's here," she said unnecessarily.

He moved, and it hurt to the extent that if he had the strength to scream, he might have, but he didn't.

"What are you going to tell him?" he asked.

She turned back from the window, her face a pale flash in his failing vision. "I don't know. I'll come up with something."

"I know where the money is."

Her response was terse. "Good, because this better be worth it."

* * *

It wasn't like this was a road untraveled; he just didn't like the familiar territory.

Chris watched the ambulance pull away, lights flashing but no sirens and just said it out loud. "A second shooting, it looks like a fatal one, by a county officer in just the span of a few months." He turned to Carter with a cynical and humorless smile. "How's that sound to you?"

"The perp was trying to gain access to a private residence and firing his weapon. Besides, there's no evidence yet you even hit him," his partner pointed out calmly.

"I couldn't see him." That was easy enough to admit. "And he'd have shot me if it wasn't for Reynolds being so intent, but what the press will announce is that I've been involved in the two most recent shootings involving law enforcement in this county."

"Both times you were being fired at, so Lawrence will have your back."

"So, let's organize and go look for Rhodes."

Carter nodded and so did Norris.

That wasn't what he wanted to do with his evening. A search in the cold woods didn't sound like fun, but it would wrap up this case. At least to the extent they could step back and leave it then to Norris and Wright.

He took a slim flashlight from his pocket. "Let's go."

Shadows, fecund leaves, silent trees and hanging branches . . .

The result was nothing but silence, a keening breeze and a consensus this would have to wait for morning. Too much territory to cover for casting around in the dark when he could be anywhere.

Carter was senior not just in age but experience. He took charge, which was fine with Chris. "All we can say is this is over for tonight. Let's go home and regroup in the morning."

Norris and the deputy departed in separate vehicles while Chris and Carter lingered.

They were waiting for Mick Reynolds to figure out how to cover the gaping hole that used to be French doors leading onto his back deck. Since he'd just moved in, he really wasn't all that unpacked. It looked like some of the emptied moving boxes and duct tape was going to be the solution.

Rhodes was still at large so they could hardly stay here, but Ms. Davidson had a house in town. It was minus the security system, true, but better than just cardboard between them and a determined killer.

It was clear Rhodes was rogue and on the run. Why he hadn't participated in the attempted invasion of Reynolds's home was a mystery, but that bold move might just have been Whitman's choice and he didn't agree with it, or he could have hung behind to ensure a quick exit.

But he was gone. Whitman's vehicle was there parked in a semi-hidden spot on the roadside in a grove of trees and at the moment deputies were scouring the woods for the fugitive.

They waited just in case Rhodes came in guns blazing like Whitman because it was clear enough both men had derailed.

"I don't believe Mrs. Rhodes," Chris mused out loud. "He has children. Jack can't simply run. He came home last night, just didn't go to work this morning. She's lying to us."

Across from him on a comfortable leather couch, Carter looked skeptical. "You have an idealistic view of the world, my friend. Many a man — or for that matter a woman — have chosen to run rather than face the music even if it meant cutting ties with everyone they knew."

"Yes, but he's not good at this."

Carter paid attention, but he always did, whether he agreed or not. "Go on."

"I think Whitman really played Rhodes. My impression is that he's backhanded and manipulative. How he convinced him the only way out of whatever they are wading waist-deep in was murder, I don't know, but he did."

"He's right." The quiet sound of a feminine voice was composed, and yet there was a quiver in there. "I was hardly eavesdropping but overheard anyway. No matter what has happened, Shawn is responsible."

It wasn't like he and Carter didn't know Samantha Davidson wasn't Whitman's biggest fan. It seemed like even his death didn't win him any amnesty. She stood there in the doorway, those green eyes shadowed and her expression remote. She added with a wan smile, "I'm not glad he's dead but won't miss not ever having to deal with him ever again."

She was clearly shaken, and he didn't blame her, for when the smoke cleared nothing was left but the stark reality. Chris asked, "He certainly made some interesting choices. If you had to call it, where would Jack Rhodes go?"

"Home." She said it simply, going over to sink into a chair. "I don't know what Jack has or has not done, but I think Patti and his kids are all he has."

At that moment Chris's phone rang. He glanced at it and didn't recognize the name but answered anyway. "This is Detective Bailey."

"This is Dr. George Reese." There was a slight pause. "My sister is Patti Rhodes. She told me that would ring a bell with you."

It did. He straightened away from the mantel where he'd been leaning, his fingers tightening around his phone. "It does. We've met. What can I do for you?"

"I just treated my brother-in-law for a gunshot wound to the chest. He refused the hospital, which is where he should have gone, but he is currently at home. I'm afraid that's all I can tell you because it is all I know."

"I believe I know who shot your brother-in-law. I am on my way."

He ended the call and said to Carter, "Well, we know where Rhodes is at the moment. Let's go."

* * *

Her house was quiet and dark, and Sam let them in with Mick's arm around her waist, his protective stance amusing in a not so funny way. She switched on the lamp on the hall table. "I think we are all clear. You can let me go."

He looked around. "Well, I didn't expect to revisit an old street in Tombstone, Arizona, tonight in my kitchen. I like holding on to you anyway."

Psychologically he had to be in an interesting place. His friend of decades was dead, he didn't even know if he'd killed him, the man who had murdered his sister likely on the loose . . .

She turned and pressed her palm against his chest and looked into his eyes. "I'm sorry."

His voice softened. "Sam."

"I'm a little in the same place. Apparently, I didn't know Jack either."

"It's . . . I don't know, for lack of a better word I'll use disturbing. You saw through Shawn. I didn't."

"You didn't want to."

"That's true enough." He gestured toward the kitchen. "The universal solution for any chaotic evening? A glass of wine maybe?"

She really didn't have much to offer in the form of food, but wine and cheese and crackers were a possibility, and they could order a pizza when it came down to it. "Yes to the wine. Let me get the glasses."

He started the fireplace, which was a nice and normal warm touch in an otherwise abnormal evening. That they didn't know what to say to each other was hardly a surprise, because what did two people say to each other after sharing this particular evening?

She wasn't sure.

"Why is it I feel like I should apologize to you somehow like this is a really bad date, or something?" Mick poured merlot into two glasses and went to sit on the couch after handing her glass to her.

"It doesn't feel like any of it could ever happen, so I admit bullets and police officers do constitute a bad date, but hardly because you planned it that way. Someday we can tell our children about it, like some lurid fairytale."

"Are we?"

She stopped, her glass halfway to her mouth. "What?"

"Having children?" He merely raised his brows. "What were you thinking? Maybe three? At least three, right? Two isn't enough."

He was his parents' only surviving child. Sam blinked rapidly. "I agree."

"Then you'll marry me?"

"I would have married you six years ago."

He contemplated his wine glass and took a moment. "That's humbling, because you are the most intelligent, beautiful, interesting woman I've ever known. Maybe those six years were worth it, because I think I took you a little for granted back then. With an arrogance that I never even saw, I expected you to love me, which is unforgivable. You did us both a favor when you didn't follow me to Chicago. I assumed you would. I was affronted when you didn't and then gradually understood it was my mistake. Whatever happens from now on, I promise to talk to you."

As far as she was concerned, that was a lot better than bended knee. Her voice was misty with emotion. "I promise to talk to you too."

"That's a deal then."

"I think so."

So she was getting married.

To Mick Reynolds.

Maybe he was right, and those six years really were worth waiting for this moment because they were no longer impetuous young lovers, feeling their way through life without the benefit of at least some experience, growing apart rather than together. If she had kept him from going, he wouldn't be back. If she had gone, she would have hated it and maybe even him for forcing her to leave. As it stood, they both understood with a greater clarity at least the foundation of their relationship.

"You have a couple of rings to choose from." He looked ruefully amused. "I would theatrically offer you one like I'm supposed to do, but they are back at my house. I didn't propose properly either, but this hasn't been an ordinary evening so far."

That was putting it mildly. "You did fine," she informed him.

Amanda would have been so happy for both of them. Neither one of them said it, but she knew they were both thinking it.

Mick slowly swirled the liquid in his glass, his expression shuttered for someone who had just committed to the promise of what hopefully was a lifetime. "This thing with Rhodes . . . please tell me for all of his closemouthed ways, Bailey will at least let us know what is going on."

"I would hope so. But then again, I wouldn't necessarily count on it. If I had to define it, I'd say that man always has a clear focus. It's the angle that is the mystery."

"I'd agree with that." His mouth quirked.

She regarded him gravely. "What do you think happened?"

Mick thought about it, his long legs extended, those hazel eyes reflective. "I think tonight was a prime example of Shawn Whitman's attempt to cut his losses. He shot Jack Rhodes because he was a liability. He tried to come after us because we were a perceived threat, just like Amanda. I think anyone who knows him for what he is — or was — is considered the enemy. Him against the world his whole life. In retrospect, what I thought was competitive spirit was just a giant chip he carted around on his shoulder."

It wasn't like she disagreed. "I can't excuse Jack because he's a grown man and made his own decisions, but the truth is, Shawn destroyed his life."

"It seems to me they destroyed each other."

"At a great cost to other people."

"Yes."

She knew he was thinking of his parents. "I know."

His phone pinged. Mick picked it up and glanced at it, then looked at her. His voice was absolutely without emotion. "That's Bailey. Jack Rhodes is dead."

EPILOGUE

Quiet spring evening.

Mist over the water drifting in ghostly patterns, diaphanous and surreal like detached spirits.

Booted feet up, Chris listened to the car pull in and waited, watching the lazy wind of the river.

When the phone call had come, he'd been specific about where he'd be, so he wasn't surprised to hear light footsteps come down the stairs to the small deck overlooking the river.

"Detective."

He did get to his feet, because politeness was ingrained in him, and as far as he could tell Mrs. Rhodes was a nice enough woman who had been dealt, in his estimation, a raw hand.

But maybe not. Even the FBI couldn't find the money, though Jack had made several transfers. Offshore banks. Someone benefited.

Phone records showed Natalie Fields had been contacted by both John Newsome and Amanda Reynolds, and at some point Amanda had called the firm where Jack Rhodes and Samantha Davidson had their offices. Probably because she wanted Rhodes to help her nail down his client and assumed he didn't realize the financial information was falsified.

Her fatal mistake.

There was no other way to look at it except that Chris had done his job, which was unravel the murders and, more importantly, stop the killing spree. The rest was up to the feds.

There were two chairs on the small deck. He gestured at one. "Ma'am."

"Thank you." Unlike the first time they met, she was dressed in a straight skirt and a patterned blouse, a loose, long, gray sweater over her shoulders, her hair tidy and straight.

She did not look like the wife of a murderer.

Actually, she was the widow of a murderer.

Jack had at least done that for her. Put the pistol he'd used for the murders in his mouth and ended the problem when he'd learned Chris and Carter were on their way and that Whitman was dead.

Game over.

He wasn't positive what she might have left to say, but there was no doubt he was interested.

"Nice view." She took the chair next to his and looked over the water. "Peaceful."

He sat back down. "Well, the cabin itself isn't exactly the Ritz, but I don't think that establishment has quite the same ambiance either. Sometimes I need peaceful."

"I can understand that."

He waited. Carter would never support the idea he was good at waiting, but now and then he was patient. As far as he knew, there was nothing at stake here any longer, so that just meant she had something to say and needed to say it.

It took a moment and she hesitated, but finally, she said, "I came here to tell you a story. Don't get your hopes up for a happy ending, but I think it will help me to tell it, and maybe if it could give you some insight, I'm hoping that it might be useful in the future to others."

It really was a nice spring evening, a blanket of stars above.

She took in an audible breath. "There once was this little boy. His parents didn't get along at all. He frequently saw his father hit his mother. He was sad. Then one night when he was ten years old, his father got extremely angry, took out a handgun and shot his mother. He saw it. Even after she fell, he kept shooting her. And when he picked up her lifeless body to carry her away, her shoe fell off. The little boy kept it. It was his secret. He couldn't tell anyone what happened, but he always had that shoe."

That there was a reason behind the ritualistic killings didn't precisely surprise him, but the human psyche was always fascinating.

With feeling, he said, "I feel very sorry for that little boy."

"Jack was always understandably afraid of his father. He didn't tell me the story for the longest time. We'd been married at least close to ten years. He left out where his mother's body had eventually been found, but when he started acting so strange and there were all these killings, I started to wonder. And yes, she'd been left in the cemetery, just dumped there."

Chris searched for something to say and simply settled for the obvious. "I think your husband was a man with a haunted past."

"Me too." She stood. "Thank you for listening to me, Detective. Please understand. I felt like I needed to tell you that."

When she left, he walked back up to the cabin. Anna was inside, her expression inquiring as she stirred something that smelled fantastic on the dilapidated old stove. "What was that all about?"

"Closure, I think."

Her dark eyes were suddenly luminous. "You certainly gave that to Mrs. Dunn. Thank you."

"No one deserves it more, so no thanks needed. I'm a sucker for sweet old ladies." He smiled down at her. "I'm kind of partial to the feisty young ones too."

"I have to ask. Did Sheriff Lawrence share the autopsy results with you?"

Anna was never one to be shy with hard questions, so he'd expected this one. He shrugged, recalling the conversation. "In Whitman's death, the cause was determined to be multiple gunshot wounds."

She took it in. "So you have no idea who actually—"

He interrupted. "Killed him? It appears Lawrence has chosen to handle it this way. He's a wise old bird, and it's for Reynolds. Norris and I were just doing our jobs. I think Reynolds would like to be the one who delivered the kill shot, but in truth, could he live with it?"

Anna looked at him. "Do you think he could?"

"This way he never has to find out."

THE END

ALSO BY KATE WATTERSON

DETECTIVE CHRIS BAILEY SERIES:
Book 1: THE LAKE HOUSE
Book 2: THE WOODS AT DUSK
Book 3: NO ONE TO HELP HER

Thank you for reading this book.

If you enjoyed it, please leave feedback on Amazon or Goodreads, and if there is anything we missed or you have a question about, then please get in touch. We appreciate you choosing our book.

Founded in 2014 in Shoreditch, London, we at Joffe Books pride ourselves on our history of innovative publishing. We were thrilled to be shortlisted for Independent Publisher of the Year at the British Book Awards.

www.joffebooks.com

We're very grateful to eagle-eyed readers who take the time to contact us. Please send any errors you find to corrections@joffebooks.com. We'll get them fixed ASAP.